SHE TOLD A LIE

ALSO BY P.D. WORKMAN

Zachary Goldman Mysteries

She Wore Mourning

His Hands Were Quiet

She Was Dying Anyway

He Was Walking Alone

They Thought He was Safe

He Was Not There

Her Work Was Everything

She Told a Lie

He Never Forgot (Coming soon)

She Was At Risk (Coming soon)

Reg Rawlins, Psychic Detective

What the Cat Knew

A Psychic with Catitude

A Catastrophic Theft

Night of Nine Tails

Telepathy of Gardens

Delusions of the Past

Fairy Blade Unmade

Web of Nightmares

A Whisker's Breadth

AND MORE AT PDWORKMAN.COM

SHE TOLD A LIE

ZACHARY GOLDMAN MYSTERIES #8

P.D. Workman

pd workman

ISBN: 9781774680049 (IS Hardcover)

ISBN: 9781774680032 (IS Paperback)

ISBN: 9781774680056 (Large Print)

ISBN: 9781774680001 (KDP Paperback)

ISBN: 9781774680018 (Kindle)

ISBN: 9781774680025 (ePub)

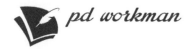

God bless the rescuers,

even when they are doomed to fail.

CHAPTER 1

Zachary tried to stay in the zone he was in, just on the border between sleeping and waking, for as long as he could. He felt warm and safe and at peace, and it was such a good feeling he wanted to remain there as long as he could before the anxieties of consciousness started pouring in.

The warm body alongside his shifted and Zachary snuggled in, trying not to leave the cozy pocket of blankets he was in.

Kenzie murmured something that ended in 'some space' and wriggled away from him again. Zachary let her go. She needed her sleep, and if he smothered her, she wouldn't be quick to invite him back.

Kenzie. He was back together with Kenzie and he had stayed the night at her house. It was the first time he'd gone there instead of her joining him in his apartment, which was currently not safe for them to sleep at because the police had busted the door in. It would have to be fixed before he could sleep there.

Kenzie lived in a little house that was a hundred times better than Zachary's apartment, which wasn't difficult since he had started from scratch after the fire that burned down his last apartment. While he was earning more as a private investigator than he ever had before, thanks to a few high profile murder cases, he wasn't going to sink a lot of money into the apartment until he had built up a strong enough reserve to get him through several months of low income.

Zachary had been surprised by some of the high-priced items he had seen around Kenzie's home the night before. He supposed he shouldn't have been surprised, given the cherry-red convertible she drove, but he'd always assumed she was saddled with significant debts from medical school and that she would not be able to afford luxuries.

Maybe that was the reason that she had never invited him into her territory before. She didn't want him to see the huge gap in their financial statuses.

Once Zachary's brain started working, reviewing the night before and considering Kenzie's circumstances as compared to his, he couldn't shut it back off and return to that comfortable, happy place he had been just before waking. His brain was grinding away, assessing how worried he should be. Did any of it change their relationship? Did it mean that Kenzie looked down on him? Considered him inferior? She had never treated him that way, but did she think it, deep down inside?

Once he left her house, would he ever be invited back? He had only been there under exceptional circumstances and, while he hoped that it was a sign that Kenzie was willing to reconcile and work on their relationship again—as long as he was—he was afraid that it might just have been one moment of weakness. One that she would regret when she woke up and had a chance to reconsider.

With his brain cranking away at the problem and finding new things to worry about, Zachary couldn't stay in bed. He shifted around a few times, trying to find a position that was comfortable enough that he would just drift back to sleep, but he knew that it was impossible. His body was restless and would not return to sleep again so easily.

He slid out of the bed and squinted, trying to remember the layout of the room and any obstacles. The sky was just starting to lighten, forcing a little gray light around the edges of Kenzie's blinds and curtains. Enough to see dark shapes around him, but not enough to be confident he wouldn't trip over something. Zachary felt for the remainder of his clothes and clutched them to him as he cautiously made his way to the bedroom door and out into the hallway.

He shut the door silently behind him so that he wouldn't wake Kenzie up. There was an orange glow emanating from the bathroom, so he found his way there without knocking over any priceless decor. He shut the door and turned on the main light. It was blinding after the night-light. Zachary squeezed his eyes shut and waited for them to adjust to the light that penetrated his eyelids, and then gradually opened them to look around.

Everything was clean and tidy and smelled fresh. Definitely a woman's domain rather than a bachelor pad like Zachary's. He needed to upgrade if he expected her to spend any time at his apartment. He'd used her ensuite the night before rather than the main bath and, even though it was more cluttered with her makeup and hair and bath products, it was also cleaner and brighter than Zachary's apartment bathroom.

He spent a couple of minutes with his morning routine, splashing water on his face and running a comb over his dark buzz-cut before making his way to the living room, where he'd left his overnight bag when he and Kenzie had adjourned for the night. He pulled out his laptop and set it on the couch while it booted up, wandering into the kitchen and sorting out her single-cup coffee dispenser to make himself breakfast.

CHAPTER 2

It was some time before he heard Kenzie stirring in the bedroom and, eventually, she made her way out to the living room. She had an oriental-style dressing gown wrapped around her. She rubbed her eyes, hair mussed from sleep.

Kenzie yawned. "Good morning."

"Hi." Zachary gave her a smile that he hoped expressed the warmth and gratitude he felt toward her for letting him back into her life, even if it was only for one night. "How was your sleep?"

"Good." Kenzie covered another yawn. "How about you? Did you actually get any sleep?"

"I slept great." Zachary wasn't lying. He didn't usually sleep well away from home. For that matter, he didn't sleep that well at home either. But after facing off with

Lauren's killer and dealing with the police, he had been exhausted, and the comfort he had found in Kenzie's arms and the luxurious sheets in her bed had quickly lulled him to sleep. There was a slight dip in the middle of her mattress, testifying to the fact that she normally slept alone, and that had made it natural for them to gravitate toward each other during the night. It had been reassuring to have someone else in bed with him after what seemed like an eon of lonely nights.

It was the best night's sleep he'd had in a long time.

"You couldn't have slept for more than three or four hours," Kenzie countered.

"Yes... but it was still a really good sleep."

"Well, good." She bent down to kiss him on the forehead.

Zachary felt a rush of warmth and goosebumps at the same time. She didn't appear to regret having allowed him to stay over. "Do you want coffee? I figured out the machine."

"Turn it on when you hear me get out of the shower. That should be about right."

"Do you want anything else? Bread in the toaster?"

"The full breakfast treatment? I could get used to this. Yes, a couple of slices of toast would be nice."

Zachary nodded. "Coffee and toast it is," he agreed.

He saw her speculative look, wondering whether he would actually remember or whether he would be distracted by something else.

"I'll do my best," Zachary promised. "But it better be a short shower, because if it's one of those two-hour-long ones, I might forget."

"I have to get to work today, so it had better be a quick one."

* * *

He did manage to remember to start both the coffee and the toast when she got out of the shower, and even heard the toast pop and remembered to butter it while it was hot. He had it on the table for Kenzie when she walked in, buttoning up her blouse.

"Nice!" Kenzie approved.

"Do you want jam?"

"There's some marmalade in the fridge."

Zachary retrieved the jar and made a mental note that he should get marmalade the next time he was shopping for groceries. If that were her preferred condiment, then he should make an effort to have it for her when she came to his apartment. He tried to always get things for her when he was shopping because, as Bridget put it, he ate like a Neanderthal. Not one of those fad caveman diets, but like someone who had never learned how to cook even the simplest foods. Most of his food was either ready to eat or just needed to be microwaved for a couple of minutes.

Or he could order in. He could use a phone even if he couldn't use a stove.

"So, your big case is solved," Kenzie said. "What are your plans for the day?"

"I still need to report to the client and issue my bill. Then I've got a bunch of smaller projects I should catch up on, now that I'll have some more time. And I need to get my door fixed. I wouldn't want to impose on you for too long."

Kenzie spread her marmalade carefully to the edge of the toast. "It was nice last night. I'm glad you called."

Zachary's face got warm. All they had done was to talk and cuddle, but he had needed that so badly. He had been concerned that she would be disappointed things had gone no further, so he was reassured that she had enjoyed the quiet time together too. Their relationship had been badly derailed by the abuse Zachary had suffered at Archuro's hands, which had also brought up a lot of buried memories of his time in foster care. However much he wanted to be with Kenzie, he couldn't help his own visceral reaction when things got too intimate.

"Hey," Kenzie said softly, breaking into his thoughts. "Don't do that. Come back."

Zachary tried to refocus his attention on her, to keep himself anchored to the present and not the attack.

"Five things?" Kenzie suggested, prompting Zachary to use one of the exercises his therapist had given him to help him with dissociation.

Zachary took a slow breath. "I smell... the coffee. The toast." He breathed. "Your shampoo. The marmalade. I... don't know what else."

His own sweat. He should have showered and dressed before Kenzie got up. Greeted her smelling freshly-scrubbed instead of assaulting her with the rank odor of a homeless person.

Kenzie smiled. "Better?" She studied his face for any tells.

Zachary nodded. "Yeah. Sorry."

"It's okay. It's not your fault."

He still felt completely inadequate. He should be able to have a pleasant morning conversation with his girlfriend without dissociating or getting mired in flashbacks. It shouldn't be that hard.

"Are you going to have something to eat? There's enough bread for you to have toast too," Kenzie teased.

"No, not ready yet."

"Well, don't forget. You still need to get your weight back up."

Zachary nodded. "I'll have something in a while."

* * *

He still hadn't eaten when he left Kenzie's. She was on her way into work, and he didn't want her to feel like she had to let him stay there in her domain while she was gone so, by the time she was ready for work, he had repacked his overnight bag and was ready to leave as well. She didn't make any comment or offer him the house while she was gone.

"Well, good luck with your report to Lauren's sister today. I know that part of the job is never fun."

Zachary nodded. "Yeah. And then collecting on the bill. Sorry your sister was murdered, but could you please pay me now?" He rolled his eyes.

Kenzie shook her head. "At least I don't have to ask for payment when I give people autopsy results."

They paused outside the door. Zachary didn't know what to say to Kenzie or how to tell her goodbye.

"Call me later," Kenzie advised. "Let me know whether you got your door fixed or not."

Zachary exhaled, relieved. She wasn't regretting having invited him in. She would put up with him for another night if he needed her.

"Thanks, I will."

Kenzie armed the burglar alarm on the keypad next to the door and shut it. Zachary heard the bolt automatically slide into place.

"See you," Kenzie said breezily. She pulled him closer by his coat lapel and gave him a brief peck on the lips. "Have a good day."

Zachary nodded, his face flushing and a lump in his throat preventing him from saying anything. Kenzie opened the garage door. Zachary turned and walked down the sidewalk to his car. He tried hard not to be needy, not to turn around and watch as she backed the car out onto the street, checking to see whether she were still watching him and would give him one more wave before she left. But he couldn't help himself.

She waved in his direction and pulled onto the street.

* * *

Late in the afternoon, Zachary headed back to his apartment, hoping to find when he got there that the door had been repaired and he could feel safe there once more. Of course, if the door had been fixed, he would need another reason to go back to Kenzie's. Or he could invite her to join him and they could go back to their usual routines. Just because she had allowed him over to her house once, that didn't mean she would be comfortable with him being there all the time.

But he could see the splintered doorframe as he walked down the hall approaching his apartment. The building manager had promised to make it a priority, but it looked like whatever subcontractor he had called hadn't yet made it there. Zachary pushed the door open and looked around.

Nothing appeared to have been rifled or taken in his absence. Of course, he didn't have much of value. He'd taken all of his electronics with him and didn't exactly have jewelry or wads of cash lying around. Anyone desperate enough to rifle his drawers and steal his shirts probably needed them worse than he did.

Though he hadn't thought about the meds in the cabinet. There were a few things in there that might have some street value.

Zachary started to walk toward the bedroom, but stopped when he heard a noise. He froze and listened, trying to zero in on it. It was probably just a neighbor moving around. Or a pigeon landing on the ledge outside his window. They spooked him sometimes with the loud flapping of their wings when they took off.

He waited, ears pricked, for the sound to be repeated.

Could it have been a person? There in his apartment?

The last time he'd thought that someone was rifling his apartment and had called the police, it had been Bridget. She'd still had a key to the old apartment.

She'd checked in on him at Christmas, knowing that it was a bad time for him, and had cleaned out his medicine cabinet to ensure that he didn't overdose.

It wouldn't be Bridget this time.

She didn't have a key to the new apartment, though he would have been happy to give her one if she had wanted it. Bridget was no longer part of his life and he needed to keep his distance from her, both to avoid getting slapped with a restraining order and because he was with Kenzie, and he needed to be fair to her. There was no going back to his ex-wife. She had a new partner and was pregnant. She didn't want anything to do with him.

There was another rustle. He was pretty sure it was someone in his bedroom. But it didn't sound like they were doing anything. Just moving quietly around.

Waiting for him?

He hated to call the police and have it be a false alarm. But he also didn't want to end up with a bullet in his chest because he walked in on a burglary in progress.

Unlike private investigators on TV, Zachary didn't carry a gun. He didn't even own one. With his history of depression and self-harm, it had always been too big a risk.

Zachary eased his phone out of his pocket, moving very slowly, trying to be completely silent. He wasn't sure what he was going to do when he got it out. If he called emergency, he would have to talk to them to let them know what was going on. They wouldn't be able to triangulate his signal to a single apartment.

Just as he looked down at the screen and moved his thumb over the unlock button, it gave a loud squeal and an alert popped up on the screen. Zachary jumped so badly that it flew out of his hand, and he scrambled to catch it before it hit the floor. He wasn't well-coordinated, and he just ended up hitting it in the air and shooting it farther away from him, to smack into the wall and then land on the floor.

CHAPTER 3

He froze. His brain seized up.

He didn't know whether to turn around and run out the door or stay where he was and hope that the burglar hadn't heard him. He could dart across the room and pick up the phone. If he didn't, he had no way to communicate with the outside world and with the police in particular.

He could hear footsteps crossing the bedroom, turning into the hallway and coming toward him.

He swore under his breath, still not sure of the best course of action, then finally staggered across the room like a drunken penguin and snatched up the phone.

The alert was still showing on his screen—a message from Rhys Salter. With the screen lock engaged, it wouldn't show what the actual message was. He had been in too many situations where a suspect seeing his incoming messages could have been disastrous.

He wondered fleetingly what Rhys had said, and if it would be the last communication that ever passed between them. He spun around, trying to press his thumb over the unlock button.

How long would it be before the cops could get there?

Assuming he could even manage to call them.

The burglar strode out of the hallway.

CHAPTER 4

Zachary nearly collapsed with relief.

The loose-limbed black teen looked at him and raised his eyebrows questioningly. He spread his hands out in a 'what's up?' gesture.

Zachary fell back onto the couch, putting his hand over his pounding heart.

"You scared the heck out of me, Rhys! How did you get here?"

Rhys seemed unperturbed. He pointed at the broken doorframe. Then he indicated a student bus pass that hung around his neck.

"You could have told me you were coming over here. I thought you were some serial killer."

Rhys raised his own phone and turned his phone screen toward Zachary.

Zachary couldn't see what was on Rhys's screen from that distance, but he looked down at his own phone. Rhys had messaged him. He finally managed to unlock it and tapped on the notification to bring up the message that Rhys had sent to him.

An animated gif of Charlie Brown knocking on the roof of Snoopy's dog house. Rhys's way of letting Zachary know that he was there at his apartment.

Zachary shook his head. "Sheesh. You gave me a turn. Come sit down."

Rhys complied, sitting in the easy chair. He pointed again to the broken door and lifted his eyebrows.

"I had... well, it's a long story. The police broke in."

Rhys gave a short laugh.

"I wasn't doing anything," Zachary told him. "I mean, they weren't breaking in because of something I did. There was a guy here... a murderer, and he was... well..." Zachary shrugged helplessly. "He was going to kill me."

Rhys settled back in the chair, folding his arms and giving a little lift of his chin. Oh, is that all.

Zachary chuckled. "I was glad the police came. I didn't even care that they broke the door. Except that I couldn't stay here last night."

Rhys made a kissing noise. Zachary's face got hot. He tried to appear casual. "Yes, I stayed with Kenzie."

Rhys nodded, his eyes dancing. Clearly worth it to have his door broken down if it meant Zachary got to spend the night at Kenzie's. Zachary suspected Rhys had a crush on Kenzie. He never failed to ask about her.

Rhys leaned forward again. The amusement left his eyes. He tapped his phone screen, looking for something. Rhys had come to the apartment for a reason. He clearly hadn't told Vera, his grandmother, that he was going to see Zachary, or she would have driven him rather than his taking the bus. If she approved of his going to Zachary's, which she probably didn't. She preferred for the two of them to meet at her house rather than anywhere they might be seen together. People might misunderstand their relationship.

Zachary moved down the couch, closer to Rhys, and leaned in. Rhys tapped a picture and turned the phone around for Zachary to see.

She was a pretty girl. A teen around Rhys's age, cute, dark-haired, smiling at something off-screen. She didn't look like she had been aware that her picture was being taken. There was no attempt to ham for the camera. Most of the phone pictures of teenagers Zachary saw posted on social media had them posing, making faces, or had some popular filter or photobooth alteration.

Zachary nodded. "Is this your girlfriend?" he asked, and then made the kissing sound that Rhys used to designate Kenzie.

Rhys shook his head, serious. His mouth turned down naturally. He always looked sad, and Zachary knew that, like he did, Rhys struggled with depression and his traumatic past. There had been too much violence in the Salter family, and it had left its mark on Rhys. He rarely spoke more than a word or two and, even when communicating using his phone, usually avoided even written language, falling back on memes and gifs that the recipient had to interpret.

"What is it?" Zachary asked.

Rhys looked at his phone again. He tapped and swiped to find another picture, then turned it to Zachary again.

This time, the girl was smiling at the camera, her lips bright red. She hung on the arm of a tall, blond boy. He was a little older than she was. Maybe still a teenager, maybe twenty. He wasn't looking at her or the camera, but off to the side, eyebrows down like he was worried or suspicious about something.

"Is this her boyfriend?" Zachary asked, though he already knew the answer.

Rhys nodded. He turned the phone back around to look at the picture himself and, for a while, just sat there, quiet and unmoving, contemplating the picture.

"Did something happen to her?"

Rhys nodded. His dark eyes were full of sorrow. Zachary reached out and touched Rhys's shoulder.

"What is it? What happened?"

Rhys made a 'blowing up' movement with his fingers, flicking them all outward. At the same time, he puffed up his cheeks and blew the air out in a 'poof.'

Zachary searched Rhys's face, wishing he could read the interpretation there. The gesture had not been violent, so he didn't think it was an explosion. More like a puff of smoke. A magician. Now you see it, now you don't.

Zachary considered, biting his lip. "She disappeared?" he asked finally.

Rhys pointed at Zachary, nodding.

"And the boy?"

Rhys continued to nod.

"You think he had something to do with her disappearance?"

Rhys's eyes closed and he nodded again. Zachary could feel Rhys's pain and anxiety over her disappearance like it was centered in his own chest.

"How long has she been missing?"

Rhys held up four fingers, then five, then made a wobbling motion with his hand. Four or five days, more or less. Long past the 'I was just at a friend's house' period.

"Have you asked what happened to her? Do you know?"

Rhys's lips pressed together into a thin line and he gave a slight head shake, brows drawn down. Zachary had broken a cardinal rule of their communication system. Never ask more than one question at a time.

"Sorry. Do you know what happened to her?"

Rhys shook his head slowly. The slowness of it and the tension in his expression told Zachary that he didn't know for sure, but he had his ideas.

"Did you talk to her family?" He had to bite his tongue to keep from asking more follow-up questions. There was an urgency to their conversation. He wanted to move it along faster. But communications with Rhys could not be rushed.

Rhys shook his head.

"Have the police been called? Is she a missing person?"

Rhys gave a wide shrug.

Zachary was impatient, but he waited, analyzing their conversation and thinking about the pictures and about Rhys being there, waiting for him.

"You want me to look into it?"

Rhys smiled, nodding emphatically.

Zachary nodded and sat back, thinking about it. There was certainly no problem with his making some initial inquiries. Maybe her parents could tell him what had happened to her. Hopefully, there was an easy explanation for her disappearance. Maybe she had gone to visit a sick relative or her parents had put her into a better school. There were lots of reasons a teenager might be at school one day, and then not show up again.

"Okay, yeah. Can you give me her name and anything you have about her? Contact details?"

Rhys tapped away at his phone and, in a moment, Zachary had her name, phone number, and a couple of social network names in his messaging app.

Madison Miller.

"Got it. And can you send me those pictures?"

Rhys nodded and sent them over as well.

"Do you have others?"

Rhys was still. He considered the question. Zachary furrowed his brows.

"If you want me to find out about her, then I need whatever you've got."

Rhys shook his head. He pushed his phone into his jeans pocket.

Zachary looked at him. "What's going on here, Rhys? What aren't you telling me?"

Rhys motioned to Zachary's phone. He had the information he needed. But Zachary knew, going into it, that he didn't have everything. Rhys was keeping something from him.

"Are you worried it would get her into trouble? With her parents or the police?"

Rhys shook his head. But his expression was still veiled. Zachary didn't know if he were telling the truth. There was definitely something that he wasn't prepared to reveal.

"Rhys... I understand that you're trying to protect her. But you know... sometimes not knowing what I'm walking into can be hazardous. I don't want to get hurt, and I don't want anyone else to get hurt because of what I don't know. You know that... I've had some dangerous cases lately."

Rhys shook his head and drew a straight horizontal line with his hand.

"Nothing unsafe?" Zachary asked, to be sure of Rhys's meaning. "I don't need to worry about what I might be getting into here?"

Rhys gave a single nod and pointed at Zachary. His sign for 'you got it.'

Zachary looked back down at Madison's information and sighed. "I'll do what I can," he promised. "Now... we'd better get you home. Your grandma doesn't know you're here, does she?"

Rhys's hand made a wobbly side-to-side shake. Well...

"Yeah. That's what I thought. Ask me to come to your place next time. She doesn't want you coming over here. If you call me, I'll come."

Rhys shrugged. Zachary was left wondering how much else he was trying to get away with behind Vera's back. It wasn't likely the first time that Rhys had hopped onto a bus and gone somewhere other than home or school.

CHAPTER 5

Zachary believed that Rhys didn't think he was getting Zachary involved in anything dangerous to himself or to Madison. Still, he had enough experience as a private investigator to know that Rhys could very well be wrong. He hadn't given Rhys any particular timeline for the investigation. After he had dropped Rhys back at home, he went to a coffee shop and opened his computer to see what background he could find on Madison Miller.

Was she really missing? If she were, did anyone have any idea where she was? Was she just staying with friends somewhere, or had something happened to her? Vermont was not known as a high-crime area, but that didn't mean they had escaped the seamy underworld. There was still plenty of violent crime, drug trafficking, and street life. Even postcard-perfect

Vermont couldn't escape that, as Zachary had personally experienced.

Madison Miller's social networks seemed pretty clean. Only the occasional posting, mostly selfies or memes shared with friends.

At least, her social accounts that Rhys had known about.

Facial recognition searches led Zachary to several other user accounts that Rhys had not known about, and which were not quite so squeaky-clean. Zachary scrolled through several racier pictures of Madison and her boyfriend. Nothing X-rated. No nudes. But maybe not pictures she had wanted her parents or casual friends to see.

There was ample evidence Madison was drinking. Zachary wasn't as sure about smoking or drug use.

There were hints of it in Madison's posts, but sometimes kids bragged about things like that when they never would have even considered using.

Going back through her history, it looked like Madison and the boyfriend had started showing up together about two months previously. While there was nothing overtly wrong in the new accounts, something about them rang alarm bells for Zachary. He couldn't put his finger on anything specific. But something wasn't right.

Maybe it was because Rhys seemed so young. He didn't seem like the kind of kid who would be interested in the drug culture and had always denied any interest in having a girlfriend. Zachary didn't want to believe that he or any of the kids his age were old enough to get themselves into that kind of trouble. Rhys was clearly not telling his grandmother about his concerns or about going to visit Zachary to ask him to investigate Madison's disappearance.

How much else was going on that Vera wasn't aware of? She hadn't handled her daughters' rebellion or mental illness well. She had denied everything for as long as she could.

Zachary made notes about Madison's activities and user names as neatly as he could so he'd be able to read them when he went back over them later.

* * *

Zachary's door was not fixed that night, so he spent another night with Kenzie—which really didn't hurt his feelings at all. Not totally exhausted when he got there like he had been the previous night, he took a few minutes while Kenzie was making dinner to explore the house.

In addition to the master bedroom with the ensuite where Zachary had spent the night before, there was one room that appeared to be a cross between storage and a home office, and there was a third bedroom, neat as a pin, set up as a guest bedroom. Zachary glanced over it and shut the door quietly, grinning to himself. When he had called to ask Kenzie whether he could stay with her while his door was being fixed, she had denied having a guest room, using it as an excuse to invite him into her own bed. He was delighted to learn that it had been a lie. She could have put him up in the guest room as a friend, but had chosen not to. He didn't need to feel like he was imposing himself on her. He was right where she wanted him to be.

Zachary returned to the living room and sat down on the couch with his computer, glancing into the kitchen to make sure that his absence hadn't been noticed.

Kenzie gave no sign that she realized he'd been anywhere but the bathroom.

"Do you need help with anything?" Zachary offered.

"Do you actually know how to cook?"

"Well... no. But I'm pretty good at putting plates on the table."

Kenzie laughed. "Okay. Set the table."

He got up and looked through the cupboards, working around her, to find the plates, glasses, and cutlery, which he laid out neatly on the table. He even grabbed a jug of juice from the fridge and put it on the table. Kenzie looked up from the bubbling pot of sauce on the stove.

"You actually know which side the fork goes on," she observed in a surprised tone.

Zachary tried to restrain a smile. "I did remember some of the lessons my foster moms tried to drill into me."

"Didn't any of your foster families try to teach you to cook?"

Zachary shrugged. "That required a bit more sustained focus than setting the table. It never went very well."

Kenzie nodded. "Well, it's never too late to learn."

Zachary looked down at the pots on the stove. "Pasta?" he guessed.

"Yes. And this is something that is certainly within your capabilities. It doesn't take much to boil pasta and warm up some bottled sauce, if you don't want to learn to make your own sauce."

"On a good day," Zachary said. "But you have to remember to take the pasta off before the pot boils dry."

Kenzie raised her brows, chuckling. "Well, yes, that's true."

"It makes a terrible stink when it starts to burn."

"Really. So you have tried."

"Once or twice. I'm better at the frozen stuff you can just stick in the microwave."

"As long as you remember to take it out," Kenzie teased.

Zachary nodded. He had warmed up meals and then forgotten them in the microwave more times than he would like to admit. His meds tended to suppress his appetite, if not make him nauseated, so eating meals was more of a chore for him than a pleasure. Something that was easier to forget or not get around to.

A timer buzzed, and Kenzie took the lid off of the pot of pasta and tested it. "What do you think? Look good?"

Zachary nodded. "Looks fine to me."

She shook her head. "I have a feeling you'd eat it whether it was over- or undercooked. What are you thinking about?"

Zachary realized he'd been staring off into middle distance, reviewing the information he had on Madison Miller. "Oh... just a new case. Maybe."

"What is it?"

"Missing girl. You haven't had any teenagers in the morgue in the last few days, have you?"

"No. It's been pretty quiet, thank goodness. Have you checked around? Jail? Hospital?"

"Not yet. Just started with some background today. See whether she was likely to be involved in anything criminal or being bullied."

"And?" Kenzie removed the pot from the burner and poured the pasta into a strainer sitting in the sink.

Zachary remembered trying to juggle a hot pot and get out a strainer at the same time. One of the problems with cooking was that the recipes didn't remind you to do things like that. Put a strainer in the sink before you start. Set a timer when the water starts to boil. How to coordinate everything so that the sauce and the pasta were both done at the same time. Kenzie seemed to flow through the meal preparations easily. Zachary's executive skills had never seemed to be quite up to snuff for the myriad individual steps required for cooking.

"She has some alternate profiles. Not quite so innocent as her standard ones. But still… I don't see anything criminal or really bad. I'll get in touch with her family tomorrow and find out what they know. Maybe she isn't even missing at all."

"Who's hiring you, if not the family?"

"A friend."

"Oh, okay." Kenzie nodded. "Well, I hope there's nothing wrong. A lot of times, kids are just staying over with friends and didn't bother to tell Mom and Dad. They had a fight and didn't feel like going home.

Or things are too strict at home and they want more freedom."

Zachary didn't bother to point out that he was a private investigator and this wasn't his first gig.

He was fully aware of the reasons kids ran away from home. Or walked away.

He'd been one of those kids more than once. He'd normally stayed wherever social services had placed him, but there were times when it had been too much, and he had bolted. And times when he had just lost track of time and supervisors had called the police.

But Madison had been gone for too long. She hadn't just lost track of time.

CHAPTER 6

The call to Mr. and Mrs. Miller had been awkward, since they hadn't been the ones to contact him about Madison's disappearance. But they agreed to see Zachary and made time for him.

Zachary arrived at the house and took a minute to consider the home and the neighborhood before going in. It was a nice suburban area. Not a slum and not a gated community. Just the kind of neighborhood with white picket fences and a basketball net on the outside of the garage. Playgrounds close by. Madison went to Rhys's school, which Zachary had been to before. It was a nice place. No graffiti and only low-key security. They had a football team and a basketball team. He imagined they had girls' teams too, but he hadn't taken the time to find out.

Probably both Madison's parents worked. Office jobs or blue collar, enough to pay the mortgage for a nice house. Madison hadn't listed any siblings on her main social profile, so she was probably an only child.

Zachary got out of his car, locked it, eyed the locks to make sure the lock had engaged, then tried the handle. He armed the security system and forced himself to move on. The lawn in the Millers' front yard was neatly trimmed. There were a few spring flowers along the sidewalk and some flowering bushes at the front of the house.

He didn't have to ring the doorbell when he got up to the house. They were watching for him, and Mrs. Miller opened the door as soon as he reached it.

She looked him over. Zachary had been sure to shave and wear a neat, clean, collared shirt so that he was presentable. He was still not the best-looking guy. Too short. He still hadn't been able to gain back enough weight after his last major depression, so he looked gaunt and he frequently had bags under his eyes from chronic lack of sleep. Hair kept short in a buzz-cut so that he didn't have to worry about maintenance.

He nodded at Mrs. Miller and held out his hand. "Mrs. Miller? Zachary Goldman."

She shook his hand. She was taller than he was. Curvy, but not dressed provocatively. Medium length blond hair in a 'mom' style.

"Of course. Come in, Mr. Goldman."

"Please, just Zachary," he told her, stepping over the threshold.

She escorted him into the living room and motioned to an easy chair. Zachary sat down, leaning forward instead of lounging back. Mr. Miller entered the room, and Zachary jumped back to his feet to shake his hand. Mr. Miller was a young-looking man, his hair receding but still dark and not quite what Zachary would consider balding. He was a bit taller than his wife, in good shape, with a strong handshake. They all sat down.

"So… you're a police detective?" Mrs. Miller asked tentatively.

Zachary shook his head. "I'll coordinate my investigation with the police, but I'm a private investigator."

"But we didn't hire you. And if you'll pardon me saying, we're not going to pay you," Mr. Miller said bluntly.

"No. One of Madison's school friends asked me to make some inquiries. He's a family friend, so I said I'd find out what I could for him."

Mr. Miller still looked suspicious, like he was sure Zachary was going to try to take them for something, but he shrugged and sat back.

"What friend?" Mrs. Miller asked.

Rhys hadn't said to keep his name out of it, but Zachary decided to give him at least a semblance of privacy by not mentioning his last name. If the Millers really wanted to, they would be able to figure it out.

"His name is Rhys. He goes to school with Madison."

They both looked at Zachary blankly, not recognizing Rhys by name.

"She's never mentioned him," Mrs. Miller said.

"Does she talk to you a lot about her school friends?"

Mrs. Miller's lips pressed together. "I'm not sure I like what you are implying."

"I'm not implying anything. Just asking whether she talks about everyone she knows by name."

"No. Not necessarily. But we have a good relationship with her. We're a close family."

Zachary nodded. He pulled out his notepad and watched for their reactions as he opened it to a blank page. They didn't object.

"I assume, since you haven't told me that Madison is just out of town visiting relatives or going to a new school now, that she <u>is</u> missing."

Mr. and Mrs. Miller looked at each other, weighing their responses. It was Mrs. Miller who finally spoke.

"We reported Madison missing."

"So there has been a police report made?"

"Yes."

"How did they respond? Have they reported any progress?"

Both parents shook their heads. "They think she's a runaway," Mr. Miller growled. "We told them she isn't that kind of girl. She wouldn't run away. We didn't have any problems."

Zachary nodded encouragingly.

"We have a good relationship with her," Mrs. Miller confirmed. "She isn't the rebellious kind. She wasn't into drugs and parties. There isn't any abuse. She isn't that kind of kid."

"How were her marks at school?"

"They were good. She's always been a good student."

"No changes lately? The last couple of months?"

Mrs. Miller looked at her husband, asking a question with her eyes. He was reluctant, but eventually nodded. Anything to get her back.

"She's had a rough time the last little while," Mrs. Miller admitted. "She said that the work was getting really difficult. And it was too advanced for either of us to help her very much. I don't remember how to do quadratic equations and I was never good at essays. We were getting her tutoring. But she was very busy; it was hard to fit it into her schedule."

Zachary made a couple of notes, waiting to see if she would add anything else.

"What was she busy with? Did she have a lot of afterschool activities?"

"Kids are so busy these days."

There were a few moments of silence. Zachary looked up from his notebook, raising his brows.

"There are clubs and sports, doing things with friends, all of the homework. Special projects for some of the classes. And part-time jobs."

He noticed that she didn't say that Madison had all of those things. Only that kids in general did.

"Where did Madison work?"

"She had a job at the mall. A sales clerk in one of the stores. You know, folding shirts, running the cash register..."

"Which store?"

"Pedal Pushers."

Zachary hadn't been in there, but he knew the name. A sports clothing and bike equipment store. He made a note of it.

"So that kept her pretty busy? Did she have enough time for her schoolwork? Socialization?"

"Yes, of course. We told her that if it interfered with her schoolwork, she'd have to give it up."

"And you didn't think that her drop in marks was anything to do with her work?"

"She said it wasn't. She said it was just that the work was harder."

"But she couldn't fit in time for a tutor."

"We would have managed it."

Zachary nodded. They saw what they wanted to see. Even though they had told her that the job couldn't interfere with her schoolwork, they weren't willing to enforce it and make her drop the job.

"How often was she at Pedal Pushers?"

"Most afternoons after school let out. And on the weekends."

"When did she do her homework?"

"There was time between school and work. Or sometimes it was quiet at work and she could do it there."

"How late did it go?"

"I don't see what this has to do with her being missing," Mr. Miller interjected.

"I'll need to track her movements. Find out where she was when. Who might have watched her or had contact with her. When she was last seen."

"She is usually home by nine," Mrs. Miller said. "They close at eight, then she has to help with cleaning up, clearing the till, all of that. Then she comes straight home. That still gives her time to do homework after she gets home too. She doesn't go to bed until eleven."

"And weekends?"

"Nine-thirty until five."

"And then she comes home?"

"No, sometimes she has other things to do. Hang out with her friends. Maybe go out to eat, watch a movie. Sometimes she had a sleepover. But she'd still get into work the next day. I never heard any complaints about her missing. And they had my phone number in case there were any problems, I made sure of that."

"You knew the people she worked with? Did you ever stop by to drop off lunch or pick her up after work?"

"I met her manager, the girl who hired her. I don't go by there. You know, teenagers are embarrassed by their parents. They want to pretend they don't exist. Like all kids don't have parents too."

Zachary nodded.

"When did she disappear? Can you give me the timeline?"

"It was... Saturday or Sunday. She was sleeping over with friends Friday night and Saturday night. She said she would still get to work. I don't think she worked both days, maybe just Sunday. But she never came home. We couldn't reach her or her manager. I tried her friends... the ones whose phone numbers I could find. They didn't know where she was."

"Do you know who she slept over with?"

Mrs. Miller shook her head slowly. "She was always very responsible," she said guiltily. "She'd tell us when she was going out and when she would be back. She'd usually say whose house she was going to, but it was so routine that... I didn't always listen. I don't know if she told me who she would be with. I'm sure she did. But it didn't register and I didn't have any reason to be concerned. And if I was trying to reach her, all I had to do was call her cell phone. It wasn't like when we were kids, and you had to have the family's land line."

"You never found out who she was with those nights?"

"No. I don't know if the police found out. They were going to make inquiries. But they haven't told us anything. When we call and ask about it, they just say it is under investigation and that they'll let us know when they find anything significant."

"And you don't know if she was at work on Sunday?"

"I tried and tried to reach the manager, but I couldn't. I tried the store and they said it was the wrong number. The police..."

"Said they would follow up on that as well," Zachary supplied.

Mrs. Miller nodded. "It makes us sound like irresponsible parents, but I can assure you that we are not. We always kept track of what she was doing, made sure that everything was okay with her. She wasn't neglected or abused. She wasn't bullied at school. She had good marks and a good job, and kids like that don't just run away." Her voice cracked, and she dabbed at tears leaking out of the corners of her eyes.

Mr. Miller sat there stoically, not crying. But that didn't mean that he didn't feel the same way as his wife. He wore a stony expression that told Zachary that he was doing his best to suppress his own emotions and show his wife a strong, supportive front. His throat worked and he stared down at his hands.

"I don't think you're irresponsible parents," Zachary soothed. "This kind of thing could happen to anyone. I wonder if I could see Madison's bedroom?"

"The police wanted to look at it too, but they didn't find anything." Mrs. Miller stood to show him to Madison's room. "Of course she didn't leave her phone or her computer at home. She took those with her."

"Did she take anything else?"

"Well… she was supposed to be away for a couple of nights, so she took changes of clothing, her toothbrush and deodorant. All of the usual things a girl needs if she's going to be away overnight."

"Nothing that surprised you?"

"No."

She opened the door and motioned Zachary into the bedroom. It was a typical girl's bedroom. Pastel colors from when she'd been younger, with band posters and other memorabilia pinned or taped up. No more frilly princess bed. A plain blue bedspread, neatly made. A desk to study at. Shelves with a mixture of middle grade and reference books. A few prized dolls and stuffies still kept close to the bed. And a closet bursting with clothes.

Zachary looked around. He walked toward the closet. "Who made the bed?"

Mrs. Miller blushed. "It was me," she admitted. "I hate an unmade bed. And I knew the police would want to come in here."

"But she didn't sleep here Friday or Saturday. So it was unmade from Thursday night."

"Yes."

"Did she ever make it?"

Mrs. Miller raised her hands, palms up. "She was a teenager."

Zachary turned his attention to the closet. If she had taken two or three changes of clothing with her, it was not obvious from the contents of the closet. It was nicely appointed with a couple of hanging rods, a shoe rack, and boxes on the shelf, but it was jammed too full of clothing to remain neat and tidy.

"She liked her clothes."

"Yes. That's most of what she spent her money on. I told her she had to put half of her money into savings for school, but she could spend the rest on what she wanted. I'm not one of those parents who demands rent just because she started working."

Zachary nodded. "Was she putting money away?"

"Yes."

"You checked her bank account?"

"No. But she told me she was putting money away."

Zachary spun in a slow circle, looking around the room. "Did she have a boyfriend?"

"No. I told her she was too young for a boyfriend, and she agreed. She said that the girls at school who had boyfriends just ended up getting stressed and distracted, and she didn't want to have to deal with that. She was much better off waiting until after high school to start dating."

"She said that?"

"I said she was better off. She said that she didn't want a boyfriend while she was still in school."

"Didn't she go to dances? Movies? Places where she would be expected to have a partner?"

"A lot of kids her age don't date yet."

"No, that's true." Zachary certainly hadn't. Even if he had wanted to, he had moved from one school to another too often and was too shy or anxious to ask a girl out. Sometimes they flirted with him, started conversations with him, or even asked him out. Girls were sometimes attracted to the new boy, the shy boy, or one who was clearly the underdog. But he'd always been too awkward to follow through.

"You have the names and numbers of some of her friends?"

"Yes… I'll write them down for you."

CHAPTER 7

In the car, Zachary made a few more notes for himself. He wasn't a fast writer and wanted to get down as many of the thoughts and questions that were floating around in his brain as he could, before they flitted away. He turned to a new page and used the car Bluetooth to place a call to his friend Mario Bowman.

"Police Department, Bowman here."

"Mario, it's Zachary."

"Oh," Mario's voice warmed. "How's it going, Zach? I should come by and see the new apartment, now that you've had time to settle in."

"Sure," Zachary agreed. "Except the door was broken in by the cops this week, so I'm not there until it gets fixed."

"Oh, heard about that. That woman who was killed."

Zachary nodded. "Yeah. So that case is all wrapped up, and I'm onto something new today..."

"What is it this time?"

"Missing girl. Madison Miller."

He could hear Mario's keyboard clicks and pictured him hunched over at his desk, pecking away with two fingers. Bowman had been a good friend to Zachary, letting him stay at his apartment for months after Zachary's apartment was burned down. Much longer than the few days that he had initially agreed to. And when he'd helped Zachary to move in at the new apartment, he'd provided him with all kinds of kitchenware, towels, and other bits and pieces that he would need starting from scratch.

He was Zachary's go-to guy in the department to let him know what was going on with any cases he was involved with. Who was on a file, how to encourage them to cooperate, all kinds of little things that smoothed Zachary's way.

"Madison Miller. You're in luck, Campbell's got that one."

Joshua Campbell had been good in the past about the cases Zachary was investigating. He wasn't like some of the cops who had it out for any private citizen who might conceivably interfere with their cases. Zachary was careful not to get in the way of the police department and kept them informed about what he was doing. Campbell had given him a couple of tips in the past and put up with Zachary's questions and requests.

"Great. Thanks, Mario. I'll give you a call once I'm back in my apartment and we'll watch a game."

Not that Zachary was that interested in professional sports. But he enjoyed hanging out with Mario occasionally. He hadn't had many friends growing up, and consequently didn't have a lot as an adult. He needed to make sure he nurtured the friendships he had.

"I'll hold you to it," Bowman returned. "Talk to you later."

Zachary disconnected and tried Campbell. There was a click as it was picked up, then a pause before Joshua Campbell spoke.

"Zachary Goldman," he greeted. "Private eye."

"Yes," Zachary agreed. "I'm calling to interfere with another of your cases."

Campbell snorted. "Nice when everyone is upfront about everything."

"I've been asked to look into a missing persons case. Mario said it's on your desk. Madison Miller."

"Madison. Yes. Not much there, I'm afraid."

"She is missing."

"Well, she's not at home with her parents. I'm not sure that she's missing or that any law has been broken."

"What have you found?"

"It's all pretty run-of-the-mill. No indication of foul play. Looks like she just took off with the boyfriend."

"So there is a boyfriend."

"Mom and Dad told you that there wasn't one, didn't they? I suspect they didn't know. Madison kept it on the quiet. Parents weren't involved enough to know any better."

"Did you identify him?"

"Name is Noah. No last name, unfortunately. He didn't go to school with her, so no one could tell us his full name or any contact info. But her friends are all on the same page. She had been seeing him for a few weeks or a couple months. Spending more time with him and less with them or at school. It looks like she decided to take off with him."

"You don't think he did anything to her?"

"Nothing we've been able to find. Her car is gone. Backpack, electronics, toiletries, and clothing. That looks voluntary to us."

"But she is a minor."

"She is. And the file remains open. But I don't think she's going to be found unless she wants to be found. Maybe if they get tired of each other after a while, she'll show up at her parents' home again. Until then… we'll keep our ears to the ground. But we can't do anything without any evidence."

"No one at her work knew anything? When was she last seen? Mrs. Miller wasn't sure whether she had worked Saturday or Sunday."

"There is no job."

Zachary raised his eyebrows and stared at the radio. "There is no job?"

"Nope. Madison pulled one over on Mom and Dad. She never worked at Pedal Pushers. They'd never even heard of her. No application, no paychecks."

"Mrs. Miller said that she met Madison's supervisor. Had her phone number."

"Yeah. It was all a setup. I don't know who Mrs. Miller met, but it wasn't Madison's supervisor at Pedal Pushers."

Zachary tried to marshal his thoughts. He scribbled on his notebook, trying to break something loose. "Then where did she work?"

"She didn't. Her friends said she didn't have a job."

"Where was she spending her time, then? With this Noah?"

"Yep."

"Where was she getting money for clothes?"

"Couldn't tell you. This was a girl with secrets. She did <u>not</u> want her parents to know that she had a boyfriend. She built up all kinds of stories to keep them from finding out. In the end, she probably saw that the house of cards was going to come tumbling down, so she decided to get out while the getting was good."

Zachary nodded. "Yeah. Did you look at her social networks? Was she into drugs?"

"According to her friends, she liked to party. They're pretty tight-lipped about what that meant. Drinking?

Drugs? It pretty obviously meant spending time with this boy."

"Her social networks show her drinking."

"Not the ones I saw. They were squeaky clean."

"I managed to find some that her parents probably didn't know about."

Campbell blew out his breath. "Of course you did. You want to shoot those my way?"

"Sure." Zachary was happy to share whatever might help them to find Madison. "I'll email you. You didn't get any from her friends?"

"Certainly not. They probably figured they're doing her a favor, keeping her out of trouble. I'll have a little chat with them about obstructing the investigation."

"You want to hold off on that for a day or two? So I can talk to them first and see if I can get anything out of them? Sometimes kids are more likely to talk to someone… unofficial."

"I'll give you a day," Campbell said grudgingly. "But I can't be seen as letting this investigation slip. There's not much for us to go on, but if people think we're just letting it go cold, they get a little anxious."

"I'll try to catch them at school this afternoon."

"Be careful hanging around schools asking questions. People will think you're a pedo and we'll get calls…"

"I'll get the school's cooperation. Mr. and Mrs. Miller can confirm that I'm on the case."

"They hired you?"

"Uh… no."

Campbell waited for a further explanation.

"You remember the boy in the Salter case?"

"The mute. Sure."

"He goes to that school. He was friends with Madison. Or at least... had a crush on her."

"Ah. You're not making him dig into his college fund to pay you, are you?"

"No. Just a favor for a friend."

"Good for you. But don't take too many pro bono cases. Even you have to eat now and then."

Zachary had to chuckle at Campbell mothering him. He was not the motherly type. "Yes, sir."

Campbell laughed at himself. "Well, you've got the bones of the case. Anything else?"

"You'd tell me if there were some leads. Any indication of where she and Noah might have snuck off to?"

"No, probably not. We'd be following them ourselves."

"Yeah. Well, let me know if there's anything you think I should know."

"And you let me know if you make some headway. This is a police investigation."

"We have parallel investigations," Zachary corrected. "I will definitely tell you if there is anything you should know."

Campbell cleared his throat. It wasn't the first time the two of them had danced around the details of who was required to tell whom what.

"We'll be in touch, Zachary."

"I'll get you those social network profiles. Maybe you'll see something that I missed."

"Thanks. I'll be looking for them."

CHAPTER 8

Zachary talked to Mrs. Miller and had her call the school to explain who Zachary was and to ask them to cooperate with his investigation. The school was well within their rights to refuse but, in Zachary's experience, they would usually do whatever they could when the health and safety of one of their students were at stake.

But he still knew that they might shut him down as soon as he got there. Then he would have to stay outside of the school boundaries and figure out how he was going to get in contact with Madison's friends to ask them questions. Maybe Rhys would be able to help him.

He parked in the public parking, went through the main doors, and headed directly for the office so that he wouldn't set off any alarm bells. The school was far more likely to be well-disposed toward him if he were completely upfront about what he was there for than if he snuck around and tried to get a look around or started asking questions before checking in with the main office.

The secretary at the front desk had apparently been warned about his visit and knew what Zachary was there for when he gave his name.

"The principal will see you in just a moment. Have a seat, please."

Zachary sat on one of the uncomfortable seats in the waiting area, mentally sliding back to the many times as a child and teen that he'd had to wait in the office for a principal or guidance counselor or school resource officer to talk to him. Or to meet his social worker or to explain to a foster parent why he was in trouble yet again. A lot of uncomfortable chairs in a lot of school administrative offices.

A young woman approached Zachary, and he stood to shake her hand and greet her, expecting her to introduce herself as a student teacher or aide. But she introduced herself as Principal Lakes, surprising him. She looked too young to be the principal.

Lakes led him into her office and offered him a seat. The more comfortable chairs. If anyone were ever comfortable sitting in front of a school principal. Zachary always felt like he was a kid again, trying to explain why he couldn't keep out of trouble. He wondered if other adults felt the same way. Normal adults who hadn't spent so much time in the office as kids.

Principal Lakes looked Zachary over carefully. She smiled and cocked her head slightly. "You don't know who I am, do you?"

Zachary was taken aback. He shook his head. "Uh... principal of the school. That's... that's all."

"My predecessor here was Principal Montgomery."

Zachary blanked on the name. He thought about it for a minute, trying to place who Montgomery was and why he or she was so significant.

Then he remembered Rancheros, the cowboy bar. Sitting and watching a blond, middle-aged principal connecting with her date, an underage student from her school. Zachary felt the blood drain from his face.

"Oh."

Lakes nodded. "Yeah. Her. I recognized your name when Mrs. Miller called. I am very happy to have the chance to meet you."

Zachary nodded as if he were greeting her for the first time. "I… I'm glad to meet you too."

"It has been an uphill battle getting parents and students to trust me, after what Principal Montgomery did."

"I can imagine. But you've stuck it out."

"I have. And I think that, generally speaking, I've succeeded in earning their trust."

"Good for you."

"So," Principal Lakes leaned back in her chair, twirling a pencil between her fingers. "You're looking into what's happened to Madison Miller."

Zachary nodded. "Did you know her?"

"I try to know all of my students by name. Some of them I know better than others."

Zachary's face warmed. He had a feeling she sensed he was one of those students she would have known pretty well. "So tell me about Madison."

"She was a good student. Bright. Good worker. Friendly. Not mean or cliquey."

"Did anything change in the last couple of months?"

"There were some concerns expressed by her teachers. Her marks were down. She wasn't handing in homework. Was distracted in class." Lakes shrugged one shoulder. "It's not all that unusual. Adolescence is a hard time. Shifting hormones. Peer pressure. The work can be very difficult. Often there are family problems that the teachers are unaware of. Kids have a lot of responsibilities on their shoulders."

"And in Madison's case?"

"We talked to her parents. They said she was having difficulty with the school work. They were arranging tutors."

"And then she didn't show up for school this week."

"Yeah. We had the police here before school even started, asking questions and asking to speak to Madison's teachers and friends. Anyone who might know where she was or have some insight."

"I'm going to want to talk to the same people."

Lakes shrugged. "We'll do what we can. But we can't compel anyone to talk to you. It will be up to them."

"Of course."

"Did the police talk to Rhys Salter?"

"Rhys? Why would they talk to him?"

"He knew Madison."

"He might have known of her. Lots of people knew who she was. But he wasn't… in her circles. And as far as talking to the police… I don't know how much you know about Rhys, but he isn't verbal."

Zachary nodded. "I know him. But he can communicate, even if he can't usually speak."

Lakes grimaced. Zachary got the feeling that she hadn't spent much time trying to communicate with Rhys. "At any rate, the police did not ask to speak to him, and we didn't give them his name. Like I say, he wasn't in her circles. He might have had some classes with her, but they weren't close friends."

"I understand. If you could get me a list, and I could maybe start seeing some of them this afternoon before school lets out..."

"We can't pull kids out of classes."

"Can't you? When one of your students may be in danger?"

"The police didn't think she was in any danger. There was no indication of foul play. I really didn't get the idea they could do much of anything."

"What did you think? Did you think it was in keeping with Madison's character to disappear like this?"

"I thought it was strange," Lakes admitted. "But like I say... things had been a little rocky lately. It wasn't the first thing that was out of character."

"What else?"

"Like I said, her marks. Being inattentive in class. She just seemed... her demeanor was different. I don't know how to describe it. More secretive. Agitated. Mmm..." Lakes squinted her eyes and pursed her lips, looking for a word. "More intense. Emotional."

"Did you consider drugs or alcohol?"

"It's one of the things we're trained to watch for, so of course we considered it. Asked her if she needed any assistance or counseling in dealing with substance abuse issues... That didn't go anywhere. We didn't have any evidence."

"Did you know she had a boyfriend?"

Lakes frowned. "In the school?"

"No. The police said he didn't go here."

"Then I really wouldn't have any way to be aware of it. Unless he came into the school."

"She was dating him during the period when her marks dropped and these other changes occurred."

Lakes gave a small smile. "Boyfriends can be distracting. And relationships can be so intense at that age. They can be all-consuming. And you can't tell a teenager that in a year she won't even care about him anymore, but her school performance is something that will impact her path for years to come..."

"But it's pretty hard to convince someone to give up a romantic relationship for the longer-term good," Zachary suggested.

"Or even just to cool it a bit. Yes. I've learned that you can't talk kids out of these first loves, even in cases where they are clearly incompatible or abusive."

"Did you think Madison's boyfriend was abusive?"

"I didn't know he existed, so no." Lakes considered the question. "I don't recall ever seeing Madison with bruises, or hearing any concerns about abuse from her teachers. But there are a lot of kids in the school, and we can miss the signs."

"Did you have any other concerns about her? Just her academic performance?"

"Yes, that was the only thing that had been expressed. Her disappearance took me completely by surprise. I didn't know of any problems she was having at home. But even the most together student can be masking serious problems. Sometimes they can be homeless for weeks before someone realizes there is a problem. Reputation is paramount to teens."

Zachary could remember the fear of being different, being bullied because he was in foster care or a group home, because his clothes were worn or out of date, having gone through several kids before he inherited them, of being on meds, having ADHD, PTSD, and learning disabilities. He would have given anything to be normal, whatever he thought that was. As an adult, he didn't worry as much about how he looked to others. But he also wasn't in close quarters with a few hundred critical peers every day.

"If you think of anything else, will you give me a call?" Zachary put one of his business cards on her desk.

"Of course."

* * *

The first interviewee was Madison's homeroom and English teacher, who happened to have a prep period when Zachary began his interviews. Mrs. Wright was an older teacher, gray hair pulled back from her face in a ponytail.

She studied Zachary intently, and he worried for a moment that she might have been one of his teachers decades ago. Then she relaxed.

"I've never met a private investigator before."

"Well... I'm just an ordinary guy. Like anyone else. In real life, private investigators aren't usually hard-boiled, gun-toting womanizers."

"You've ruined my fantasies."

Zachary smiled. "I know you've already talked to the police, but I was hoping you wouldn't mind going over some of the same ground again."

"I would like to help you find Madison and make sure she is okay."

"That's what it's all about. Had you noticed any changes in Madison lately? Did you have any concerns?"

"She was definitely going through changes… but I didn't have any reason to think that it was anything other than the usual adolescent stuff. Development is so rapid at this age. They're bouncing between childhood and becoming responsible adults, and that's a big gap. Add in hormones and increasing scholastic demands, and lots of kids lose it."

"Did you think Madison was losing it?"

"I knew she was having problems. Her marks had dropped quite drastically. She was not turning in her work. She was distracted in class."

"Her parents said that they would get her tutoring?"

"That was what they said."

"Did you think that was a good solution?"

Mrs. Wright considered the question. "No, I was not confident that was going to solve the problem. I didn't think it was just a matter of her not understanding the work and needing to be walked through the process."

"What did you think the problem was?"

"I thought she was… experimenting. Some kids go off the rails, rebelling and trying out the things that their parents have told them to stay away from. It can be a long journey back when they get too deeply into drugs or some other alternative lifestyle."

"You thought it was drugs?"

"That was just one possibility. There are many of them. Lots of ways to self-destruct." She narrowed her eyes at him. "I imagine you have explored some of them."

"A few," Zachary admitted. He'd made some fairly disastrous choices in his life.

"She was tired in the middle of the day. Sometimes dozing off, particularly after weekends. Mondays you might as well give up on trying to reach her."

"Could it have been her job? Working too much in addition to school?"

"Could have been. Her parents threatened to make her quit if she didn't straighten up. I got the feeling that there was an emotional aspect to it."

Zachary frowned. "What does that mean?"

"Hard to explain. It wasn't just that she was tired and not doing her homework. She was… emotionally labile. Anxious, angry, defiant… and then other times, silly and giggly. Showing off her latest fashion statement. It was more than just being overtired. If it was because of work… then I would wonder whether she was being bullied or harassed at work. She was so distracted and emotional."

That sounded about right for a teenager. Zachary had felt out of control all the time, unable to corral his brain or his emotions to be a calm, productive student like so many of his peers seemed to be. But then, he had been bullied and harassed almost constantly, both at school and in his various homes.

He made a few notes in his notebook, trying to capture the thoughts and questions that flitted around his brain. It gave him a chance to breathe and distance himself from the childhood memories.

"Madison didn't ever talk to you about what was wrong, or say anything that gave you a clue. Maybe you overheard her talking to a friend, but didn't hear the rest of the conversation. Just... some sense..."

"I'm afraid not. I wish she had come to me. I would have done whatever I could to help her. But I don't know what was wrong or why she disappeared. I'm sorry."

"You've been very helpful. Thanks for answering my questions. And let me know if you think of anything, or happen to hear anything. Keep your ear to the ground…"

"I'll do my best," Mrs. Wright promised, and gave him a brief smile. "Thank you for taking this on. I hope you're able to find her."

CHAPTER 9

Madison's three best friends were apparently joined at the hip. They came together into the conference room that Zachary had been allowed to use, and wouldn't be divided.

"I'd really like to talk to you separately," Zachary told them. "I'm sure the police interviewed you separately, didn't they?"

"You're not the police," the redhead challenged him.

Zachary shook his head. "No. I'm a private investigator. It would be most helpful to me—and most beneficial to Madison—if you would talk to me one at a time. Sometimes there are little things that you remember differently, and they wouldn't come out if you all talk to me together, because your recollections color each other's memories. I don't get three individual stories; I get one blended-together story."

"We're meeting together," the tallest girl, a brunette, declared, and she put her arms around the waists of her two friends. They, in turn, threaded their arms around her, so that they were all holding on to one another. Zachary looked at them helplessly. He didn't have any authority over them. He couldn't force them to talk to him, much less to do it separately. He counted himself lucky that all three had agreed to meet with him at all. He had expected at least some pushback, with one of them saying that Madison deserved her privacy and if she wanted to run away, he should just stay out of it.

The girls looked satisfied that they had talked him into it, and each took a chair.

"What are your names?" Zachary asked with a sigh. He felt overwhelmed and outnumbered. Another reason he didn't interview witnesses together was that it was so distracting to have to watch three different people and their reactions at the same time. It was hard enough to keep his thoughts and questions straight when he was only talking to one person. Three felt a little like trying to hear all of the words of a three-part round at the same time.

"I'm Josette," the redhead offered.

Zachary wrote it down.

"I'm Leila," the taller brunette said.

"And I'm Katelyn." The smallest girl, another brunette.

"How long have you each known Madison?" Zachary puzzled over whether to assign each girl a page in his notebook and flip back and forth as they answered, or whether to make three columns, one for each of them, or just to try to tag each note and keep track as they went along.

Josette and Katelyn had known Madison the longest, since some time in the early elementary school grades. Leila had gone to a different elementary school and didn't know Madison until she graduated to middle school.

"So you know each other pretty well."

They all nodded their agreement. Zachary tried to peg their moods before getting deep into the interview. They were more cheerful than he would have expected. With Madison missing, he would have expected them to be sad, maybe tearful. They weren't laughing and smiling, but they didn't seem to think that anything bad had happened to Madison.

"What's been going on with Madison lately?"

They exchanged looks, questioning each other with their eyes. Zachary could feel the communications passing between them, even if he couldn't interpret each look.

"What do you mean?" Josette asked.

"Several people have said that Madison was having trouble lately. Schoolwork, inattentive, and now this… you didn't notice anything different about her?"

More looks, trying to decide what they should tell Zachary. They clearly knew plenty, but they weren't sure that they wanted to divulge anything to him. They were closing ranks on their friend, shielding her from the investigation. Did they know where she was? Had they been in communication with her or had she told them ahead of time that she was planning to leave?

"She was good," Katelyn said. "Really. Maybe she wasn't doing so good with her schoolwork, but who does? I mean, it's hard, and where is it going to get us? Does it really matter how we do now? No one is going to be looking at these marks when they're deciding whether we can get into college or be hired for a job. All they'll be looking for is a diploma. Maybe SAT scores for college. That's all. No one cares what you got in high school English."

"It would be a problem if she failed."

"She wasn't failing. She was still passing. And the final exam is half the mark, so you can totally coast during the semester, as long as you do well on the final."

"So you think she wasn't doing well just because she didn't care about marks? She figured she could just study for the final and be okay?"

Katelyn shrugged. "I don't know. It isn't like we talked about it. We didn't talk about marks and studying. Sometimes we worked on homework together, but most of the time when we were hanging out, it was to have a good time together, not to do work."

Zachary nodded encouragingly. "What did you like to do together?"

"Go to the mall and shop. Girl talk. Internet stuff. Chill out bingeing on TV series. Whatever. Normal stuff."

"Did you spend a lot of time outside of school together?"

"Yeah, sure." Katelyn looked at the other girls for their reactions, and they nodded to back her up.

"Sure," Josette agreed. "Every day. We were like the four musketeers."

"What about her job?"

A more significant shared look. They knew that Madison didn't really have a job. But they didn't know that Zachary knew.

"Yeah, we all have jobs. But we make it work. We're not working all the time. Our parents wouldn't let us. It's just a few hours. You have to leave enough time for homework and socializing."

"Where did Madison work?"

"Pedal Pushers," Leila said instantly. They didn't have to look at each other for that one. They had the story established already.

"Are you the one who pretended to be her supervisor at Pedal Pushers?"

"What?"

"When her mother met the supervisor and got her phone number. Was that you?"

Leila looked at Zachary with wide eyes. She didn't look at the others, realizing that he was already on to them and knew at least one of the secrets.

"I don't know what you're talking about," Leila said in a thready voice. She swallowed and swiped at her eyes like she was crying, but Zachary didn't see any tears.

"Madison didn't work at Pedal Pushers. That's just what she told her parents."

"She did!" Leila insisted.

Zachary shook his head. "She didn't. Even if I didn't figure that out, the police have already checked. There is no record of Madison working at Pedal Pushers. Or of the girl she said was her supervisor."

They all just sat there, looking at him. Zachary wrote down a few notes and cleared his throat. "Lying about it isn't going to help Madison. If she's in danger, I want to help her. If you think it's going to get her in trouble, then tell me that. I'm not stupid. I'm not going to tell her parents or the police something that's going to get her in trouble."

Leila's head was bowed as she looked down at her hands, but she raised her eyes to Josette to see what she thought.

"Fine," Josette said in an exasperated voice, like Zachary was the one being stubborn instead of them. "She didn't work at Pedal Pushers."

"One of you acted as the supervisor?"

"No. Mrs. Miller knows all of us. We got someone else to do it. Someone she hadn't met. And we're not turning her over to you. She didn't have anything to do with Mad disappearing."

"But you were all in on it. You all knew that it was just an act that Madison was putting on for her parents and schoolteachers."

"Yeah."

"Why did she do that?"

"So she could spend time with her friends."

Katelyn spoke up. "Parents think it's okay to spend twenty or thirty hours a week at a job, but they don't like you spending that much time with your friends. They start to complain that you're not putting in the effort. So Madison wanted to keep her parents off her back. Make them think that she was working hard, instead of hanging out with friends." Katelyn gave an unconcerned shrug.

"So you want me to think that she was hanging out with you," Zachary said. "With her girlfriends."

"Yeah. She was," Josette said challengingly, looking Zachary in the eye. Her eyes stayed steady, as if she weren't lying. But he knew better.

"She wasn't with you. She was with Noah."

That got all of them. Their eyes widened and they looked at each other for help again. They put their heads together and there were furious whispers between them. Arguing about who had told, who had given it away. Somebody must have, for Zachary to know.

"She didn't hide it that well," Zachary said. "She was with him quite a bit. The police know his first name, but not his last name." Zachary looked at each of them. "Do you know Noah's last name?"

There was no need for them to check in with each other for that answer. They all shook their heads independently.

"None of us know his last name," Josette asserted. "I don't know if Madison even knew it. He was sort of... an enigma." She liked the word. He saw her smile, enjoying the chance to use it.

"An enigma," Zachary repeated. "Is that what he called himself? Or was that Madison's word?"

"Madison's, I guess. I don't think he ever called himself that." Josette wrinkled her nose. "It's not the kind of thing you can call yourself, is it? It's like saying that you're the smartest one in the room. You don't get to choose what other people call you."

"And Madison said that Noah was an enigma."

Josette nodded. The other girls followed suit.

"He was so hot," Leila said, and giggled.

Josette and Katelyn elbowed her. "Leila!"

"Well, he was—don't tell me that you weren't both thinking it. He was so..." She shrugged, having difficulty expressing it. "He was older, and he was good looking, and no one knew where he had come from or why he hooked up with Madison. He just... no one had ever seen him before, and then suddenly, he was there, and he and Mad were getting really hot and heavy, but it was like they'd always known each other. He really loved her."

"You didn't know him before? None of you did?"

"No. None of us."

The others both confirmed.

"Where did they meet?"

"Just..." Leila looked at the others for help. "Just here, right?" she made a motion to encompass the school. "He was just, like... there one day. Outside the school, like he was waiting for her. He knew her name. Stopped her to talk to her..."

"He said that he'd seen her at a party," Josette offered, inserting her memory. "At a party or a football game; I don't remember. Just that he already knew who she was, because he'd seen her before, but none of us knew him. He was just there. Out of the blue."

"Like an angel who fell from heaven," Leila said in a dramatically dreamy voice, and then laughed. The others made motions for her to stop and settle down.

"Leila!" Katelyn said in a low, stern voice.

"You don't know where he had seen her before?" Zachary looked at them each in turn. Leila sobered, putting on a serious expression, and they each denied knowing where Noah had seen Madison before.

"So, he approached her. Just called her name. And then suddenly, they were boyfriend and girlfriend?"

"Well... pretty much," Katelyn admitted. "I don't remember where he took her the first day. Out for ice cream, I think. Something like that. Something nice and sweet. And he was. He was always treating her like she was something special. Opening doors for her and taking her out."

"And buying her things," Leila added. "He, like, was always giving her something."

"Clothes?" Zachary suggested. "Handbags? That stuff?"

The three girls nodded. If anything, they looked jealous. They wished they could have had a boyfriend like Noah. A sweet, handsome older guy who liked to buy them things. What girl wouldn't like that?

"How much older than Madison was he?"

"Mmm… I don't know." Katelyn looked at Josette. "Did she ever say? I don't think she knew. None of us did."

"But he was for sure?" Zachary checked.

"He didn't go to school here, and this is the only high school in the area. So he must have graduated."

"Or dropped out," Leila added.

"He didn't drop out," Katelyn said, rolling her eyes. "He was smart. And he had a job. He must have, right?

Otherwise, how could he get her all of those presents? And it had to be a good job, because some of that stuff was really pricey. No high school guy can afford to spend that much on his girlfriend."

Zachary nodded and wrote down a few details. He had seen some of the labels on the clothing and, as a private investigator, he'd learned clothing brands and designers in order to be able to tell how much people were worth. Or if they were suddenly spending more than they should. The brands he had seen in Madison's closet had been big names. And those were the ones she had left behind.

CHAPTER 10

"What did the two of them do together?" Zachary asked. "You said that they were getting pretty serious."

They avoided his gaze, each pretending to be looking at something else in the room. The light. The table. Her fingernails.

"How serious were they?" Zachary asked. "From the pictures I saw, I'm guessing they were spending a lot of... intimate time together."

"What pictures?" Josette demanded. Her eyes were blazing. "What pictures are you talking about?"

"Pictures that other people took of her. And pictures she took herself and posted on social media accounts." He paused. "Not the ones that her parents knew about."

Leila started to flush. She rubbed her forehead. She turned her face away from him, shielding it with her hand, as if she could keep Zachary from seeing she was blushing.

"Yeah, well, her parents wouldn't have wanted to see that, would they?" Josette said in a hard voice, like if Madison's parents thought they had anything to complain about, they should just get over themselves. "She had to keep it a secret."

"They were pretty heavily involved."

"They were together. A couple. That's what couples do."

"High school couples?"

"Sometimes, yeah. Why would they be any different than adults?"

"On the weekend, Madison had a sleepover Friday and Saturday nights," Zachary said.

"Yeah, so?"

"She wasn't sleeping over with one of you, was she?"

"The cops already asked that. And they would know, wouldn't they? They could look at her phone records or something. They'd know she hadn't been with one of us."

"Besides," Leila said. "Her mom already called everybody. None of us knew where she was. If she'd been with one of us, Mrs. Miller would have figured it out."

"Unless Madison told you not to let her mom know."

Leila shrugged.

"So she was with Noah," Zachary said.

None of them argued with him.

"How often did she stay overnight with Noah?"

They all looked down, silent. Not telling Madison's secrets.

"Every weekend?" Zachary suggested.

She was with him every day after school when she was supposed to be at work. Every weekend when she was supposed to be at work. All of those nights that her parents thought she was sleeping over with girlfriends. He had worked his way into her life so that she was spending every spare moment with him.

"How much time did she spend hanging out with you the last few months? The four musketeers?"

Katelyn was sniffling and wiping her nose. The first of them to show any emotion. "Not very much anymore," she admitted. "We were always telling her that she needed to spend some more time with her sisters. I mean, boys come and go, right? But your girlfriends. They're your real friends."

"It bothered you that she wouldn't spend time with you anymore?"

"No," Josette said. "We all would have done the same, if Noah had picked us. It's stupid to say that we wouldn't. If we wanted her to spend time with us, it was just because we were jealous and didn't like to see her with him all the time."

"No," Katelyn sniffled. "It wasn't just that."

Zachary let them sit and stew for a few moments. He scribbled in his notepad. Not because he had anything to write down, but because he wanted them to think about it for a bit. He didn't want to rush the questions. They would tell him more if they volunteered it.

"It wasn't just because we were jealous," Katelyn repeated. "She was... different."

"Yeah, because she had a boyfriend," Josette declared.

"No. It wasn't just that. I mean... she was..." Katelyn's forehead wrinkled. She tried to tease the emotion out. "She wasn't always happy. You know. If I was with a guy like Noah, I'd be over the moon. I'd be happy all the time. I'd be gloating to my girlfriends about how awesome the sex was and how great the clothes he bought me were. I'd be bragging to everyone about him."

"And Madison didn't?"

Katelyn shook her head. The other girls didn't disagree.

"Why do you think that was? Was it just her personality? Maybe she was shy about it?"

"No. Maybe. Who knows what's inside people's heads. Maybe she felt guilty for being with him. Because her parents wouldn't have liked it."

"Or...?" Zachary let the word hang, hoping one of them would take it and come up with some ideas. Because he had no idea how teenage girls talked with each other about their boyfriends. He thought it was unlikely that Madison would be happy all the time. She had trials and troubles just like any other teenager. Even with the perfect boyfriend, she still had to deal with school and homework and her parents. With parents who wanted her to straighten up and start working with a tutor to improve her marks, when all she wanted was to be with her boyfriend.

Both the principal and Mrs. Wright had said that Madison had an attitude. That she had mood swings. They thought that something was wrong. Not that she was spending too much time with her boyfriend. But that she was using drugs or was upset by something going on in her life.

"If it was me, with a boyfriend like that, I wouldn't be complaining," Josette said.

"What did she complain about?"

Josette considered. She rubbed the center of her forehead, frowning. "She'd say that she had to go out with Noah. Act like she didn't want to. If it was me, I'd want to. No one would have to convince me of it. And after a weekend together, she'd be, like, all crabby and tired. She'd say how exhausted she was, and we'd be like, we know why you're so tired. And she'd just... be all mad about it."

"Was he possessive of her? Forcing her to go with him?"

They looked at each other, shaking their heads. "He was always really soft-spoken in front of us," Katelyn said. "She never said that he was making her. But she was... sometimes she'd act like she was having the time of her life. There were the new clothes, and booze, and parties, and she'd be on top of the world. She'd post selfies all over and make everyone jealous. And then she'd be down in the dumps, complaining about how we didn't understand what it was like, and she just wanted to stay home for once, or hang out with us girls. But she had to go with Noah, because he was her boyfriend."

"She scared me sometimes," Leila said. "She'd get really dark moods, say that she was no good and her life was crap and that if her parents knew what was going on, they'd kill her. We all tried to get her to just chill. You know, who cares what parents think? In a couple of years, they won't be able to dictate any rules. They'll be calling us, begging us to come home and spend time with them. They'll forget all about anything we did soon enough."

"But she'd get really down," Katelyn agreed. "You couldn't talk her out of it. I thought..."

Zachary waited for her to finish, raising his eyebrows expectantly.

"I guess I thought it was the alcohol," Katelyn said. "Some people are really downers when they've had a lot to drink. Or maybe she was using something else, and felt bad when she came down off of it."

"Was she using drugs?"

None of them volunteered any knowledge of Madison's drug use.

"I figured she probably was when I saw some of the pictures on her social media," Zachary said. "She looked pretty out-of-it in some of those pictures. Glassy-eyed."

"I don't know." Katelyn shrugged. "She never said she'd tried any hard stuff with me. Just alcohol. Maybe some pot. Nothing much."

"None of you knew if she was taking anything else?" Zachary looked from one to the other, but couldn't detect any signs they were lying. "Okay. So we don't know. Maybe she was, maybe she wasn't."

He was silent, letting the minutes tick by. The girls were moving around restlessly, uncomfortable. No longer united on all points. Thinking their own thoughts and what they ought to tell.

"What do you think happened to Madison?" Zachary asked finally.

"I don't think anything happened to her," Josette said loudly. "I think she just decided not to go home. She'd had enough of being harassed by her parents and teachers, and just decided to stay with Noah. Why not? What could anyone else offer her? She had it good with Noah. Had everything she could possibly want. Why torture herself by going to school and putting up with her helicopter parents?"

Zachary didn't answer. He looked at the other girls, waiting for their responses. Would they just follow Josette's lead? Or would they venture opinions of their own?

"Yeah," Katelyn agreed, in her small, sniffly voice. "I don't think anything happened to her. I'm sure she's okay, wherever she is. She's just with Noah somewhere. She didn't want to come back. Like Josette said."

"Find Noah and you'll find her," Leila agreed.

But no one knew where to find Noah. No one even knew his last name.

CHAPTER 11

Zachary talked to Madison's guidance counselor about the boy. He kept the rest to himself, but he wanted to hear what Mr. Carlton thought about Madison's romantic relationship.

"I never saw her around the school with any boy," Mr. Carlton declared, running a hand through the hair on top of his head to make sure that the thinning strands were all arranged with the maximum possible coverage. "I wouldn't have guessed that she had a boyfriend."

"Apparently, he was older. He didn't go to the school."

"Oh. Well, that explains it, then."

"But he picked her up here. And when he originally sought her out, it was after school, when she was just leaving here. He told her that he knew her from somewhere."

"Maybe he did," Carlton agreed with a shrug.

"You don't find it disturbing that he would hang around the school grounds looking for her? Don't you have security out there, keeping an eye on things, making sure that there aren't strangers loitering around eyeballing the kids?"

Carlton grimaced. "It isn't like it's an elementary school, with creepers coming around to try to snatch little kids. It's not like that at all. Our students are almost adults. They're old enough to look after themselves. And to tell us if there is anyone hanging around that they feel threatened by. We don't exactly have security or supervisors patrolling the school grounds, chasing off anyone who doesn't look like they belong."

So the answer was no. They didn't have any security protecting the students from predators who might be looking for a mark.

"But you said that she's been dating this guy for a couple of months," Carlton pointed out. "If he was some creep or she was getting a bad vibe from him, she wouldn't have kept going out with him for months. She would have told him to take a hike. Told the staff if he was hanging around here when she didn't want him to. Our kids get lots of instruction on being assertive, speaking up, not staying in an abusive relationship. We have whole courses of study on it."

Zachary didn't point out that, trained or not, a teenage girl was not necessarily mature enough to recognize red flags in a relationship and know how to get out safely if something didn't feel right. Children were socialized to do what they were told. Not to rock the boat. To get along and not hurt people's feelings. All of those lessons were deeply ingrained and at odds with whatever relationship training the school was trying to do once they thought the students were old enough to make some of their own life decisions.

By the time Madison realized that she wanted out of the relationship, she might have been in too deep to get herself out.

* * *

With Rhys's permission, Zachary filled Vera in on the fact of Madison's disappearance and his agreement to do some inquiries to see if he could find out what had happened to her. Rhys sat cross-legged near the fireplace, staring down and running his thumbnail through the nap of the carpet while Zachary and Vera sat on the couch.

Vera's eyes got wide as Zachary gave a broad outline of the case. "Is that what's been bothering him?" she murmured, looking at Rhys. Rhys could clearly hear them, but he gave no sign that he knew he was being talked about. Vera looked back at Zachary, shaking her head. "I knew something was on his mind, but there are so many things for teens to worry about. I just didn't know what it was."

Zachary nodded his agreement. Neither of them said the obvious—that it was that much harder with a teen who was mute. Even when he wanted to share something, it was an effort for him to get his point across. His grandmother understood him better than anyone, but there was still a communications gap.

"I wanted to talk to Rhys about it some more," Zachary told her. "Just the two of us... but I didn't want you to wonder what was going on. I thought maybe we could go out for pizza, but you don't like me taking him out..."

Vera was too worried about rumors getting started about Rhys. A white man who had been in the news too much recently taking out a vulnerable black teen would be an easy target for gossip.

"You can order pizza here," Vera suggested. "The two of you can hang out in the kitchen or wherever you want. I'll give you guys your space."

Zachary knew that was as good as he was going to get. And, all things considered, it was probably better than going out. In a pizza joint or arcade, there would be a lot of distractions, things that could interfere with the already tricky flow of information between the two of them. Rhys could feel safe and secure in his own territory. It wasn't the casual environment that Zachary had initially envisioned, but maybe it was better that way. Zachary's questions were going to be far beyond casual.

He nodded. "That would be great. Sound good, Rhys?"

Rhys nodded, not looking up.

Vera quizzed him on what kind of pizza he wanted, but Rhys waved off her questions and pulled out his phone. He waggled it at her questioningly.

"Fine, order it on your app," Vera agreed.

Rhys tapped away at the phone. He pointed to Vera and raised his eyebrows.

"I'll have some of whatever you get. I'm not picky."

He switched his gaze and his pointing finger to Zachary.

"Same here," Zachary said with a shrug. "I'll eat whatever you get."

Rhys held his gaze. He knew from past experience that Zachary wasn't likely to eat much.

"I promise I'll eat a slice of whatever kind of pizza you get."

Rhys held up two fingers. Vera chuckled.

"Okay, two slices," Zachary agreed. He hoped that it wasn't a huge pizza, where each slice was the size of a personal pizza. He'd be hard-pressed to get through one of those, let alone two. He was on meds that took away his appetite and left him nauseated much of the day, so trying to gain back the weight he had lost was a constant battle.

Rhys bounced his hand, emphasizing the two fingers.

"Yes, two slices," Zachary repeated.

Rhys went back to his phone, tapping in whatever information the app needed. Eventually, he got up and walked over to Vera, showing her the screen. She took the phone from him, adjusting the distance and squinting at it. She didn't take a long time to read before handing it back. "Yes, that looks fine, Rhys."

Rhys held it up for Zachary. He didn't want to take the time he would need to read through the long list of toppings densely listed on the screen. He glanced over it for anchovies or hot peppers, but it didn't really matter even if Rhys had added them. Zachary had grown up eating different foods at each home he went to, and had become an expert at forcing down what he didn't like. What was the point in fighting with a foster parent or supervisor when all he had to do to show compliance was swallow a bite or two of the meal?

"That looks great," he told Rhys, handing it back to him.

Rhys frowned, and Zachary knew that he had responded too quickly. Rhys knew he hadn't really read the list of toppings. He turned the phone back around, craning his neck to look at it and point out one word to Zachary. Zachary followed Rhys's finger. He smiled.

"Yes, I'm okay with pineapple on pizza."

Rhys turned the phone back toward himself, grinning. He tapped through the next few screens to place the order.

CHAPTER 12

Zachary chatted with Vera while they waited for the pizza, with the occasional contribution by Rhys. Zachary was waiting until they had the pizza and Vera was out of the room to ask Rhys more questions about Madison.

When an extra-large, steaming, fragrant pizza arrived at the door, Rhys set it on the counter in the kitchen and got out a stack of paper plates.

"Oh, I can wash a few dishes," Vera protested, heading toward the cupboard.

Rhys shook his head, handed her a paper plate, and pointed her in the direction of the pizza. <u>No dishes. Your night off.</u>

Vera made a few further noises of protest, but they weren't genuine objections, and she helped herself to one of the large slices.

"I'm going to use a TV tray and put on a movie for myself," she informed Rhys. "A grandma movie that wouldn't interest you. You boys keep the food in here so I don't have to clean it out of the carpet or the bed. Put the leftovers in the fridge."

Rhys nodded obediently, giving her a little grin. After Vera left the room, he grabbed a couple of cans of soda out of the fridge and handed one to Zachary. They sat down at the table with their paper plates and Rhys took his first piece. Zachary tried to pick out the smallest piece of what remained. They were definitely too big for him to eat two full slices, but he would do his best. If he left part of the crust of the first and ate a few bites of a second piece, then he would make good on his promise to have two slices, even if he hadn't actually eaten more than one slice. He took his first slice of loaded pizza and had a bite.

"Mmm. Very good," he told Rhys. It was a privately-owned pizza restaurant rather than one of the big chains. "I can see why you picked them. Really good crust, too."

Rhys nodded. He mimed stirring and then tossing a pizza.

"Hand made?" Zachary guessed. "Made fresh?"

Rhys nodded and pointed at Zachary.

Zachary took another bite. He didn't pull his notepad out. If he did, he was sure to get food on the pages. But he didn't really need his notes to start the conversation with Rhys.

* * *

"So, I talked with some of Madison's teachers and friends today."

Rhys nodded. He'd obviously already been aware of that. Zachary had intentionally not interviewed Rhys at the school at the same time as he had conducted interviews with her other friends. From what he had seen and heard, Rhys and Madison had not been close friends, and certainly not boyfriend-girlfriend, and he didn't want to shine a light on Rhys and cause people to speculate as to what his relationship with the missing girl was.

"I'm getting a better picture of what was going on with her before she disappeared."

Rhys continued to eat. Zachary hadn't yet asked him a question, and he didn't have anything to agree or disagree with.

"You had concerns about Madison."

Rhys nodded.

"Before she went missing."

Rhys paused in his consumption of the pizza, then nodded again, slowly.

"What, specifically, were you concerned about?"

Rhys thought about it, chewing and taking another bite. Zachary didn't rush him. They had all the time they needed. Eventually, Rhys pulled out his phone. While he ate, he paged backward through photos. Zachary couldn't see any dates or anything that would tell him the timeline Rhys was browsing through.

Eventually, Rhys found the picture he was looking for and brought it up on the screen. He slid it across the table to Zachary.

Zachary looked down at the picture. It was just Madison. No Noah in the picture. No laughing friends. Not a posed family picture. But it didn't look like a selfie, either. Rhys had probably taken it himself and, since Madison was not looking directly at the camera, it had probably been a candid shot that she was unaware of.

"Okay." Zachary slid it back across the table after studying it for a moment. The Madison in that picture looked like any other student. Calm, pleasant, just a student sitting at her desk on a regular day. She was wearing jeans and a simple peach blouse. Not one of the designer items that Noah had given her later.

Rhys flicked through the photo album again, moving forward this time. He found another picture and slid it in front of Zachary.

It was another picture of Madison at her desk, from the same angle. She and Rhys apparently attended a class together, and both shots were taken while they were in their assigned seats. In the second shot, Madison had her head down on the desk, sleeping.

There were other subtle differences.

She had on quite a bit of makeup. In the first picture, she'd had some on, but it had been understated. It was much more dramatic and noticeable in the second picture. Her clothing was different. The camera angle didn't make it easy to identify, but Zachary could tell by the stitching around the shoulder that it was a higher quality product. Not something produced in a factory in huge quantities. Designer. He remembered the pictures he had seen on her social networks. More daring outfits. Off the shoulder or strapless, short skirts or shorts, cleavage. Formal cocktail dresses and sporty shorts and halter-top sets.

She didn't have the same glow in the second picture as she'd had in the first. Maybe it was just because she was sleeping, her face slack, not much of it visible to the camera. He wouldn't call her gaunt, but it looked like she had lost weight. She looked worn. But maybe she was just tired from a weekend of partying.

Zachary nodded at Rhys. "Her teachers said that she was tired, particularly after weekends. She wasn't going home. Her parents thought she was sleeping over with her girlfriends, but she was with Noah. You think she was partying too much?"

Rhys shrugged. He took the phone back. He didn't look at Zachary as he fiddled with it some more. He eventually handed it back to Zachary.

The triangle in the center of the screen told Zachary that it was a video. He tapped it and watched. It was a noisy environment. School had let out, and there were kids everywhere, chattering and on the move. The camera centered on a female figure, and Zachary realized it was Madison. She was walking more slowly than the other girls she was with, hanging back from them slightly, looking tired and sore like she'd been working out. There was a part in the crowd and Madison's friends moved out of the way as Noah came onto the scene. Zachary saw Madison flinch when he reached out to her. He put his arm around her waist and, at first, she looked like she was going to pull away from him. He moved his arm up to her shoulder and pulled her closer, squeezing her against his side. Madison's arm went around his waist and they kissed.

Madison, looking over Noah's shoulder, saw Rhys. "Are you recording me?"

Noah turned around. His face got red. "What the...? You can't go around recording people! Put it away, retard!"

"Noah!" Madison reprimanded. "Don't call him that!"

He glared down at her. "We don't want that idiot recording us. Why does he always have to be around you? Tell him to take a hike. You already have a boyfriend."

Madison looked at Rhys, warning him with her eyes. But also apologetic. "You better go, Rhys."

The video ended.

Zachary dragged the time indicator back to the beginning of the video and watched it a couple more times. He looked up at Rhys. "Do you think he was abusive?"

Rhys spread his hands wide.

"Did you ever see her with bruises? Do you think he was hurting her?"

Rhys shook his head.

Zachary pondered this. "Is there anything else?"

Rhys considered. The fact that he didn't answer immediately told Zachary that Rhys still hadn't shared everything he knew or was concerned about. "If you want me to help Madison, you have to tell me what you know."

Rhys took a big bite of his pizza and chewed it. Zachary rolled his eyes.

"It's not like you can't talk with your mouth full," he pointed out.

Rhys grinned broadly and covered his mouth to keep from spitting any of the pizza back out. He touched his phone, not doing anything at first, just considering it. Then he picked it up. Zachary watched him quickly finding the app he wanted and looking through a list. Eventually, Rhys pushed it back toward him. Zachary saw the messaging app that Rhys often used to communicate with him. But it was Madison's name up at the top of the screen.

Zachary saw a cartoonish puppy—Rhys seemed to have a thing about dogs—with the words 'you okay?' scrawled across the bottom of the graphic. He scrolled down and saw Madison's answer on the left side of the screen.

Rhys, I can't talk to you. You need to stop messaging me.

There was a single word question from Rhys. Safe?

And Madison's reply. I don't want you getting involved. Leave me alone.

Zachary looked at the date stamp on the message. The Friday before Madison's disappearance. He slowly pushed the phone back to Rhys. "You haven't heard from her since?"

Rhys shook his head.

"Tell me what you think."

Rhys just pointed to his phone, raising his brows. He shook his head.

Zachary sighed. Rhys couldn't tell him what had happened to Madison. He'd done everything he could to keep track of what was going on with her and to try to help her, but she had turned him away. He was the only one who had reached out to her personally, but she had refused.

"I'll do my best. If you have any ideas of where she might be, I need to know. It's already been a few days… the police didn't find anything and the trail is cold."

Rhys picked up his phone and returned to the video of Madison and Noah together. He pointed to Noah.

"They'll be together," Zachary agreed. "But no one knows who Noah is. They don't even know his last name."

Rhys pointed at Zachary. He was the private investigator. He should be able to find Noah. Rhys was counting on it.

CHAPTER 13

It had been a long day. Zachary was determined to spend the evening relaxing with Kenzie, not thinking about the case. He couldn't work twenty-four hours a day to find Madison. As much as he wanted to find her and make sure she was safe, he couldn't be expected to find her the first day. It was going to take some time, and he would be more likely to make the proper connections if he got the rest and regeneration he needed than if he ran himself into the ground.

Kenzie had texted him to let him know she was on her way home and he could come over any time. Zachary stopped in front of her house and waited a few minutes, breathing deeply and trying to put all of the squirrely thoughts trying to distract him to the side so that he could focus on his girlfriend. If he was going to repair the relationship with Kenzie, he needed to give her the time and attention. Ignoring her or piling all of his troubles onto her wouldn't help them.

When he got into the kitchen, Kenzie was making a sandwich. She smiled over at him.

"You should probably eat too. You can handle making a sandwich, can't you?"

"I already ate."

"Sure you did. I mean a real meal."

"I did. I had pizza with Rhys." Zachary put a hand over his aching stomach. "He forced me to eat way too much."

"He forced you, did he?"

"I'm not used to eating that much. You wouldn't believe the heartburn I've got."

"Well, it's probably a good thing. You need to get fattened up."

"Mmm. Not like this."

"Have a seat. I won't make you eat, but you do have to visit."

Zachary was happy to sit down at the table with her.

"How's the case going?" Kenzie asked.

"I probably shouldn't talk about it. Why don't you tell me about your day?"

She sat down and took a big bite of her sandwich. "Why shouldn't you talk about it? Confidentiality? You already told me who it was."

"I just think... I shouldn't just talk shop. We should spend time together, talking about something other than work."

Kenzie chewed, considering. "I've always enjoyed talking shop together. There aren't too many guys that you can discuss corpses with."

Zachary snorted. He covered his mouth and cleared his throat. "Is that the only reason you want me around? So you can talk about corpses?"

"Well, it's a definite draw."

"I don't have any to talk about yet. And hopefully... I won't on this case."

Kenzie sobered. "Yeah, I hope not. That would not be a good resolution."

"But you could tell me about your bodies if you want to."

"With how much you've eaten, that might not be a good idea."

Zachary touched the notepad in his pocket. After fiddling with it for a moment, he pulled it out and looked at it. "I haven't had a chance to gather all of my thoughts and process everything yet."

"Do you have any good leads?"

"I don't know yet. The boyfriend is definitely key. But no one knows his full name. He didn't go to the school. He just showed up one day and… picked her up."

"She must have met him sometime before that."

"He said that he recognized her from a party. But her friends had never seen him before, so how likely is that to be true? If she'd been at a party, they would have been with her. And she didn't remember him. If they'd hit it off at a party, wouldn't she have remembered?"

"Depends how drunk she was at the time."

"I don't think they'd met before."

"So, what...? You think that he was lying? Why?"

"I think it was just a line. He wanted to pick her up."

"Possible," Kenzie agreed. "But why? He had to have seen her somewhere before. Then we're back to where."

Zachary shook his head. "I don't know. That's one of the questions to be answered. Along with his name. And where they have disappeared to."

"Do you think it was foul play?"

"Rhys doesn't think that Noah was hurting her. So that leaves... either she went off with him of her own free will, or he kidnapped her. I talked to Campbell. They didn't come across anything in their investigation that suggests there was any coercion or violence. And I didn't find anything like that either. So that means she chose to go."

"Girls do. All the time."

"Her parents have been calling her. The police have been calling her. Why hasn't she answered her phone? Why haven't the police tracked the signal to figure out where she is? Did she ditch it?"

"How about Rhys? Has he tried to call her? Or her girlfriends. They must have at least tried to find out if she was okay and what they should tell her parents."

"She told Rhys not to contact her anymore. He'd apparently... stepped on some toes. Hers or Noah's, I'm not sure which."

"So he didn't try to get her when she didn't show up on Monday and the police said she was missing and started asking questions?"

"Not that he told me. I'm not sure that's the same as no."

Kenzie nodded her agreement. She had a drink of water and another bite of her sandwich. "Does he know more than he's telling you?"

"I think that's true of every teenager. And every client, for that matter. They almost always have something they are hiding. And even if they are not being deceptive... they still know something they don't realize they know." Zachary flipped to random pages in his notebook, not reading anything. "I think that he's told me everything he believes is relevant."

"So, what's your next step? Or do you know yet?"

"Not yet. I need to think about it. Sleep on it."

"We'll have to make sure you get some sleep tonight, then," she teased.

"We could go to bed now and get a head start."

"Let's not move too fast," Kenzie warned, putting the brakes on.

Zachary should have been happy about that. He was the one who had been feeling uncomfortable with too much intimacy and needing more time. He was the one who had held back and caused the separation in the first place. But he felt a twinge of anger and frustration at Kenzie's words. She had been ready for more. She was the one who had gone to Zachary's foster father, Mr. Peterson, to ask him personal questions about Zachary's previous relationships and the possibility of past abuse. She was the one who had gone to Zachary's ex-wife to ask her about how he'd been between the sheets—specifically, whether he had dissociated when they had been together.

And now she was putting on the brakes?

Even though he knew it was a good idea for them to go slowly and take things one tiny step at a time, it still made his already-sore stomach feel tighter and heavier.

He picked up his notepad and held it in front of his face to hide any change in his expression from her. She had become too proficient at reading him.

"I might be able to track some mutual friends. Madison mostly spent her time with Noah, but the girlfriends were invited to a couple of parties and remembered the names of a few other people who were there. I might be able to connect through a friend of a friend of a friend."

"Uh-huh."

"And I have a couple of pictures with his face. I'll run facial recognition and see if I can track down his social media. Even if he's using a pseudonym, that might give me his friends or followers list, and I can get closer."

"Yeah."

Zachary looked at Kenzie. She was watching him closely. Serious again. Zachary cleared his throat and closed the notepad. "So, that was my day. You get anywhere with the stiffs you work with?"

Kenzie gave a forced laugh, and launched into a description of her day and the various puzzles and problems that she had run into. Zachary watched her eyes and her mouth as she spoke, hearing very little of what she said.

CHAPTER 14

While he had expected Kenzie to want to spend all evening together, she suggested that they take a break so that she could read her personal email and check a few things off of her list.

Zachary was very bad at keeping lists, but it had been a while since he had touched base with Lorne Peterson, an old foster father, so he decided to take the opportunity to see if he was at home. He didn't have the energy to deal with a Skype call, so he just dialed the number on his phone and stretched out on the couch, listening to the line ring.

It was only a few rings before Mr. Peterson—Zachary still had trouble thinking of him as Lorne—picked up. "Zachary! Good to hear from you," he greeted cheerfully.

"I know it's been a few days," Zachary admitted. "So I didn't want to let it go too much longer."

"How are you keeping? Everything good?" the older man asked tentatively.

"Actually... I'm calling from Kenzie's house."

"Kenzie's?" Lorne's voice was surprised. "Well, that's a surprise. The two of you decided to give it another try?"

Zachary shrugged, his face heating. He was glad no one could see his face. "Yes. I tried giving Kenzie a call when I needed a place to stay for the night, and she accepted..."

"Nothing like the direct route."

"I didn't know if she would say yes. She didn't want to talk about getting back together before. But..."

"But obviously you managed to talk her into it. So does that mean you're officially back to being a couple again...?"

"I don't know what it means... I guess so. We're giving it another try."

"Well, you don't know how glad it makes me to hear that. That's fabulous news."

"Yeah, I'm pretty pleased about it."

"The two of you make a good couple. You really seem like you're good for each other."

"I don't want to jinx anything, but I think... I don't know. I'm hoping."

"Now you make sure you talk," Mr. Peterson's voice took on a stern, fatherly tone. "You can't communicate and keep your relationship healthy if you don't talk to each other. Even when you don't feel like it. You know you tend to bottle things up and not talk when you need to."

"Yeah."

"You could try some family therapy. Get a good couples counselor. Or a group. Or just ask your regular psychologist. But someone else in the equation could help the two of you to connect better with each other. Figure out what things need to be brought out in the open."

"I don't know if Kenzie would want to do that."

"Do what?" another voice asked.

Zachary's eyes flew open. He hadn't realized that Kenzie was walking by while he was talking on the phone. He choked, looking at her, trying to figure out what story to tell her.

"I, just... I was just talking to..."

"Tell her the truth," Mr. Peterson said in Zachary's ear.

Zachary licked his lips, considering. There was only one way to find out whether Kenzie would object to couples counseling or not.

"Lorne said... we should do some... therapy together."

Kenzie nodded. "Not a bad idea," she agreed. She continued on her way into the kitchen. "Say 'hi' for me."

Zachary breathed out. His eyes burned with tears and there was a lump in his throat. He coughed, trying to maintain his composure. Kenzie really didn't need a man who burst into tears at the slightest provocation.

He swallowed and tried to continue the conversation with Mr. Peterson.

"Yeah, she says she'd be okay with that. She says 'hi' to you and Pat."

"There, you see? All you had to do was ask. Pat...?" he called to his partner somewhere else in the house. "Kenzie and Zachary say hi."

There was an answer from far away, casual and faint. Then Zachary heard a clear 'wait a minute!' The next time Pat spoke, it was obvious he was right next to Mr. Peterson. "Kenzie and Zachary? Together?" His tone was eager and excited.

"Yes. Zachary is at Kenzie's house as we speak."

"Well, that's awesome! Congratulations, Zach!"

Zachary murmured his thanks, blushing even more than he had when he had told Mr. Peterson that he and Kenzie were back together. He listened to Pat and Mr. Peterson banter back and forth for a minute, and then Pat departed to go back to whatever project he was working on.

"As you can tell, we're both just tickled that the two of you are trying again," Mr. Peterson said. "That's really good news."

"No guarantees," Zachary warned. "I really want it to work, but I can't guarantee everything is going to work out like I want."

"I know, Zach. Trust me. I've been through my own relationship issues. When Lilith and I split… well, you know how hard that was. I knew that it wasn't going to work, that I was just lying by staying in the relationship. But it was so hard to admit it and leave a relationship that I'd been in for so many years."

Zachary remembered showing up on the Petersons' front steps to get some help developing his photographs—something Zachary was allowed to do even though it had been a long time since the Petersons had been his foster parents—and Mrs. Peterson informing him that Lorne no longer lived there. It had been a huge shock. He had known they weren't well-suited to each other but he'd never thought that they would get divorced.

None of it had made any sense until he had met Patrick Parker and realized that Mr. Peterson had, as he had said, been living a lie for all of those years.

But Lorne and Pat had now been together for over twenty years, and it was hard to believe that there had ever been a time when Zachary had thought that Lorne and Lilith Peterson had belonged together.

"I'm going to do my best to make it work," Zachary repeated.

"Good. How about the two of you come down for Sunday dinner this weekend? It seems like forever since we have seen you, and as for Kenzie, I'm not sure if we've seen her since Christmas."

"It hasn't been that long," Zachary protested. He thought back, trying to think of each time that he'd been down to visit Lorne and Pat. He was sure Kenzie had been there at least once since Christmas, but Mr. Peterson was right, it had been a long time since she'd taken the trip with him. "I'll ask her if she's free."

CHAPTER 15

Noah was a ghost. Zachary did several image searches to find him on the internet or track down his social profiles, and couldn't find him. He tried the image alone and in combination with the name Noah, but probably Noah wasn't even his real name.

It seemed highly unlikely that a boy of his age would not have any social networking profiles. But of course, some parents refused to let their kids set up social network profiles while they still lived at home, and people advised that young people not use their own pictures for the profile pics. Gamers liked to use avatars. But Noah didn't strike Zachary as the gamer type. Gamers didn't generally show up at high schools to pick girls up. They were the ones at home, leveling up virtually rather than in real life.

Zachary switched to looking at photos on the school's website. Kids who had participated in special events, spectators at football games, everything he could find. Maybe he had been a student teacher, and they had misjudged his age. Anything was possible.

That led to another thought, a leap that Zachary hadn't taken before. He dialed up Campbell's number and lucked out when Campbell answered.

"Zachary. What's up? I wasn't expecting to hear anything from you so quickly. You haven't found our missing girl already, have you?"

"No. Working on it, but I'm not even close yet. I had a question, but I suspect it's one that you can't answer."

"Why don't you call someone who knows, then?"

"I think you know; I just don't think you can say."

Campbell laughed shortly. "Okay, exactly what does that mean?"

"I'm trying to track down Noah. Anything about him. But I'm not pulling anything up."

"Welcome to the club. We weren't able to get an ID on him either."

Zachary considered that for a moment. But Campbell wasn't necessarily telling the truth.

"It occurred to me that it's possible he's an undercover cop."

"A cop? No."

"Is that a real 'no,' or just an 'I can't tell you that' no?"

"It's a real no. As far as I am aware, Noah is not an undercover officer." There were a few seconds of silence from Campbell. "But it's not an avenue that we considered. I haven't contacted any feds about whether they have someone in the area. Could he be DEA or another branch? I have no idea. I can put out a query, but chances are, they won't answer me."

"Yeah." Zachary leaned back in his seat, a less-than-comfortable chair at a diner, stretching. "They aren't generally too forthcoming about that kind of thing."

"You giving up?"

"No. Just rethinking. I can't find a social profile. But he's out there somewhere. Someone has seen him. What about traffic cams or surveillance at the school? Did any of them capture him? His license plate?"

"It's on the list of things to check, but it takes a lot of man-hours to go through video logs, if they caught anything, and if they were kept. We can't check every license plate of every car spotted in the area. We have to see one of the two of them getting into the car or driving it."

"I have the phone numbers of a couple of her friends. I can see if any of them can tell me what kind of a car he drove."

"I think I have that in here somewhere. Hang on a moment."

Zachary could hear Campbell rifling through papers and a few key clicks as he looked for the information. It was a few minutes before he came back on.

"Yeah. White late model Subaru is what I've got."

"So you wouldn't have to look for any car, just the white Subarus."

"Or anything that looks like a Subaru. Because witnesses honestly are not that good with cars. And there's always a possibility that he changed what he is driving, too. If they planned to disappear, he might very well have swapped for something else to lead us in the wrong direction."

"True," Zachary admitted. "But it wouldn't hurt to check the white Subarus."

"We will if we have the time and manpower. Until then, it's going to have to wait."

"If he took her, or if she went with him, then his address is the best place to look for her. Unless you've got some good leads in another direction. Without his name or identity, the best bet is to find his license plate."

"We'll get to it when we can," Campbell repeated.

"But you don't think there's anything to worry about. You think she's just shacked up with this guy somewhere."

"There's no law against disappearing."

"There is for sheltering a runaway."

Campbell grunted. "Not worth our while."

Zachary cast around for some other way to find Madison. "How do the phone logs look? She must have called this guy a lot over the last couple of months. So you must know his cell number."

"Looks like he's changed it a couple of times. My guess is that he's buying burners and not refilling the minutes. Use one up, switch to a new one."

"Are they registered?"

"Fake info. No joy there."

"What about location? Can you see where his phone was most of the time? You must be able to narrow down the location he lived and worked in by where the phone is most often."

"Need a warrant to get that kind of information from the phone company. And who knows how long it takes them to get it to us. Or how useful it will be once we get it. It's not like we live in a big city. It's not going to narrow the search radius much."

Zachary sighed. "Well, I'll keep up the search the best I can."

* * *

The only concrete information Zachary had on Noah was what he looked like. He had pictures of the boy's face. An internet search had not turned up anything, but that didn't mean it was a dead end. Zachary messaged Rhys to send him all of the pictures he had of Madison and of Noah.

Of course, Rhys wouldn't send him everything. Judging from what Zachary had seen so far, Rhys had a lot of pictures of Madison. He'd been watching her for a while, maybe for months before Noah showed up on the scene. Since the school year had started, if not before that. As far as Zachary could tell, Rhys had a crush on Madison and had demonstrated some borderline stalkerish behavior in taking candid pictures and videos of her.

Zachary could understand it. He'd had problems of his own with letting Bridget go after they had broken up. And with having to keep tabs on where Kenzie was and what she was doing when they had first started to go out together. Since he had gone back to therapy and had some med changes, he'd been able to curb most of those impulses.

Most of the time.

So he knew that Rhys wasn't going to send him everything, but Zachary needed as many pictures as he could get.

Rather than trying to send them all individually, Rhys set up an online album and shared it with Zachary, which allowed him to browse through them and pick out the ones that would work best for his purposes. Armed with several different shots of Noah and Madison, he started his search near the school, working in an outward spiral.

He approached everyone on the street or in the commercial establishments that he could, showing a couple of pictures of Noah and asking whether they knew him or had seen him around.

There were plenty of 'no's,' people who avoided him, and those who wouldn't look at the pictures. But he did get a few who looked at the pictures and thought that they had seen Noah around, or who identified other people in the pictures that they knew or had seen around. Zachary noted the information in his notepad, along with a list of addresses where people had recognized him. He would plot them all when he got back to his computer and, hopefully, there would be some clusters that would help him to nail down where Noah lived or worked or hung out. People had to know him.

If the police had thought that there was foul play, then they would have at least published Noah's picture to ask for information on him as a person of interest. But they didn't think that Madison was really missing. Putting Noah's picture in the paper, under those circumstances, could be considered inflammatory. It could ruin the reputation of a young man who was innocent of any crime.

At a bodega half a mile from the school, the elderly man at the counter frowned at the picture Zachary showed him and used his fingers to zoom in on Noah's face, and then on Madison's and each of the other people in the background of a party shot. Hopefully, people Noah and Madison hung out with on a regular basis. Eventually, the man put the phone down on the counter. He jabbed a finger at Noah's face.

"I know this boy. He comes from the neighborhood. Been here a few years. The girl, I don't know her. Not one of the ones I have seen him with."

Zachary was a little surprised by that. "You've seen him with other girls?"

"He's been here a few years," the man repeated. "He has one girlfriend all that time?"

"No," Zachary agreed that wasn't likely. Noah had only been with Madison for a couple of months. If he'd been there for a number of years, then of course he'd gone through a string of other relationships. "No, just the last little while."

"I have not seen him for a long time. Maybe a year. Used to be here all the time, when he was younger. Some of these other boys," he poked his finger at some of the other faces in the party crowd. "Some of them, I know. Seen them here. Not in here," he clarified, indicating his store, "out there... other places. On the street, in cars, in bars. Not a good crowd."

A knot tightened in Zachary's stomach. He nodded his understanding. "Do you know where any of them live? Any idea, even if it's not a particular building, just the area...?"

"Him... used to live with his grandma. Red brick building a few blocks down." He gestured in the direction of the building Noah had lived in with his grandmother. "But no more."

"Does she still live there? His grandmother?"

"No. She died. Then he was gone, not living here anymore. But then I started seeing him again. Maybe he was back for a while."

"With these guys?" Zachary suggested, indicating the other young men in the picture.

The old man scratched his bristly chin, thinking about it. "Yes, maybe. Them or other boys like them. Trouble."

"What kind of trouble?"

He shrugged. "Can't say. I'm not looking for any trouble."

"What are they? A gang? Friends? Organized crime?"

He shrugged his shoulders. "I keep my head down. Don't make waves. But that doesn't mean I don't have eyes. These boys are trouble. If he is in with them now..." He looked down at the picture. "Looks like he is. That means he's trouble too."

"Okay. I appreciate it. You know where any of the others live?"

"Don't know. Come back at night, check out the bars and clubs, maybe you see some of them. But you be careful. They hear you're asking questions..." He trailed off and grimaced. "I don't think you want to be on the wrong side of that crowd."

Zachary nodded. "Thanks. I'll be careful." He hesitated. "The girl, though, you've never seen her?"

"I don't remember. Not a good idea to stare at girls you don't know."

CHAPTER 16

Kenzie wouldn't like the idea of Zachary going back to bars and clubs at night to find known troublemakers related to the missing persons case, so he didn't tell her. He said only that he had to go out to do some interviews.

If she knew, she would have told him it was stupid to go into a dangerous situation without a gun or some kind of weapon to protect himself. But Zachary would never carry a gun, and he knew that whatever weapon he took into a situation could potentially be used against him. There wasn't any point in trying to explain that to Kenzie. She already knew, but that wouldn't stop her arguing about it.

His guts were in knots as he got out of his car to check out a few of the hot spots. He could have taken a tranquilizer, and it would have helped to settle him down, but he didn't. There were some situations in which hypervigilance and his ADHD distractibility were advantages rather than disabilities. He needed to be aware of everything going on around him. He needed to key in on everything that was off by the slightest bit. Every detail could be significant. Any change in the environment, every person approaching him, could be a danger. And he would be aware of it all.

He took a few deep breaths before going into the first club. His chest and abs were tight with tension. He tried to look casual and relaxed, to smile and slouch and mask the anxiety. He circulated for a few minutes before going up to the counter. Took the temperature of the room, walked to the men's room in the back in order to scout out any extra security, any private areas in the back. He wasn't part of the club scene and, even if he had been, he probably would have avoided the area.

There weren't any obvious hazards. It might be a slightly tougher crowd than he was accustomed to, but there weren't obvious weapons or illegal activities going on. Any drugs were below the tables. Any illicit business being conducted there was quiet, not out in the open. After checking out the bathroom, Zachary wandered out to the bar. He ordered a beer because ordering a soft drink when he was there by himself might be suspect. He wouldn't do much more than wet his lips; it was only a prop.

He turned on his stool as he raised the glass, looking around. He had a good memory for faces, so he didn't need to refresh his memory looking at the pictures he'd already looked at a hundred times that day as he canvassed. He scanned faces, not meeting anyone's eyes or looking in any one direction for very long.

He saw one young man he recognized from a picture of Noah partying. Just one, but that was a good start, especially when it was the first place he had entered. He sipped the beer and put it down on the bar. There was a mirror on the wall behind the bar, and he used it to spy on the boy without looking directly at him.

He was loud. His manner confident, almost bullying. But not quite. He behaved pleasantly toward the small party he was in and toward the wait staff. Brash and full of smart comments and stories. Enjoying himself. Unconcerned with anyone outside of his bubble.

He downed several drinks before having anything to eat. Zachary suspected he was already high on something. Loud and talkative, having a great time.

There were mostly men in the group. A lower percentage of women, not a one-to-one ratio like there would be if they were all couples. The women with them were young, dressed well, showing plenty of skin and acting happy and eager to please. They all had drinks.

It wasn't easy to nurse his one beer for long enough to keep an eye on the party. Zachary ordered wings and fries and a coke as well, eating slowly, pretending he was using social apps on his phone and enjoying himself.

The girls weren't paired with specific men, but slowly circulated among them. They danced several times, different songs with different men. They sat in different seats, carrying on conversations with different members of the group. They walked down the hallway that led down to the bathrooms in the back at different times, in various combinations.

Zachary sighed, eating a few more fries. Something was going on and, as the old man at the bodega had pointed out, if he got into the middle of it and started asking questions, he was going to get in trouble.

* * *

It was late when Zachary got home. He counted himself lucky that his door had been fixed and he was back at his own apartment instead of Kenzie's house, and therefore wouldn't have to explain where he had been all night.

Until he got to his door and saw a sticky note on his door, Kenzie's way of warning him that she was there, so he didn't have a heart attack or call the police when he realized someone else was in the apartment. He smiled at the little heart that she had drawn on the note, and tried to pretend that her presence there hadn't just added additional weight to the already heavy burden he was carrying. Which felt like it was right in the center of his chest and stomach instead of on his shoulders, where people normally talked about responsibility or emotional burdens. He felt more like a heavily pregnant woman looking like she was about to burst with all of the additional weight he was packing. The stomach cramps only added to the mental image.

Zachary shook his head, trying to shake the distracting thought of Bridget and her pregnancy out of his mind. He didn't need that interfering with his life too.

He tried to be very quiet so he wouldn't wake Kenzie up. They hadn't talked about getting together. He had thought that she would be happy to have her space back to herself after a couple of nights with him.

Apparently, she wasn't looking for space.

He didn't turn any lights on, feeling his way around and occasionally using his phone screen for a bit of light if he needed it. He got ready for bed, plugged his phone in on the bedside table, and slid into the bed as quietly as possible. Kenzie tended to sprawl right in the middle when she was asleep, but this time she was keeping to her own side of the bed.

"I didn't expect you to be so late," Kenzie whispered. She turned over to face him.

Zachary's heart thumped. He didn't want to have to explain all that he'd been doing that night to her. As far as she knew, he could have ended up doing surveillance for the night. He didn't always come home.

"Oh, hey. You didn't stay awake all night, did you? Have you had some sleep?"

"Yes, a little. Pretty restless, though. I was worried about you."

"You don't need to be worried. Everything is fine."

She reached out in the darkness, feeling for his body, and put one arm gently around him, cuddling up to his chest. Zachary relaxed, letting go of the tension. He put one protective arm around her and sighed. He loved when she snuggled up to him like that. He breathed in the scent of her body and her shampoo, resting his face against her head.

"I do worry. I know you said that you were going to be out doing some interviews tonight, but I thought... that would just be during the evening. Unless you're interviewing someone on night shift."

"Some interviewing. Some investigating. Watching people, trying to sort out what's going on."

"Mmm-hm." Her voice was sleepy. "Did you figure anything out?"

"I think so. But I'm still not sure where to go from here. I will have to think about it."

"Sleep on it," Kenzie murmured.

"Yeah." Zachary kissed her hair. "That's what I need to do."

He listened to her breathing, long and regular. She was soft and relaxed in his arms, slipping quickly back into sleep.

But for him, sleep was always elusive, even when it was late and he was tired. Rather than clouding and slowing down when he got tired, his brain seemed determined to jump into a higher gear, worrying over everything that was on his mind; the case, his relationship with Kenzie, anything he had said or done during the day, whether he had made any mistakes, if he had failed to do something he was supposed to. If he was a good enough human being.

Some days, just the part about being a human being was hard enough.

He lay there holding her and tried to slow his breathing down to match hers and join her in sleep.

CHAPTER 17

Despite how late he had been getting home, Zachary was up in the morning before Kenzie. He was having his second cup of coffee and poring over pictures of Madison and Noah when she got up. Kenzie rubbed her eyes, yawning.

"Don't you ever sleep in?" she complained.

Of course, she already knew the answer to the question, and they had discussed it many times before. Zachary did go through periods of depression when his body and brain wanted to nothing but sleep, or when a stressful situation became too much and he just shut down, but the rest of the time... sleep was elusive, and didn't stay for long.

But Kenzie wasn't actually looking for an answer.

"What time did you get in last night?" she asked after pouring herself a mug of coffee from the carafe sitting on the burner. "I know it was late, but I didn't look at the clock."

"I'm not sure. Maybe two."

"Too late. At least I got back to sleep after that. Sometimes when I wake up at night, my body decides it's time to get up, and I have trouble settling in again."

"Mmm-hm."

"What about you? You must have been exhausted. Did you fall right asleep?"

She probably already knew the answer to that one too.

"No. Took a while."

"You should have stayed in bed a while longer."

"Wouldn't have been able to get back to sleep. I would have just kept you awake tossing and turning."

"Maybe I could have helped you relax and get back to sleep." She put an arm around his shoulders, bending down to brush his cheek with a kiss. Zachary turned his head to kiss her on the lips, which tasted like morning breath and coffee. He closed his eyes and savored her closeness.

"I wasn't expecting you to be here."

"Well, my place felt so empty after you left. I decided I didn't want to knock around there alone."

"So you ended up knocking around here alone instead."

"I wasn't expecting that, but it was okay. When I'm here, I can still… feel you around me. Because this is where your stuff is, you kind of… leave an imprint here. But at my house, there isn't enough of you there to feel that."

Zachary considered the comment. Did that mean she wanted him at her house more often? That she wanted him to leave some of his things in her closet, drawers, and bathroom? That she wanted him to move in?

He tried to cut off the train of thoughts. He didn't want to push the relationship too fast. They would just end up derailing again.

Kenzie sat down on the couch and pulled a blanket throw around herself. "Did you make some progress last night, then? Was this on your missing persons case, or something else?"

"The missing person. I... have some thoughts about it. Spotted a couple of people that she or her boyfriend partied with. Watched them for a while."

Kenzie nodded. "Did you ask them if they had seen her? I suppose you would have started with that if they had said so."

"I didn't approach them. Just watched."

Kenzie raised an eyebrow. "You can't get very far if you don't ask. You didn't think it would be productive?"

"I was warned—and I could see—that they were not the kind of people who would want to share anything with a private investigator or the police. You have to be careful who you talk to."

"Yes, you do," Kenzie agreed, with a direct gaze that reminded him he had done just that when trying to track down Jose. He had not been as careful as he should have been. He had walked into it as if none of the people he was talking to might actually be dangerous.

Lesson learned.

He ducked his head, trying to suppress the red flush he knew was spreading across his face. As if he could prevent it just by trying.

“I’m glad you’re being careful,” Kenzie said. “I don’t want you to get hurt.”

Zachary nodded.

Kenzie leaned forward, looking at Zachary’s screen. “Is this her? Do you mind if I look?”

Zachary considered, then decided it was okay. Kenzie helped him out with other cases. They were used to bouncing ideas off of each other. He got up from his desk chair, disconnected his laptop, and took it over with him to sit beside her on the couch.

"I'm looking at the pictures of her and her boyfriend, looking for people who reoccur across several pictures, and also looking for clues in the pictures as to where they were. The more information I can get about where they were spending their time, the more easily I'll be able to find where they are now. Chances are, they will have gone to places convenient to her house, the school, or his place. There should be two or three clusters of locations."

"And whichever one is not close to her house or the school should center on his place."

Zachary nodded. "Unless he is also close to the school. It sounds like he grew up close to there, but I don't know if he still lives in the area. And Madison doesn't live far from the school. So I might just end up with one big cluster."

"Nothing is ever for sure," Kenzie agreed.

"Yeah."

Zachary swiped to the next picture in the gallery. They both studied the faces and any location clues. Kenzie pointed to a window, through which a two-color neon sign was visible.

"That looks like it's close to Old Joe's Steakhouse."

Zachary closed his eyes, picturing the street and everything he could construct around it. Kenzie was right. There was a bar on the same street with a similar two-color neon sign. He wrote down the photo number and a notation next to it. "I'll check that out."

Kenzie had her phone with her. She tapped at it, zooming in on the steakhouse on a map until she got down to street view. She panned around, looking for the neon sign and for what was across the street from it.

"If it's that sign, then that was taken in something called Union Public House."

Zachary added this to his note. "Never been there. Have you?"

"No. Kind of a seedy place, if I remember right. Not the kind of place I'd hang out with the girls."

Zachary nodded. The bits of the interior caught in the pictures were not fancy. Dim lights, black and white photos on the wall, not a trendy place you might expect young adults to go. "They seem to show up in a wide variety of places. Some of them higher-class, and some of them… cesspools."

Kenzie laughed. "I guess young people are always trying out new places, experimenting, seeing where they are comfortable. Playing different roles. Trying to find out where they feel comfortable. What fits."

"Yeah."

Zachary swiped to the next picture. In each one, they looked for clues about the location.

"These aren't all pictures you got from Rhys, are they?" Kenzie asked, frowning.

Zachary immediately understood her concern. Rhys was especially vulnerable. And too young to be attending at bars and clubs.

"No. I pulled a bunch of them from Madison's social networks. Selfies that she or her friends took. She shouldn't have been there either... must have false ID."

Kenzie nodded. "I'm just glad Rhys wasn't."

* * *

By the end of the day, Zachary had identified as many locations as he could from the pictures. Some of them helpfully had geographical locations in the metadata, but most of the ones that Madison had taken did not. She or someone else had been smart enough to shut off geolocating on her phone.

He reviewed the different locations, trying to identify clusters that would help him to track her down. The pins were scattered much more broadly across the city than he would have expected. It was only a small city, not a big metropolis like in other states, but he still hadn't expected Madison to have had the run of the whole city.

There were also a few people who he had spotted in a number of pictures. There were, of course, several with the friends that he had interviewed at school. But there were also a handful of men Noah's age or older who made repeat appearances at different parties or clubs. Zachary tagged the various subjects. He'd try finding all of their social networks and then comparing friends lists. "Probably time to put those away," Kenzie commented when she saw Zachary rubbing his eyes. "You remember how late you worked last night. You need to give your body and brain a rest tonight."

"Every day that I let pass without finding her..."

Kenzie's lips pressed together. She nodded. "I know. I don't like thinking of her out there alone. But remember... the police don't think she was kidnapped.

If she's just somewhere with this boy… then it's not like when Bridget was missing, or when you were… you know."

"But we don't know that."

"I know. But at least you've made progress."

Zachary nodded. He wasn't going to be able to go on another bar crawl looking for Noah and the other men and girls that appeared in the pictures. If he didn't get enough rest, his brain would let him down. He wouldn't be alert enough to spot danger or clues. He wouldn't be able to make the split-second decisions that might be needed to save his own life or Madison's.

CHAPTER 18

Zachary knew that it was probably too early in the day for Madison and Noah to be out and about. If they were spending a lot of time partying, they probably slept until noon or later. But that didn't mean he couldn't look around and ask questions at some of the locations around the clusters he had identified. If he were lucky, maybe he'd be able to get a line on them before they even woke up.

People were not nearly as willing to help him as they had been when he had canvassed around the school. He met with a lot of blank stares and clenched jaws, and more than one person told him to get lost. Though not that politely.

He was glad he was there in the morning instead of at night. Experience told him that this was probably not a neighborhood he wanted to be wandering after dark. Not without a posse of his own.

He approached a woman sweeping the sidewalk in front of her store. "Excuse me, ma'am? I'm looking for a missing girl..."

She rested, leaning on the broom, looking at him. Zachary approached with his phone held low, so she wouldn't think he was trying to make some kind of move on her. Both hands visible, no weapons. Nothing threatening. He was glad in such situations that he was so short and slight; it would have been a lot harder to portray a nonthreatening appearance if he were six feet tall and two hundred and fifty pounds.

She studied his face for a moment before looking down at the phone, still wary, but willing to look.

"She's been missing almost a week," Zachary explained. "There have been some sightings in the neighborhood; I'm trying to find out where she might be staying."

"Staying? If you think she's just staying somewhere, why are you looking for her?"

"She might be in danger. I don't know whether she is being held against her will. If she is... I want to help her."

"And if she isn't?"

"Then I'll just talk to her. I'm not here to cause trouble, just to give her a hand, get her reunited with her family if she wants."

The woman studied Madison's picture. "I don't know. She looks like a lot of girls. They come and go."

Zachary nodded understandingly. "Is there someplace they tend to live? Maybe an apartment where a few of them share the rent, different girls rotating in and out?"

She started to sweep again, moving slowly, the movements of the broom short. Away from his feet, but Zachary still felt like she was trying to shoo him away.

"Who knows where they go, or why?"

"Right. So you don't know? Maybe a building you've seen girls at before? Young girls like this?"

She had been with other girls in the pictures. New friends, not the girls from school. Drinking buddies. Party girls. A new lifestyle. One that didn't fit with her home life.

"I didn't tell you anything," the woman muttered.

Zachary looked at her in confusion for a moment. "Okay," he agreed. "You didn't tell me anything. Send me on my way."

She nodded. Her eyes flicked down the street. "The brick apartment building down there. That's where they go. That's where I see them."

Zachary didn't turn his head. He looked out the corner of his eye. "I'm just asking!" he said in a louder voice, one meant to be overheard by any watchers.

The woman batted at his shins with the broom. "Just get out of here. I don't know anything."

He withdrew, not looking her in the face again, muttering under his breath about crazy old bats and striding across the street, shaking his head.

He stopped there, taking a deep breath. He pulled a water bottle out of the courier bag over his shoulder and took a drink, taking a glance down the street at the building she had referred to.

Was the woman overly cautious about reporting anything that went on in the neighborhood? Or were they being watched? Was she aware of something going on with the girls in that building and didn't want to be seen tipping him off?

There were plenty of old women who were just paranoid or delusional. She might be one of them. But she was not that old. And she had seemed to have it together. She hadn't been warning him about squirrels or unicorns or Martians trying to monitor their brainwaves.

Zachary took a few more swallows of his water, looking around for anyone who might be paying attention to him. He didn't see any watchers. But that didn't mean that there weren't any. They could be inside the buildings, watching through cracks in the blinds. They could be out of sight, listening and monitoring everything going on in the neighborhood. Zachary put his water bottle back away and walked down the street. He stopped to tie his shoelace, looking around from another angle. He went into a convenience store and bought a chocolate bar. He didn't ask the man at the counter about Madison. He didn't announce himself as a private investigator. He was just a guy having a chocolate bar for breakfast.

The owner or manager of the store didn't say anything to him. Watched him, but didn't comment on him being new to the neighborhood or warn him to stay out of business that had nothing to do with him. Just another guy, slaving away in a convenience store, making sure that he didn't get ripped off by a shoplifter or armed robber.

Zachary wandered back out to the sidewalk, unwrapping the chocolate bar slowly and eating it. He watched the birds, the clouds scudding across the sky, the few people who were out on the sidewalk waiting for buses or going about their own private business, heads down, paying no attention to anyone else.

As far as he could tell.

After consuming the chocolate bar, he proceeded down the street, still alert for anyone who might be following or watching him. Everything seemed peaceful and nonthreatening. The woman had just been a crazy old woman. Playing cloak and dagger with him. A little excitement to spice up her day. Something to tell her husband when they saw each other at the end of the day. Something to laugh about.

He crossed the street again when he reached the building she had indicated. Red brick. Old. Not exactly dilapidated, but not quite middle class, either. The type of place Zachary might have moved into. Something cheap, without a lot of amenities, that fell within his budget. And if there were several kids living together, they could split up the rent into something that was manageable for entry-level, minimum-wage workers.

He entered the front door alcove. The same as any apartment building entryway. A little glassed-in area with a button panel on the wall, some of them with names scribbled on labels or tape beside the buttons. Room numbers, last names, crossed-out previous occupants.

The easiest approach in an apartment building was just to press all the buttons. Most people would ignore it, or would answer in irritation, or sleep through it. If no one answered the first time, he would try again. Eventually, someone would just give up and press the door release because they didn't want to be bothered anymore.

He looked at the handwritten labels as he pressed each button in sequence. He didn't see a Madison, Miller, or Noah. But he didn't know Noah's last name and probably neither of them would want their name on a button. Did they have friends who came to see them? Or was it just a place to crash? There was no guarantee that it was Madison's building. In fact, the odds were against it.

Zachary continued to press buttons and ignore the irritated answers, until he heard the buzz of the door release. He pushed through it and started down the hall. The building was pretty quiet. It was too early for night-dwellers, and those who had stores to open or nine-to-five office jobs were gone.

A man opened one of the doors into the hallway, looking out blearily. He had an unkempt beard and long hair. He was shirtless, but at least had boxers and a dingy robe wrapped messily around him, showing plenty of curly dark chest hair. He had dark skin and very dark eyes. They looked completely black in the dim wattage of the hallway.

"Who are you?" he demanded. He scratched under his arm. "You don't belong here."

"Where is she?" Zachary returned, as aggressively as he could manage. He pointed his phone screen at the man, closing in way too fast on his head so that he was forced to rear back before he could see it. "Dumb broad stiffed me! She stiffed me! I'll teach her she can't do that!"

The man seemed to be having problems focusing his eyes. He looked at the screen, blinking, moving in and out to get it at the right distance. He raised his eyebrows and shot a glance farther down the hallway, and up. Like he was looking at a room on the second floor.

"How do I know?" he protested. "Hasn't got anything to do with me, man!"

"You think it's good business to go around cheating people out of their money? I paid cold, hard cash. I should call the police. I should teach her a lesson she won't forget!"

"Hey, chill, man," the man said, his voice low and warning. "Look, if you weren't satisfied, then take it up with her manager. Don't go causing trouble. You'll get the wrong end of that stick."

"Her manager? She wasn't with anyone. Just by herself. She thought I wouldn't be able to find her. Well, I have my ways! I knew where to find her!"

"You've got the wrong place," the man said, shaking his head. Even so, he couldn't help looking up again. "There's no one here like that. I've never seen her before. You've got the wrong place."

"You said she was here. You said talk to her manager. Who is her manager?"

"I don't know. I misspoke. I thought you were talking about a girl at the bar down there," he motioned vaguely down the street in the other direction. "This girl? In the picture? No. She's not around here."

"You're lying."

"No, man. Seriously. Everything is cool here. No one like that around here. I don't know who told you she was here." He tried to close the door.

Zachary stuck his toe in the door, which momentarily prevented its closure.

"Is she in there with you? I'll call the cops. They'll come in there and take all your dope and they'll put her behind bars. You can't go around defrauding people like that!"

"There's no one else here." The man kicked at Zachary's shoe with his bare foot. Ugly, yellowing toenails. Dark, hairy legs.

Zachary withdrew his foot and let the man close the door. He waited for a moment, watching for other people to open their doors to see what the ruckus was all about. Or to quietly shut the doors that had been opened a crack to allow for better acoustics. There was no sound. Everyone was still, waiting to see what he would do.

Zachary muttered a few times about crazy chicks and being ripped off, retreating toward the front door.

He stopped at the stairway that led up from the tiny lobby area. No elevators. Nothing that was going to break down and need regular maintenance. People who couldn't make it up the stairs need not apply.

Zachary stuck his head into the stairway first, listening for any movement.

Manager the man had said. That threw a whole different light on Madison's situation. Maybe the crazy woman with the broom hadn't been so paranoid after all. Maybe someone asking about girls in the neighborhood was putting himself in a dangerous situation. Maybe Madison wasn't just a girl staying with her boyfriend or renting with a group of girls. A manager? That meant an organization. Probably a criminal enterprise.

So he was cautious. If the man on the main floor knew that she was upstairs, then her location was well known. And possibly guarded. If Madison were being held against her will, Zachary needed to be very careful in his approach.

He listened at the stairway for a long time. Until he heard someone coming down the stairs at a slow, heavy plod. A man with bloodshot eyes dressed in a long, dark coat came down the stairs. He looked at Zachary, wondering what he was doing hanging around in the stairwell. Zachary stepped forward to the first stair, acting casual, like he hadn't been there waiting, but was just getting home like any other day. The man's eyes flicked to him curiously, then he kept going.

Someone who lived there? Or a client? His red eyes could indicate that he was a drug user. Or that he had been up late. He could be completely innocent, nothing to do with the girls. But he didn't appear to be armed or there to guard anyone—just a guy walking down the stairs.

Zachary only went up two stairs, then turned sideways to give the man plenty of room to get by him. Polite and respectful. Actually, he just didn't want to get too far up and be knocked down the stairs by the man if he had misjudged the situation. Much easier to fall down two steps than a full flight. Less chance of breaking a bone or being put out of commission.

The man gave a polite nod of acknowledgment and walked past Zachary. He didn't pause or look back, just kept going out the door.

Zachary climbed the stairs slowly, still listening for anyone else, either coming down the stairs or waiting farther up in the stairwell guarding against intruders. He went slowly so he wouldn't be out of breath and distracted when he got up the stairs, but would be alert to any dangers.

There wasn't anyone at the top of the first flight of stairs. As far as Zachary could tell, the stairwell was empty.

He was assuming that the man had been looking up toward the second floor, and not to a higher floor. He hadn't looked way up, just at a bit of an angle, like he was looking down the hall at his own ceiling.

Just one floor up.

Zachary hoped.

CHAPTER 19

He walked down the hall.

It was quiet, like the first floor.

He could hear voices. A discussion, not a fight. Other than that, silence. No one walking around, slamming doors, or conducting business. Night people sleeping. Morning people already gone.

Zachary didn't see any signs of trouble. No guards. No threats. He looked at the ceiling. No surveillance cameras. There could be peephole cameras, but he didn't see any that were obvious. The building smelled musty and of leftover cooking smells. Not a high-class place, but not a rat's nest, either. Low class respectable.

After walking down the hall and back, he tried to decide on the best approach. Friendly like with the woman on the street? Aggressive like with the man downstairs? Waiting until the door opened to decide on an approach?

He decided to start at the apartment the voices were coming from. Might as well start where people were awake, rather than waking people up. They would be in better moods. And if the occupants could quietly point Zachary in the right direction, he wouldn't need to wake up any enforcers. They could sleep, and he could decide whether to call the police.

He went to the closed door and listened for a moment, but he couldn't make out any words. It was a woman's voice. Muted. He still didn't think it was an argument.

Zachary raised his hand and knocked on the door. Quietly, like a private caller, not like the police, hammering on the door and ready to break it down if the occupants did not comply with the initial demand.

The voices stopped. Zachary waited, listening carefully. He didn't think that he would have to run, but he needed to be ready, just in case. Not that running was his best skill. He'd never been particularly athletic and, since the car accident, he had done physiotherapy to get him walking again, but running was problematic.

There were footsteps, and then the door opened. Cautiously. Not all the way. A face looked out at him through a gap of several inches. Zachary blinked. He had not expected to see a face that he knew.

"Noah."

The boy eyed him warily. "I don't know you."

"Is Madison there?"

He looked back over his shoulder, a reflex reaction. So Madison was there. "Who are you?"

"My name is Zachary Goldman. I'm a friend of Rhys Salter's."

"Rhys." Noah shook his head, frowning, then remembered. "That re— handicapped boy? What does he have to do with it? What are you doing here?"

"Madison has been reported missing. Her parents and a lot of people are worried about her."

"Madison doesn't want to talk to anyone." Noah tried to close the door.

As with the man downstairs, Zachary already had his foot in the gap, preventing it from closing. "I'll leave if I can talk to Madison. See she's okay."

"She doesn't want to talk to anyone."

Zachary raised his brows. "She needs to talk to me so I can reassure her parents that she's okay. She's a missing person. She needs to let people know she is all right."

"She's fine. You can tell them that."

"No I can't, I haven't seen her. She could be hurt. Chained up. It could be someone else in there. I need to see her or I don't know."

Noah looked over his shoulder again, reluctant. Weighing his options.

"What's going on?" the female voice asked.

"It's some guy... friend of your buddy Rhys. I don't know how he found this place." Noah rubbed his whiskers, frowning.

"Rhys?"

There was movement behind Noah. Zachary couldn't see her yet, but she was there. Not being tortured. Not chained up. Just shacking up with her boyfriend.

Noah opened the door farther so that Zachary had a better view of him and of the room behind him. A small kitchen. A girl clad only in a long t-shirt, her hair still rumpled from sleep. Madison.

"Madison. Hi. My name is Zachary Goldman. You know your parents are looking for you?"

Of course she knew that. Did she think she could leave home and they wouldn't look for her? That they would just shrug it off? Oh well.

Madison bit her lip. She looked at Noah, then at Zachary, not sure what to say. "I just… tell them I'm okay."

"Why don't you call them? Let them know that yourself."

"I don't want to talk to them. They'll try to make me go home. I don't want to go home. I'm fine here. Just tell them that. But... don't tell them where. Tell them I want to be left alone."

She looked at Noah again. Careful. Not wanting to say anything that would upset him? Was he abusive? Was he holding her there against her will, and she was afraid to tell Zachary?

There were a lot of ways to detain someone. Ropes and chains were not the only way to keep someone captive. Zachary studied Madison's eyes. She avoided his gaze. Was she being drugged? Abused? Threatened? He wasn't sure.

"Your family wants to hear from you. They're not going to take my word that you're okay. Whatever you're running away from, it's best if you confront it head-on. If it's a problem with your family, it can be dealt with. If it's something else..." Zachary shook his head. "They want to help you, Madison. Just talk to them."

Madison shook her head. She put her hand on Noah's back. Reassuring? Stabilizing? "No. Tell them I'm fine, but I'm not going back. I'm staying here. With Noah."

Zachary looked for something that might convince her. But she was firm. And if he pushed too hard or made threats, they might run. It wouldn't be so easy to find them a second time. He reached in his pocket and brought out one of his business cards. "Call me if you change your mind. Or if you need anything."

He reached out to hand it to Madison, but Noah snagged the card out of Zachary's hand and skimmed it onto the floor of the hallway.

"Out," Noah said firmly.

Zachary withdrew his foot. He didn't want to push Noah into physical violence, either against himself or against Madison. He had already stirred the pot enough.

The door shut quietly. Not slammed. A bolt and a chain slid across.

Zachary took a couple of deep breaths, standing there and hoping that his heart rate would slow down, now that he was no longer face-to-face with Noah. There was no danger. He had communicated with Madison. He'd been told to leave. He'd withdrawn. Whatever was going on with Madison, Zachary was safe.

He picked up the business card from the worn carpet, considering it for a moment. He slid it under the crack of the door into Madison's apartment. Maybe she or Noah would just throw it away. But maybe Madison would pick it up and pocket it, and reach out to Zachary when she was not under Noah's supervision.

When he reached the sidewalk outside the building, he again stopped to breathe and relax. He had another drink to wet his parched mouth before taking his phone out. He dialed Campbell's number.

"I found her."

CHAPTER 20

Zachary had hoped that the resolution of the case would be a big celebration. He would find Madison, bring her home, and she and her family would be overjoyed. Everything would be resolved. Rhys would be happy. Zachary could go on with his other work, knowing that he had made a difference in one family's life.

But knowing where Madison was and that she refused to go home was disheartening.

Campbell sent a couple of officers over to talk to her before they could ditch the apartment and find something else. The cops confirmed what she had told Zachary. She said she was there of her own free will. She wanted to stay. She didn't want to talk to her parents.

And there was no law against leaving. She was a runaway, but she was old enough that the cops knew there was no point in taking her home. She would just leave again. There was nothing to resolve with her parents. There hadn't been a fight. She had just decided to move in with her boyfriend. Maybe in a few weeks or months, they would have a fight and break up, and maybe then Madison would decide to go home again. Until then, there wasn't much that anyone could do.

* * *

Kenzie had agreed to Sunday dinner with Mr. Peterson and Pat. There was always a discussion over who would drive. Both liked to make the drive for different reasons. Zachary because he found it reassuring and meditative. Highway driving was one of the only times that his brain slowed down and he experienced being 'in the zone,' which he imagined was what it was like in most people's brains most of the time. Able to focus on just one thing at a time, his restless brain watching the horizon and taking care of navigation, leaving the remainder of his brain to think things through.

Kenzie, on the other hand, loved her little red sports car. Zachary had to admit that it was a sweet ride and, in the summer when they could ride around town with the top down, it was an exhilarating experience. But highway driving with the top down just made the wind roar around his ears, and it was still too cold for even driving around town, unless it was an exceptionally nice, unseasonably warm day.

"How about I drive this time," Zachary suggested. "And next time we go, you can take your car. When it's warmer."

"We could go down in separate cars," she teased. "Then both of us can drive."

Zachary opened his mouth, trying to corral the one argument that would convince her that was a silly idea. If they arrived in separate vehicles, Lorne and Pat would think that they were fighting. Or that something was wrong. It would use up twice the gas. And they wouldn't have the pleasure of each other's company on the way. It just didn't make any sense.

Kenzie grinned at him. "We're not going to go in separate cars," she assured him.

"Okay, good."

"You can drive this time. But just because you seem sort of bummed out. And because next time it will be warmer, so it will be nicer in the convertible."

Zachary nodded. "Good. Thanks. Next time you get to drive for sure."

It was a couple of hours, and mostly they didn't talk, but just listened to the music on the radio and enjoyed the smooth highway under the tires. The pavement was dry, so there were no worries about having to slow down for ice. Zachary drove a little above the speed limit. Still low enough that he didn't think any cop would bother to pull him over and Kenzie wouldn't complain that he was being reckless. He was very good at driving at high speeds. It was one of the few TV-private-eye skills that he actually had. But he didn't want Kenzie to think that her life was in danger. And he didn't want a ticket or to be delayed for dinner.

* * *

Mr. Peterson greeted them at the door, giving both of them warm hugs and Kenzie a peck on the cheek. He ushered them into the house. Zachary was surprised to see Tyrrell and Heather sitting in the living room. Mr. Peterson hadn't mentioned that they would be there. But Zachary was happy to see them. It was amazing to be able to see his siblings after decades of being separated. He still couldn't quite believe that it was true. Heather's husband was also there, sitting beside her, with his arm around her. And another woman was sitting next to Tyrrell.

Zachary hadn't expected Tyrrell to bring a girl with him. He hadn't told Zachary that he was going out with anyone.

"Uh, hi," he greeted, a little awkward. He didn't know how to address her.

Tyrrell smiled, putting his hand on the woman's arm. "Zach, this is Jocelyn."

Zachary stared at her for a minute, trying to process this. Jocelyn was the name of their older sister. Tyrrell was dating a woman with the same name as their sister?

Tyrrell kept looking at Zachary, and the woman looked up at him, both of them waiting for his response.

"Jocelyn?" Zachary repeated.

She kept staring at his face. "Joss," she said.

Everything finally connected, and Zachary's jaw dropped. "Joss?" He gasped for breath, finding that all of the oxygen had suddenly been sucked from the room. "Oh my—Joss?"

When he had met Tyrrell, they had hugged each other, both eager and excited. With Heather, she'd been less certain. A reserved handshake. She'd been dealing with her own troubles, trying to figure out how to ask

Zachary for help and wondering whether he could do anything for her.

With Joss, it was like there was a wall between them. She didn't look inviting. She didn't stand up to hug him or reach out her hand to take his. She just sat there, waiting.

Zachary swallowed. "It's so good to see you, Joss. How are you?"

She nodded, a strained smile. "I'm good. Nice for the four of us to see each other again."

Zachary nodded. "Yeah. I didn't know you were going to be here. I'm sorry if I seem a little… I'm just surprised. I didn't know it was you."

He'd had practice in trying to recognize the faces of his siblings. Tyrrell's eyes had given him away, even if nothing else about him had seemed familiar. Heather looked very different, and he had trouble seeing anything of the little girl she had been. But every now and then he caught a glimpse of that little girl. One of the little mothers who had tried to look after him and keep him out of trouble before they had gone into foster care.

And Joss had been the other.

As a child, her hair had been blond, but it had darkened over time. Not the almost-black hair that Zachary and Tyrrell sported, but darker than Heather's. They were all sitting, so he could see that she was a little shorter than Heather. She looked older. The two of them were only a year apart, but she looked a decade older than Heather, at least. Her mouth was pinched, wrinkles and frown lines around it and her eyes. She looked like she'd lived a hard life. Probably a smoker. That aged the face and skin. Although she was smiling at Zachary, she didn't look even remotely happy to see him. She smile was just a mask. A social convention.

Zachary turned slightly toward Mr. Peterson, hoping for some help. Mr. Peterson was socially adept, he got along with almost everyone, and he was good at drawing people out. Zachary had no idea how to talk to Joss or what to say to her.

"They wanted it to be a surprise," Mr. Peterson said, his round face wreathed with smiles. "We know how much you can worry over things, and didn't want you to spend the last few days and your whole ride here wondering about how things were going to go. Jocelyn said she would like to meet you, so we just went ahead and set it up."

Zachary nodded as if it all made perfect sense to him. He looked for somewhere to sit down, and Kenzie steered him toward the seat on the couch next to Jocelyn. Kenzie herself picked the easy chair close by that Mr. Peterson usually sat in. Zachary wanted to move everyone around to more comfortable places. His three siblings on the couch together. He and Kenzie on the adjoining love seat. Mr. Peterson in the chair he belonged in. Everybody in the right, most comforting places. He didn't want to sit next to Jocelyn, with her fixed smile.

He swallowed, trying to think of something to talk to Jocelyn about. He should ask her about herself. How her life was now. He couldn't mention their childhood, how Zachary had destroyed the family, the abuse and hard life that each of them had suffered through as a result.

"So… really nice to see you," Zachary said, though he thought he might have said it already. "What are you doing with yourself? How are things? Are you... I don't know where you live."

"I'm on my own," Joss said, in a clipped tone. "No current spouse or partner. No kids that would claim me. Just looking after myself."

Zachary nodded. "Uh-huh. That's great. I'm... I guess you already know I'm a private investigator. Do you... have a job? Or..." he trailed off, unsure how to end that question. Was she just a bum? Living on the street or in some halfway house? Trying to get her life together? Where did he think he was going with that question?

"I have a job," Jocelyn said defensively. "I work at a restaurant."

"Oh, great. Anywhere I would know?"

"By the looks of you," she cast an eye over his narrow frame, "you don't eat out much."

"Well… now and then. Just not… very much at a time. It's my meds… they suppress appetite…"

She told him where she worked. It wasn't anywhere that Zachary knew. He shrugged. "Sounds like a nice place."

She rolled her eyes.

Zachary looked at Heather and Tyrrell for help.

CHAPTER 21

"What have you been working on lately?" Tyrrell asked.

Zachary cleared his throat and swallowed, considering how much he wanted to share—or not to share. As long as he kept names out of it, he wasn't breaking any confidences. "I, uh, just finished up with a missing persons case."

"You should tell them about it," Kenzie encouraged.

"If you finished with it, does that mean that you found him?" Tyrrell asked.

"Her. Yes, I did."

"It wasn't—not like that other case?" Heather said tentatively. "You mean that you found her and…"

"She was fine," Zachary hurried to assure her. Not like Jose. He flashed for a minute on Dimitri's bloated corpse. He hadn't seen Jose after his death, but he'd seen Dimitri. Zachary wouldn't want to bring up Jose in front of Mr. Peterson or Pat. He had searched for Jose at Pat's request, and the results had not been good. He didn't want to risk setting Pat back on the progress he had made in recovering from his friend's death. "She was voluntary—that means she had disappeared because she wanted to, not because someone had kidnapped her."

"I think we all know what voluntary means," Jocelyn said dryly. "I may have dropped out of high school, but I still know basic vocabulary."

"Sorry... I didn't mean it to sound like I was putting anyone down."

"So why did she want to leave?" Tyrrell asked. "Was this like a battered spouse, or a runaway kid, or what?"

"A teenager. Ran away to be with her boyfriend."

"Figures," Joss said. "Waste of your time."

"I guess," Zachary said. "But she could have been in danger. I'm still glad that I took the case and could make sure that she was okay. Even if she did choose to stay with her boyfriend, at least her parents and friends know that she's safe. They know that nothing happened to her."

Jocelyn snorted.

They all looked at her. Zachary wasn't the only one who didn't understand why she was being so scornful.

"Wouldn't you rather know where your daughter was?" Kenzie asked.

"Just because they know where she is, that doesn't mean that they know what's happening to her. Most parents haven't got a clue what's going on right under their own noses."

"I saw her," Zachary said slowly. "She told me right to my face that she wanted to stay there with her boyfriend."

"And you can't see what's right under your own nose, either. I thought you'd at least have some sense, after being in foster care."

"What does foster care have to do with it?"

"Lots of kids are trafficked in foster care."

Zachary stared at her. He didn't argue the point. He'd been too worried about Madison and what might have happened to her. He remembered the man in the bathrobe downstairs saying that he would have to talk to Madison's manager. Not her boyfriend, but her manager.

Madison hadn't been bruised. Her body language hadn't said that she was afraid. But Zachary had still been worried. He'd sent the police there, despite her saying that she wanted to stay of her own free will, because he wanted to make sure. If she were being trafficked for sex, he wanted to make sure that she could get out. The police wouldn't let her stay there if she were being victimized. Campbell said that his officers confirmed back that she was voluntary. She had confirmed to them, even with Noah out of the room and out of hearing, that she wanted to stay there and that she wasn't being harmed or coerced. The police had dealt with situations like that before. They had their tricks. They could arrest the girl on some pretext to get her out of there, and her pimp wouldn't know what had happened. They would think she had just been arrested. People were arrested every day in that business.

So he didn't repeat 'trafficked' like he didn't know what Joss was talking about. And he didn't say that Madison couldn't be. He just looked at her, wondering how Jocelyn had focused in on trafficking with the little he had said.

"She wasn't being trafficked." It was Kenzie who objected, not Zachary. "She had just run away with her boyfriend."

"Not her boyfriend," Jocelyn said, "her Romeo."

Kenzie frowned. "What's the difference?"

"A Romeo isn't a boyfriend. She might think he is, but he's just there to get her into the business. Romance her and make her think that they're in love, so he can get her to trick for him."

Zachary thought about this. He pictured Madison and Noah together. They had seemed like a genuine couple. But they would, wouldn't they? If that's what she was supposed to think, then that was what her body language would say. And if he had set out to play her, then he would have the act down pat.

"But they've been together for months," he said. "He wouldn't take that long to turn her out, would he? That's too long."

Joss's expression changed ever so slightly. Zachary couldn't identify what it was that changed but, for the first time, she seemed to be viewing him with some respect. Not just the tolerant older sister, there to put on an appearance and make nice. Realizing, maybe for the first time, that he was no longer the little boy who had accidentally set the house on fire. No longer the bratty little brother who didn't know anything and was always getting everyone in trouble.

"Yes, he would have turned her out by now. But she might not realize what's going on."

"How could she not know what's going on?" Kenzie demanded. She looked over at Zachary, reading his warning look. "I'm sorry. I don't mean to sound like I doubt you, I just mean I don't understand it. Please explain it to me."

Zachary hoped that was a humble enough apology for Joss to decide to forgive Kenzie's question. As he remembered it, Joss could hold a grudge. She was scary that way. She'd been in charge of all of the kids when they were away from their parents, and she could be mean. Zachary had felt the sharp side of her tongue many times, and she'd been bigger and stronger than he was too. She hadn't been abusive like their mom and dad, but she'd done everything she could to keep their little gang in line.

Jocelyn studied Kenzie for a minute, glanced aside at Zachary, then focused again on Kenzie, since she was the one who had asked the question.

"There's no way for someone like you to know what it's like to be trafficked," she said coolly. "Someone like you doesn't have any idea what it's like on the other side of the street. None at all."

Zachary expected a protest from Kenzie. Saying that she wasn't that privileged. That she knew what things were like in the real world, even if that wasn't one of the things she had experienced herself. But Kenzie just kept her mouth clamped shut and let Jocelyn speak.

Jocelyn turned her attention back to Zachary. The familiar one. It had been decades since they had seen each other, but they had some shared background. She knew how he had started out life, and it hadn't been with a silver spoon in his mouth. She had been in contact with Tyrrell or Heather, so she probably had the broad strokes of Zachary's life since then. Not privileged. Far from it.

"He'll ask her to do it as a favor. Just once. Because he's in dire straits and some leg breaker is going to come after him. Just once, and he'll be able to pay off his debt and they'll be okay. He loves her and he doesn't want to ask her to do it and he'll understand if she says no, but… it's the only way he can see out. So she does it once. Nothing kinky. Something safe and vanilla. It's over quick, and he gets a wad of cash to pay off his debts, and they're okay. He loves her for what she did for him. It's proof of just how much she really loves him. And maybe there's enough left over for a fancy new dress. And for them to go out to dinner together. He makes it nice for her. Sets up all of those reward centers in the brain to feel good. So that when she tricks for him, she feels valued and appreciated and like she's really helping out someone she loves."

Zachary swallowed and nodded. "And that's the first time."

"The first time is the biggest barrier. After that, it's easier. Could she just help him out this once? They're getting evicted and they need a new place. They need to get out of that rat hole. If she could just do a couple of guys for him, then everything would be okay. And he's nice and loving and appreciative..."

Zachary sighed.

"And pretty soon," Jocelyn said, "he'll be sure to get her hooked on something too. Maybe heroin. Maybe meth. If she ever resists him, he holds back the drugs. It doesn't take long before she's desperate, and she'll do whatever he tells her too. Doesn't matter if she's not protected anymore, if she's seeing five or ten guys a night, if she's doing stuff she never would have considered before. She needs the drugs. She craves the love and attention he showers her with when she does what she's told. She likes the fancy dresses and purses and all of the proof that she's having a good time."

"And then it's too late," Kenzie said.

Jocelyn shrugged. "It was too late the minute she met him. These guys know what they're doing. He's got a boss above him who tells him how to do everything.

Who to target, how to get her to fall for him. How to keep her on a string and to turn her out. He's given step-by-step instructions, and if he makes a mistake or she falls out of line, there's a consequence for him."

"So he's a victim too," Tyrrell said.

Jocelyn shrugged her shoulders. "There are layers and layers of predators and victims in every organization. If you've been there for a few months, you'd better be looking at who you're going to bring in. They don't want the money to dry up. It's like a pyramid scheme. The more people you can bring in, the more you get out of it. You get higher and higher in the organization. More money and power. More perks."

"What makes you think that she's trafficked and not just a runaway?" Zachary asked.

"Show me a runaway who's not being trafficked."

The knot in Zachary's stomach tightened. He didn't want to be worrying about Madison. He wanted to relax and have a nice time with his family and not to have to think about Madison again. He had finished what he had set out to do. Rhys had asked him to find Madison, and he had done so. It wasn't his fault that she didn't want to go back to her family.

"If she's being forced into these gigs, then why wouldn't she want to go back to her family? Wouldn't she get out at the first opportunity?" Kenzie asked.

"She thinks she's in love with Romeo. She wants to help him and protect him. And maybe she's addicted. And proud of her new clothes and position. And maybe someone at home is abusive, which is why she left there in the first place."

"I didn't see any sign of it," Zachary put in. "Seemed like she had a pretty good life. Parents were friendly and worried about her. I didn't get a bad vibe from them."

"But you don't know. People can put on the best show in the world for you. You would never guess what kind of creeps they are when the door is shut and they're alone with each other or their daughter. You have no idea what goes on behind closed doors. No idea. Trust me."

Zachary nodded. He'd seen how different people could be once the authorities had gone home. He'd had to live with people like that.

He still didn't think the Millers were like that. But Joss was right. You never could tell.

CHAPTER 22

"So, are you a social worker?" Kenzie asked Joss as they dished up their meals.

Pat moved back and forth between the table and the kitchen, bussing platters and deep dishes of all sorts of rich foods. It was a wonder he still looked so strong and athletic at his age. He obviously did not eat very much of his own cooking.

Tyrrell and Heather spoke a little to each other, voices lowered. It was amazing how close they had become. Zachary was between Heather and Tyrrell in age, and he thought that he should be the one with a closer relationship with Tyrrell, but since Heather had made contact with them, they had become very close. He tried not to be jealous of their relationship and paranoid about what they were whispering to each other.

"I said I work at a restaurant," Joss snapped. "You were sitting right there."

"Well… yeah, I guess you did. But you sounded like you knew a lot about trafficking, and I thought maybe you were a social worker. Before. You could be a social worker and not be working as one right now. I'm sure they get hit by the economy just like anyone else. Or get burned out and decide they can't keep doing it. I thought maybe you were a professional."

"No," Jocelyn said curtly.

Kenzie looked at Zachary and raised an eyebrow. <u>Just what's eating her?</u>

Zachary shook his head. He would have to talk to her about it later. It was obvious to him where Jocelyn's knowledge had come from. Lots of foster kids got trafficked, she had said. And she'd been a foster kid. She knew how the organizations worked from the inside out. Who knew how many years she had been caught in that life. He wasn't about to ask her. Not over the dinner table.

"It's so nice to see you again, Kenzie," Pat said, finally sitting down. "It's been too long. How have you been keeping since you were here last? Any interesting cases?"

"You should know better than to ask Kenzie about interesting cases," Zachary warned. "Most people don't like autopsy talk at the table..."

"I promise no autopsy talk," Kenzie agreed with a laugh. "How about zombies? I have some new jokes..."

* * *

"Are you okay?" Kenzie asked when they got into the car.

Zachary didn't process her words immediately. He heard the silence, and then looked at her, then ran the tape in his head back and replayed it.

"Um, yeah. I'm fine."

He started the car and drove out of Mr. Peterson's neighborhood and out to the highway. He noticed Kenzie's silence again after a while and glanced over at her.

"What? Did you say something?"

"No."

"I'm okay." He repeated the assurance. "Why? I'm just fine."

"You didn't seem yourself at dinner today. I thought you would have a good time with so much of your family there. But you hardly even talked to anyone. Half the time, I don't think you had any idea what the conversation was about."

Zachary felt the tightness across his forehead and tried to smooth out his frown. To look bland and unworried. Nothing for Kenzie to be worried about.

"No, sorry. I think… it was just too many people for me. I'm okay with a small group, but once it goes past a certain level… I just get distracted. Overstimulated. Sorry about that. I didn't mean to make anyone uncomfortable."

"What have you been thinking about?"

"Just... the usual. Old memories. The family. Cases still waiting for me when I get back home. What I need to work on tomorrow."

"You told Rhys that you found Madison?"

Zachary broke into a cold sweat. He had told the police. They had informed Madison's parents. He hadn't immediately messaged Rhys with the good news.

Maybe because it wasn't good news.

Rhys wanted to see her again. He didn't want Zachary just to find her and assure him that everything was fine. He wanted to see her. Talk to her. Know for sure that she was okay.

And Zachary couldn't tell him that. He couldn't tell Rhys that everything was fine with Madison and she had just chosen to move away and to go somewhere else.

Maybe because he still had his doubts. Jocelyn's words had not reassured him. He knew that what she said was true. For a good part of dinner, he had not been thinking about Madison. Instead, he had been thinking about Joss.

He had always been a little scared of her as a kid. She'd been almost an adult in his eyes, and she'd ruled them with an iron fist. As much as a thirteen-year-old could rule with an iron fist.

And he was still scared of her. She was a hard woman. It was obvious that she too had been through a lot both in foster care and after she had aged out. She hadn't had an easy time. He hated the thought that she had been victimized just as much as he had. Just as much as Heather.

Maybe even more.

"Do you think she'll be okay?" he asked Kenzie.

"Madison?"

"Joss. I meant Joss, but I guess Madison too. If she's being trafficked by Noah like Joss said she is… I don't know how to get her out. I already tried to get her out, and the police tried. What else am I supposed to do?"

"I don't know, Zachary. I think you have to leave it to the police. There's not much you can do, especially about a criminal organization. If you were just trying to talk her out of staying with her boyfriend, of making contact with her parents, that's one thing. But trying to get her out of there if she's part of an organization…

they won't take very kindly to people who try to take their assets."

Zachary shook his head. He pressed his foot to the gas pedal, whizzing by several slow-moving vehicles on the highway. Kenzie looked at him. Zachary eased off, letting the needle of the speedometer settle at a lower number.

"Why are you worried about Joss?" Kenzie asked. "She struck me as a person who can look after herself."

"She's always had to be grown up… but I don't think that means she can always look after herself. I think a lot of it is bluff. Trying to make other people think she's tough and in charge."

"Well, you would know better than I would, but she didn't seem like she was having any problems communicating her thoughts to me."

"That's not what I meant."

They covered the next few miles in silence.

"What did you mean?" Kenzie asked. "Why are you worried about Joss?"

"She's been through so much, and it sounds like she's just barely holding things together with her job at the restaurant. I'm just worried... things are going to go downhill."

"You guys barely even talked to each other. What do you mean about her being through so much? You mean when you were kids?"

"No. I mean what she was talking about. Sex trafficking. Being caught in that kind of business... and addicted to drugs. She can't be making very much waitressing at a restaurant, and if she relapses... it's just one step to get back into prostitution and get enough money for drugs."

"I don't think she ever said that she was being trafficked."

"She didn't have to."

"You think so? You think she was talking about herself when she was talking about what might have happened to Madison?"

"Yeah."

"Well… I suppose. There's nothing to say that she wasn't. I just figured, if she was talking from experience, she would have said so."

"When you asked her if she was a social worker?"

"Yeah. That would have been a good opportunity."

"People don't talk about that so openly. It's… it's just not done. People are ashamed. When they come out about being abused or trafficked… society doesn't treat them very well. They get bullied. People tell them that they're lying or imply that it's their own fault. They get re-victimized."

"Our society has moved forward quite a bit in the last few years. I think that with the latest developments, it's a lot more acceptable to talk about your experiences with being abused. Maybe not for men, still, but women… are allowed to be more open now. More supported."

Zachary shook his head. "No. Not really."

"You have to admit that we treat rape victims a lot better than we did back in the eighties, when Heather was a victim."

"I hope so." The photos he had seen of Heather in her cold case file were burned into his memory. He would never forget what she had looked like after the assault. And the police had still treated her like she must have asked for it. It was her own fault for dressing so immodestly and walking through the park, which was out of bounds for the school kids for a reason. "But I don't know. There are still a lot of jerks out there. Older people. Religious bullies. People who… just like to hurt others. They feel so insecure, they'll attack the weakest person in the room. Someone like Joss… she's learned to present herself as someone strong and independent, to keep people at a distance. Keep them from attacking."

Kenzie nodded slowly. Zachary was sure she had seen and heard enough examples to understand that they were still in the dark ages as far as treating victims went.

"Are you going to keep in touch, then? Let Joss know that you're available if she wants to talk about it? Sometimes, just having someone who is open to talking things through is helpful to someone... on the edge."

For some reason, her words made Zachary remember his agreement to do couples therapy with Kenzie. To somehow do something to help them to stay together and work through the difficult times. Zachary blamed himself for all of the intimacy speed bumps, but he didn't know how to get over them.

"Hey, umm..."

Kenzie looked at him, her eyes wary.

"So… I don't know if I ever said… when Bridget and I were together, we talked once or twice about doing some couples therapy. To see if we could work things out."

"Yes… good suggestion," Kenzie agreed. She sounded intensely uncomfortable. While she had been amused by Bridget at the beginning of their relationship, she had discovered over time just how twisted up over her Zachary was. How hard it was for him to separate himself from what they had been as a couple. How he was still in love with her even though he didn't want to be.

He wanted to move on and be totally devoted to Kenzie and not distracted by Bridget and her pregnancy with her current partner—after she had refused to even consider having children with Zachary.

"Sorry. I shouldn't bring it up."

"No, finish what you started. Where are you going with this?"

"Bridget... she wouldn't agree to any kind of therapy. She didn't need anything. I was the one who was broken, not her."

"And that worked out real well, didn't it?" Kenzie said with a sneer. "How can you expect to have a healthy relationship with someone if you refuse to put the effort into it?"

Zachary breathed slowly in and out. He knew that Kenzie was right, but his immediate reaction was to defend Bridget. She wasn't the one who was broken. She had put plenty of effort into the relationship, just not into therapy. She thought that Zachary needed to work harder at fixing himself. That he could choose to be healthier if he just wanted it badly enough. If he wasn't getting better, then it wasn't her fault. It was his.

They drove in silence for a while longer. It was dark, and Kenzie had her face turned away from Zachary, looking out the window into the blackness.

He watched the road and the taillights ahead of him. He knew the route; it was all automatic to him. Which lane to be in. Where the pot holes were. Where he could speed up on the straightaways, if he were driving alone.

"Zachary." Kenzie's hand was on his leg. A warm squeeze. "I think couples therapy is a good idea. I told you that when you were talking to Lorne. I should have suggested it before, instead of striking off on my own and... you know. Taking things into my own hands."

Zachary didn't nod or agree. He didn't think that would be very tactful. He didn't want to hurt her or to focus on what she had done wrong in the past. She had been trying to help him. She had been trying to find a way to make their relationship work. He had forgiven her, so he shouldn't bring it up again.

"I want us to get stronger," he said. "To grow together. Not to... end up going different directions from each other."

"I do too."

"Okay. So. I'll talk to Dr. Boyle about it. See if she'll do it, or if she recommends someone else." He looked over at her, gauging Kenzie's reaction, making sure he had understood her correctly. She thought it was a good idea. So she was prepared to go ahead with it?

Kenzie nodded. "You bet. Let me know, and we'll find a time that can work around my work schedule. I'll be there."

She would be there.

Zachary released a pent-up breath.

CHAPTER 23

Zachary was at the Salter house when Rhys got home from school. Rhys raised his eyebrows at finding Zachary in his living room. He looked around for his grandmother, but Vera had left them alone for the conversation.

Zachary stood up to shake hands with Rhys, almost always a two-handed affair, with the non-shaking hand either patting Zachary on the shoulder or wrapping around him in a hug. Rhys was less effusive than usual, waiting for Zachary to fill him in on why he was there.

"I found Madison this weekend, Rhys," Zachary told him, not wanting to draw it out painfully.

Rhys squeezed Zachary's hand tighter.

"It's okay," Zachary assured him. "She's okay. She's alive, and she's not being held captive. She's just… with Noah."

Rhys sat down on the couch with a soft thump. He held his hand over his heart, breathing out a puff of air.

"Sorry. I wasn't trying to scare you. I knew you would assume that someone had kidnapped her and was holding her…" Zachary swallowed. "Like when Gloria took Bridget."

Both of them thought about Bridget's kidnapping. Rhys had been there, trying to help her and keep her alive. Zachary had been on their trail, and the timing had been very close. A few more hours, and she wouldn't have made it.

Rhys always asked Zachary about Kenzie, but never Bridget. He knew that Bridget was Zachary's ex. He had seen the reunion when Zachary found Bridget and knew that Zachary still had feelings for her. But he had never once asked after Bridget or teased Zachary about her. Only about Kenzie.

"I'm sorry. I wish I had better news for you," Zachary apologized, sitting on the ottoman to face Rhys on his level.

Would it have been better news if Madison had been kidnapped? If it meant that she was going back to her parents and back to school, back to her old friends and to Rhys? For that to happen, Madison first would have to go through the trauma of being kidnapped and held against her will for a week. Was that better than finding out that she was gone because she wanted to be? Because she chose one boy over everything else in her life?

Rhys shook his head and gave Zachary a thumbs-up, indicating that it was a good result. He slapped Zachary on the shoulder in congratulations and smiled at him encouragingly.

It was a good result. It was good to know that she hadn't been kidnapped and held against her will or, worse yet, killed.

But was it good? If she was only in love with Noah because he was romancing her to turn her out as a prostitute, how was that different from holding her captive?

Rhys got up off of the couch and went to the kitchen. He called over his shoulder, a single word directed at the rest of the house. "Gram?"

When Vera joined them in the kitchen, Rhys had his head and half his body in the fridge as he looked through it to see what goodies Vera had put away. He turned to look at her, and motioned to Zachary.

"Can Zachary stay over for supper?" Vera interpreted. "Of course he can. If he doesn't mind warmed-up leftovers. It's my night to volunteer at the old folks' home, so we always just have something quick from the fridge."

"Uh, sure," Zachary agreed. "I'm not picky."

It was funny to think of Vera volunteering at a seniors' home when, not that long ago, Zachary had thought that she was sliding into dementia herself. Once she got off of the meds that were causing her fogginess, that had changed completely. He was glad that Rhys had a family member who was able to look after him. He had grown up in his grandma's home and she understood him better than anyone else. She was protective of him after everything he had been through, but not a helicopter parent.

Rhys started pulling bowls out of the fridge and, in a few minutes, Zachary was warming up some leftover casserole while Rhys heaped food from several other dishes onto his plate. Zachary kept an eye on Rhys, wondering how he was feeling about the news about Madison.

"So, it's good news about your friend, isn't it?" Vera said to Rhys brightly, testing out the waters.

Rhys nodded without looking at her.

"Scary to have someone just disappear like that. You're lucky Zachary is such a good investigator."

Rhys looked over at Zachary as if waiting for him to say something. But Zachary didn't want to mention the possibility of sex trafficking in front of Vera. She had enough to worry about, without thinking about how vulnerable teens Rhys's age were to predators. Rhys himself was even more vulnerable due to his communication disabilities and the loss of his mother. If he had been targeted instead of Madison…

Zachary knew that there were plenty of boys being trafficked. They were not safe from predators either. As Joss had said, he'd seen enough in foster care to know about the possibilities.

"It's good that we at least know where she is," Zachary acknowledged Vera. "Though how long they'll—how long she'll stay there, I don't know. Girls will move around when there's too much attention from the police."

Vera had just a cold sandwich for herself, and left Rhys and Zachary alone again to eat their meal while she got ready for her night out.

Rhys took his heaping plate out of the microwave and set it on the table. He sat down and tapped on his phone for a minute. He slid it across the table to Zachary.

A video. Zachary tapped the triangle and watched the same video that Rhys had shown him before. Madison and Noah together. Telling Rhys to quit taping. Zachary opened his mouth to remind Rhys that he'd already seen the video. But there was a reason Rhys was showing it to him again. Rhys knew where Madison was now. Knew that she was with Noah and that she hadn't been kidnapped or murdered. And he still wanted Zachary to watch the video.

Zachary tapped it and watched it over. Madison, looking sore and tired. Flinching and initially pulling away when Noah touched her. Noah's anger when he saw Rhys taping them.

With his elbows on the table, Zachary put his palms over his eyes, closing his eyes and reviewing the video and everything else he knew.

"I'm going out," Vera called out, as she walked by.

Zachary removed his hands from his eyes and saw her look in through the doorway. She stopped, head cocked to the side.

"Are you okay, Zachary?"

"Yeah. Just tired."

It was a good excuse, because he usually looked tired. He was chronically short on sleep. Vera nodded. "Don't keep him too late, Rhys. He needs to go home to bed."

Rhys nodded his agreement. Vera left the kitchen, and in a minute they heard her close the front door as she left the house.

Rhys motioned toward his phone, still beside Zachary's plate. Zachary pushed it slowly back toward him.

"She looks like… something could be wrong," Zachary said, not wanting to put ideas into Rhys's head if it weren't something he'd already thought of. He didn't want Rhys lying awake at night, thinking about what was happening to Madison.

Rhys nodded briefly. His eyes were on Zachary's, waiting for him to say more.

"You think this guy is taking advantage of her? That he's not... what he appears to be?"

Rhys nodded firmly. Yes. Of course. Why would he keep showing Zachary that video if he didn't think it told a story? Madison, tired and in pain from her recent activities. Flinching away from a man's touch. Pulling away from the one who was supposed to be her boyfriend. Noah's anger at Rhys catching them on video.

Did Rhys know? Did Noah and Madison realize that Rhys knew? Was that why Madison had to disappear?

* * *

Back at his apartment, Zachary scowled as he looked through the pictures he had of Madison once more, looking for signs that she was being coerced into trafficking for Noah. Or, if not coerced... encouraged.

Pushed. Emotionally blackmailed. Maybe, as Joss had said, she didn't even know that she was being trafficked. She didn't realize that's what it was. She thought that it was just her own choice to help out her boyfriend, not realizing that she was part of a larger criminal enterprise. Not understanding what would happen if she refused.

But the pictures were not a lot to go on. Rhys had seen her. He'd seen how she had changed and how she behaved around Noah. Something had struck him as being wrong, but he couldn't tell Zachary exactly what that was. He could keep showing him the same pictures and videos over and over again, but he couldn't explain what it was that he was seeing and feeling. And Zachary didn't think that was just his communication difficulties. Even if Rhys could put it all into spoken words, maybe he still wouldn't have been able to explain what it was he knew. But he knew.

He thought back to Rhys's response when Zachary had asked him, "What do you want me to do?"

Rhys had considered it for a few minutes, then he had pointed to Zachary, pointed to himself, and pointed to the video of Madison on his phone. <u>You and me go see Madison.</u>

Zachary had immediately shaken his head. He couldn't take Rhys there. He wouldn't do it. They would have to find another way to approach the problem.

He had thought that he was done with the case. He had told Kenzie that it was solved. He'd told his family that it was closed. But there he was, looking through the pictures and the notes he had written when he talked to Madison's family and the people at the school.

If Madison had been pushed into prostitution and drug addiction, then he was morally obligated to do what he could to help her. It wasn't just a matter of telling the police where she was and letting her family know that she didn't want to go back home. That didn't clear him of any obligation. It wasn't the end of the case, and he knew it.

Zachary rubbed his gritty eyes, looking for some other approach. He had talked to Madison and Noah. Of course, the next step was to approach her when she was alone. She might have a different response from what she had when Noah was there. Like in the video when she had told Rhys to stop recording and to leave her alone. That was what she had said out loud, but her eyes and facial expression had been apologetic.

She didn't like the way Noah had talked to Rhys. She hadn't wanted to tell Rhys to go away and leave her alone.

When Rhys had followed up with a message asking her if she were safe, she had told him that he shouldn't contact her again.

Noah could be controlling her use of her phone as well. He could be reading all of her messages and making sure she responded to them the way that he wanted her to. He could be controlling every aspect of her life, while she thought she was still in control.

So how was Zachary going to get her alone? That was what he needed to do. Maybe she hadn't wanted to talk to the cops even when she was alone with them. But Noah had been in the next room. He could have overheard. He could have the room bugged. If the cops had taken Madison out of there, he would have a pretty good idea that she had wanted to go. They didn't have any reason to arrest her unless she gave them a reason to.

CHAPTER 24

Zachary shifted in his chair. He had not anticipated that he would be quite so uncomfortable in his session with Dr. Boyle. He had been seeing her for a while and, although he was sometimes nervous about telling her something or exploring his deepest feelings about a problem or an incident in his past, he had been forcing himself to see her regularly and not to cancel or reschedule any of his sessions. Not like after the assault, when he had avoided going to see her for weeks, when it was probably the time that he needed to see her the most. He hadn't been able to. He'd just shut down.

But having Kenzie in the room there with him changed things completely.

He wasn't afraid that Dr. Boyle was going to reveal anything to Kenzie or break any confidences. She had already promised him that. He still had his privacy. She wouldn't tell Kenzie anything Zachary didn't want to tell her.

And he wasn't afraid that Kenzie was going to tell Dr. Boyle anything that was shameful or embarrassing. It would be easier if Kenzie talked to Dr. Boyle directly about any concerns that she had than for Zachary to have to put them into words and bring them up himself.

But he'd never had anyone in sessions with him. Not since he was a kid and had been forced at several points to do family or group therapy. Bridget had never wanted to do couples therapy. It felt wrong to have Kenzie in the room with him.

He shifted again, looking over at Kenzie, who gave him a warm, reassuring smile.

Everyone had said everything right. They had all assured him that they would be respectful of his boundaries and his feelings. But it didn't feel that way.

Dr. Boyle's door opened and she walked in. "Sorry to keep you waiting, Zachary. I had an emergency call. That doesn't normally happen."

Zachary nodded and smiled tightly, saying nothing.

"And you must be Kenzie. It's nice to meet you." Dr. Boyle extended her hand to Kenzie, and the two women shook. They didn't make small talk about how they had each heard of the other and were looking forward to the session. Both quietly professional.

Zachary shifted in his seat, looking for a comfortable position. Dr. Boyle's eyes went to him as she sat down.

"You're looking a little anxious there, my friend."

"Yeah," Zachary croaked. "Sorry."

"That's okay. This is a stressful situation. It's something new. It might feel intrusive, like Kenzie isn't supposed to be a part of this life."

Zachary nodded his agreement.

"It's okay," Kenzie said. "After we've done it once or twice, it will be natural."

Zachary tried to keep his face blank and emotionless like a mask. He didn't want the two of them reading him, discussing him with each other. He wasn't a monkey in a cage.

But he sure felt like one.

He didn't need to pound his chest like a gorilla; his heart was already doing that, pounding so hard it hurt. He knew it was just anxiety. He wasn't having a heart attack. At least, that was what they always told him. It might feel like he was going to die, but he wasn't. If he just rode it out, it would go away by itself.

Zachary wiped at the sweat trickling down his temple. He tried to meet Dr. Boyle's eyes. To look like he was calm and casual and ready to begin the session. Just like any other session. Just like any other patient she had. Totally onside and cooperative.

"Do you need a minute?" she asked.

"I'm..." Zachary swallowed. He couldn't find the right words to respond.

"Zachary, are you okay?" It seemed to be dawning on Kenzie for the first time that something was really wrong. Her voice was full of concern. Not like Bridget, who had grown to hate his panic attacks, acting like he could decide to turn them on or off.

Dr. Boyle looked at her watch. "I can give you some time, if you need it. I realize that I'm already running late, but that's not going to affect your session. I'm not rushing you into your first couples session. I want you to be ready. To be comfortable with what we're doing here. If you feel pressured, you're going to associate those feelings with our sessions, and we want this to be a safe, comfortable place for you. So take your time."

The sweat was still gathering on Zachary's temples and was running down his back in long, cold streams. He grabbed a couple of tissues from the box on Dr. Boyle's desk and mopped his face. He used his right hand, aware that his left was clenching a handful of his shirt tightly over his chest. It was like it wasn't even under his control.

"Maybe we should do some guided relaxation," Dr. Boyle suggested.

Despite all of his efforts to appear calm, Zachary started gasping for breath, unable to get enough oxygen. There were too many people in the room. Kenzie was stealing his air. His breaths were loud in the room, horrendous gasps.

"Zachary!" Kenzie moved her chair closer and grabbed his right arm to comfort him. She couldn't exactly hold his hand while it was full of soggy tissues. "Hey, it's okay. Breathe. You're all right."

Dr. Boyle stood up and hurried over to Zachary, pressing her cool fingers firmly over the pulse point on his left wrist.

"Nice long exhales," she prompted. "When people start to hyperventilate, they aren't getting rid of carbon dioxide. It isn't lack of oxygen, it's that you aren't getting rid of the carbon dioxide."

"Can't," Zachary gasped. "Can't breathe. My heart!"

"You've had panic attacks before," Dr. Boyle said calmly. "You've never had one here, but you have a history, don't you?"

Zachary nodded his agreement. The pain in his chest was like a knife. Heart tissue dying. They didn't know what it was like. He was going to die there right in front of them. While they watched. Because they thought it was just another panic attack.

"Hurts."

"I know it does," Dr. Boyle agreed. "Do you have your meds with you? Do you want to take something?"

Zachary panted. He looked at Kenzie, sweat running down his hairline, embarrassed for her to see him like that. She'd seen him have one before. But he'd been triggered by Bridget. Kenzie had been able to see that he had been provoked. It at least made sense.

For him to break down in his therapist's office because he had to do couples therapy with Kenzie would be an insult to her. She'd think that he was trying to get out of it.

"It's okay," Kenzie assured him. "You can relax. It's fine."

But he knew it wasn't fine. He wanted to get through it without taking a Xanax. He still wanted to go through with the session, and the combination of a panic attack and Xanax would knock him out. He'd be too tired to do the session. He would just want to crash and go to sleep.

"No," he told Dr. Boyle. "I'm… I'm okay."

He took a deeper breath at another stabbing pain to his heart. He held back tears, struggling mightily to keep from completely embarrassing himself.

"Can I get you a glass of water? Do you want to be alone? How can I help?"

Zachary shook his head.

Kenzie rubbed his back. Zachary could feel how his shirt was soaked through with sweat, but she didn't recoil. She acted like she didn't even notice, moving her hand in slow, firm circles. "I know it's not a flashback or dissociation, but would anchoring help?" she suggested.

Zachary shook his head. But he tried anyway. What could it hurt? "I see… blue sky outside." He tried to pick the things he saw that would normally make him feel good. "Your lipstick. B-birds. Dr. Boyle's pen." He took a shuddering breath. "Coffee cup."

"Good," Kenzie encouraged. "How about five things you hear?"

"My breathing." It was drowning everything else out. Zachary tried to hear something else. He breathed out as long as he could, getting rid of the carbon dioxide and trying to hear something other than his own rasping gasps. "My heart. There's… a phone ringing." He strained, holding his breath. "You… moving…" He swallowed. "The air."

"The air?" Kenzie repeated. "I think you're grasping. You can't hear the air."

Zachary managed a couple of longer breaths. He pressed his fist into his chest, trying to focus on slowing his heart down.

"I can," he insisted. "It's forced air heating. I can hear it."

He swallowed. His mouth was very dry from breathing so hard.

"Smell?" Kenzie suggested.

Zachary swallowed again and tried to focus his attention on his sense of smell. Dr. Boyle released his wrist and leaned back on her desk, watching him.

"Your shampoo." Despite the sopping tissues in his hand, Zachary put his hand alongside Kenzie's lowered face and pressed his face against hers, smelling not only her shampoo, but her skin and everything that was Kenzie. She didn't pull away from him, but turned her head slightly and brushed his cheek with her lips. Not quite a kiss, but close. Zachary was breathing more easily. He closed his eyes and took a couple of slow breaths, counting the intake and the exhale. The hand over his chest loosened a little. He rubbed the muscles, sore from holding himself so rigid.

"That's looking better," Dr. Boyle said.

Zachary nodded.

Kenzie sat back down, drawing away from him, but at the same time holding his hand with the balled up tissue inside her own.

"Sorry," Zachary told them both, embarrassed.

"You don't need to apologize," Dr. Boyle said. "If this was easy, you wouldn't need me. You come here together, looking for my help with your relationship, which is very important to you. You don't want to mess it up. It feels strange to have someone else here. You're venturing into the unknown."

Zachary gulped and rubbed at his face, trying to wipe all of the sweat away with his left hand this time, keeping the right in Kenzie's grasp.

"I'm nervous too," Kenzie offered. "I've never done anything like this before. I'm kind of worried about what it's going to be like. What if I make things worse? What if Dr. Boyle says we're incompatible and shouldn't be together? What if you decide you're better off without me? That it's too hard?"

Her fears reflected a lot of Zachary's.

"For what it's worth," Dr. Boyle said, "I'm not going to tell you that you should break up."

"How do you know?" Kenzie challenged. "Maybe you decide that we're not good for each other. That I'm damaging Zachary?"

"I don't think that's going to happen. If one of you is being abusive, then we'll talk about how to change the dynamic. I might recommend certain individual therapies, anger management, something like that. I don't think that any relationship is hopeless. Not when both partners come here to see me and are determined to do what it takes to make things work. You're already way ahead of the curve by coming here to learn how to deal with your differences."

"My differences," Zachary corrected.

Dr. Boyle shook her head, smiling slightly. "You are both different than each other. Yes, Zachary, you have a lot of challenges. More than the average person, for sure. But that doesn't mean that you are broken and

Kenzie and I are here to fix you. And it doesn't mean that you can't ever have a healthy romantic relationship. This is the starting line, not the finish line. You've got lots of road ahead of you."

"I can't even do therapy without having a meltdown," Zachary said with disgust.

"Really? This is the first time I've seen you have a panic attack. Which means that you can do therapy without having a meltdown. When is the last time you had couples therapy?"

"Well... never."

"So would you say it's something new?"

"Yeah."

"There are a lot of people who feel anxiety over new situations. You need to give yourself a break."

Zachary rubbed at a spot on his jeans, nodding. He looked at the clock on Dr. Boyle's desk. How much of their time slot had he wasted with his breakdown?

"We can still get started today," Dr. Boyle said. "In fact, I think it's important that we still go ahead, so that you can feel like you have achieved something today. It will make it easier next time."

"You don't think I'll have a panic attack next time?" Zachary sniffled, still trying to get his emotions smoothed down and under his control.

"I don't know. Maybe you will, maybe you won't. But even if you do, we can still achieve something, can't we? We can still move ahead with couples counseling."

"Okay."

"Good." Dr. Boyle returned to her chair and sat back, looking at the two of them. "So. What would you say are the biggest obstacles in your relationship right now?"

Zachary snorted. "Me."

"That's not helpful, Zachary." Dr. Boyle looked at Kenzie. "How about you, Kenzie? What do you see as the roadblocks?"

Kenzie let go of Zachary's hand and rubbed her palms together, then wiped them on her pants.

"The big one right now is Zachary's dissociation. His PTSD or whatever it is that's making him check out whenever we start being physical."

Dr. Boyle nodded. "How do you feel about that, Zachary?"

"Helpless. It's not like I can stop it. I want to be close to Kenzie."

"Good. I think it's helpful to label your feelings about it and to affirm that you do want the physical intimacy."

"I didn't have that problem with Bridget. So it makes me even more frustrated… I love Kenzie." He looked at her and gave a little nod to emphasize his words. "So why can't I… show her that? Why does my body and my brain have to block me from feeling that?"

"And there's the other one," Kenzie said with a sigh. "Bridget. It's like having a third person in our relationship. Whatever we do, I know he's always comparing me to Bridget. Thinking about her and about how things were when they were together. He idealizes her. Idolizes her. When she's… you would think from the way that he talks about her that she was the perfect wife. But she's not a nice person. To put it kindly."

"That's just toward me," Zachary explained. "Because of... my failings. She had to put up with a lot, and in the end, it was just too much."

"It's not just toward you," Kenzie said. "She may act nice toward other people, but you know what she's like on the inside. You know what she's like behind closed doors. You can bet that person comes out whenever she's not on public display. You're not the only one she treats like that."

Zachary furrowed his brow and shook his head. "No. She has friends who are very loyal to her. She makes friends wherever she goes. She always had more friends than I did, even in places where I had been for years. In a few minutes, she would have everyone eating out of her hand, and even though I'd been around forever, it would be 'Zachary who?'"

Kenzie rolled her eyes and shook her head.

"How do you feel about that, Kenzie?" Dr. Boyle prodded.

"Like I said, he sees her as perfect. But she's not. That's not what she's like. Did you tell Dr. Boyle about the latest developments?" Kenzie raised her brows.

Zachary appreciated that she didn't just drop the bombshell. He shook his head. "No, I didn't... I didn't think it was relevant. It's nothing to do with me."

"Something you want to share?" Dr. Boyle asked.

Zachary motioned toward Kenzie. "Go ahead. I'd... I don't even know if I could say it."

Kenzie looked at him for a moment as if double-checking, making sure that he really wanted her to say something, before it was too late to take it back. Zachary just shrugged.

"It's fine."

Kenzie looked at Dr. Boyle. "Bridget is pregnant."

"That's a complication, isn't it?" Dr. Boyle observed neutrally.

"It's nothing to do with me," Zachary repeated.

"But that doesn't mean it doesn't affect you," Kenzie said. "It obviously does."

Zachary stayed silent. He looked down at the carpet. He hadn't expected to have to talk about Bridget's pregnancy and all of the issues that it brought up for him.

"How do you feel about it, Zachary?"

"She can get pregnant if she wants to. I'm happy for her."

Kenzie snorted.

Zachary grimaced. "Okay, maybe I'm not happy for her. But… it isn't any of my business."

"When they were together, Bridget said she didn't want children," Kenzie explained. "When they had a pregnancy scare, she said she was going to get an abortion. Didn't matter what Zachary wanted. It wasn't a mutual decision. It was Bridget saying that she wasn't going to have his baby."

"Ouch." Dr. Boyle nodded. "That makes it hard to see her pregnant in another relationship, without you."

"It had to be planned," Zachary told them. "Because of her radiation, the doctor said she should have her eggs frozen. In case she ever changed her mind about having children. So… she didn't just accidentally get pregnant, and decide to go ahead and have them. She had to have in vitro. It had to be planned, with the eggs she had harvested before her cancer treatment."

Kenzie was looking at Zachary. "I didn't know that part," she said softly.

Zachary nodded.

Dr. Boyle had caught Zachary's accidental revelation. "Them?"

"What?" Zachary pretended he didn't know what she was talking about.

"You said she decided to go ahead and have them. Does that mean she's having twins?"

"I… don't know. When Gordon was talking, he said 'the babies.' Not 'the baby.' So… I guess she's having multiples. Hopefully just twins."

"So, she refuses to have your baby, but with Gordon, she'll have two," Kenzie summarized. "On purpose."

Zachary nodded. He swallowed and stared out the window.

"And how do you feel about that?" Dr. Boyle asked.

CHAPTER 25

In the car after the session, Kenzie suggested going out for ice cream. Zachary looked at her, frowning, wondering if he had misheard.

"Ice cream?"

"We deserve a treat, don't you think? Where do you want to go? If you prefer something else, I'm game."

"A treat for going to therapy?"

"Sure, why not? Didn't any of your foster parents ever reward you for going to the doctor or dentist without a fuss?"

Zachary shook his head.

"My mom always got us a treat when we went to the doctor," Kenzie said. "So I think it's time to go out for a treat. If you'd rather go for steak or Chinese, I'm game."

Zachary didn't feel like a heavy meal. He was feeling drained after his panic attack and the session, and just wanted to go home and zone out.

"Okay, ice cream," he agreed. He thought it was still a little cold out to be going for ice cream, but if that was what Kenzie wanted, he didn't see why she shouldn't have it.

"Good." Kenzie gave him a sunny smile. "I think you deserve a treat especially. I had a hard time going and not giving in to the temptation to cancel at the last minute. I know it was a lot harder for you, but look at how strong you were. I didn't even hear a word about you not going. And after your... episode... you didn't even suggest going home. You just went right into it."

"Dr. Boyle said it would be easier next time if I did."

"Yeah. But you still could have said no."

Zachary nodded, keeping his eyes on the road. "Where do you want to go for ice cream?"

There was really only one good ice cream shop in town, assuming Kenzie wanted to go for a cone or bowl of the fancy stuff, and not just stop at the grocery store for a pint. Mostly, Zachary just didn't want to keep talking about therapy.

"We have to go to the Fro Zone," Kenzie said. "No other choice."

"Okay." Zachary headed toward the ice cream shop. "What kind are you going to get?"

"I won't know until I get there. I don't know what their special is today. Or what new flavors they might have added since the last time I was there."

"Chocolate?"

"Well, something with chocolate usually wins out. But I don't know what kind of chocolate. And they could have something special in another flavor. Something really awesome, like..." Kenzie trailed off, trying to come up with an example.

"Like double chocolate with chocolate sauce?" Zachary suggested.

Kenzie giggled. "Yeah. Something like that."

Bridget would never have double chocolate ice cream with chocolate sauce. It would ruin her figure. She was meticulous about what she ate and how much so that she wouldn't put an extra ounce on her perfect figure.

Zachary wondered how she was managing the pregnancy and the extra weight that it entailed. She'd told him she was never going to ruin her body by having a baby.

Yet another thing she had told him that had turned out not to be true.

* * *

Jocelyn sounded surprised when Zachary called her. She had obviously not expected him to reach out to her after the awkward meeting at Mr. Peterson's.

"What's this about? I have to work, you know. I don't have loads of free time."

"I'll come to you," Zachary promised. He worked for himself, but that didn't mean he had loads of free time either. Especially not when he was doing the investigation for Rhys pro bono. No matter how much time he spent on it, it wasn't going to bring him in any money. "I just wanted to ask your opinion on some things."

"What kind of things?"

"On my case."

"Your case? The girl you already found?"

"Well, yes. I still have concerns. I'm not sure how to proceed."

"You proceed by leaving it alone. You did what you were asked to do, so go on to the next case."

"Could I talk to you about it?" Zachary persisted. "Could we meet?"

"Are you going to pay me for my time as a professional consultant?"

Zachary winced. He still had money in the bank due to a few of the bigger cases he had taken recently. Gordon Drake had even kicked in some money on the Lauren Barclay case—though that had felt more like hush money than payment for services rendered.

"I could give you a small stipend," he said. "I'm not making anything on this case, but I do value your time."

She thought about that for a minute. "Fine," she agreed finally. "Can't we just discuss it over the phone? Do we need to get together? You'll have to travel on top of everything else."

"I don't mind driving. And I would like to see you again. I have some pictures and videos that you could look at, give me your opinion, some insight. Things that I wouldn't know because I'm not close enough to her situation."

"Why are you still pursuing it? You think you can talk her into going home?"

"I have to try. If she's not safe, I have to do everything I can to get her back."

"And if she won't?"

"If she won't, she won't. But I'm hoping that with your help, I might be able to convince her. It will at least give me a better shot than just approaching her without any understanding of her situation. Would you have left if some random guy just told you that you should?"

"Of course not."

"So I'm going to need something. Some way to at least have a chance."

"You know I'm not going to try to help you," Jocelyn warned. "I'm going to try to talk you out of it."

Zachary laughed. At least she was upfront about it. Did he want to waste his time trying to get answers from someone who thought that the whole thing was a mistake?

He actually did. He wouldn't be walking into it blind. If Jocelyn didn't manage to talk him out of it, then he would be ready. And if she did convince him to give it up, then there were obviously good reasons to do so.

"Fair enough," he agreed. "I guess I don't have to warn you that I'm stubborn and don't always make the smartest decisions."

Jocelyn's answering laugh was more natural. Much more relaxed and familiar to him than anything else she had said or done. Joss remembered what he was like, all right. And that made him feel closer to her.

CHAPTER 26

He didn't mind another highway drive to meet with Jocelyn. It gave him a chance to try to sort out his thoughts and marshal his arguments before their conversation. Kenzie was working, so he was on his own and could drive a little faster if he felt like it.

The land surrounding the highway was turning green. The weather was still chilly, but things had started to come alive again after their long winter hibernation, and it cheered him to see it. Vermont was like a postcard in the winter, but he preferred the summer.

Would he ever consider moving somewhere that was warm all year? Somewhere people decorated palm trees or cactuses rather than evergreens for Christmas and there was no snow on the ground?

It was hard to say. He hated anything that reminded him of Christmas, but he wasn't ever going to be able to find somewhere there was no Christmas. Not in the United States.

He took the highway exit the GPS told him to, and followed its directions to the book store Jocelyn had directed him to. He thought that a book store was an odd place for a meeting, but they had a social area with a coffee shop and table and chairs, and it was clearly a popular hangout. Jocelyn didn't need to be worried about being alone with him, a man she barely knew.

She was there waiting for him, a book in hand. Zachary glanced at it but didn't recognize the cover or title. It was a thick book, and he wasn't a reader.

"Hi," Zachary greeted. He hesitated, not putting out his hand for a handshake or his arms for a hug. Jocelyn nodded and didn't offer either method of greeting, so he left it at that.

"Let's sit here." Jocelyn motioned to a table off to the side, by the window. "I ordered a couple of coffees. You drink coffee, right?"

"Sure."

"You never know these days. Health nuts, religious freaks, fair trade, blah, blah, blah. We're just talking about a cup of coffee, not a lifetime commitment."

Zachary smiled. He sat down. "If I could live on coffee, I probably would."

"Well, thank goodness for that. You really are a Goldman."

"Did you ever doubt it?"

Jocelyn shook her head. "No. You look just like I expected you to."

They waited. Zachary tried to make small talk with her and looked out the window at the people coming and going in the parking lot. Jocelyn waved to a barista who was looking around at the tables with two cups of coffee in her hands.

"Over here."

The woman saw Jocelyn's waving arm and approached them. "Jocelyn and Zachary?"

"Yes."

She put the cups down in front of them, and Zachary picked his up and took a sip, even though it was boiling hot.

"Thanks. Good stuff."

"Yeah. You bet."

Zachary sighed. He put his notepad on the table beside him. "So… you know that I'm trying to figure out how to get Madison back home."

"You should just stay out of it."

"She's only a kid. Don't you think it's best to get her out early? Before she gets in too deep?"

"No. I think you should leave her alone. It's her life, not yours. You don't have any right to tell her what to do."

"I know. I'm not trying to force her or tell her what to do, just to help her out. Wouldn't you have wanted someone to help you?"

"No. Plenty of people tried to interfere and get me to do what they thought I should be doing. And it didn't do anything but get me in grief. I just wanted everyone to stay out of it and let me live my own life the way I wanted to."

Zachary swirled the coffee cup. "But did you really know what you were getting into? Did you really understand what kind of life it was going to be? Or what kind of life you could have if you got out?"

"Life outside the business isn't all roses."

He thought about that. Zachary wasn't about to tell her that he knew better than she did. She had lived the life that Madison had been in, and she had gotten out. She was the one who had seen both sides.

"I don't know if anyone's life is all roses. Do you think things were better when you were..."

"In some ways, yes. I had drugs, and they helped me to feel better. As long as I was getting what I needed, I felt okay. I didn't have to think about whether it was right or wrong, or whether I could be doing something else or living another life. None of that came up while I was high. I could… be what I was, and no one cared. Least of all me."

"But that does things to your body. Makes you sick. Could kill you."

"But I didn't care. That's the magic of it. I knew I was living a crappy life and I wasn't going anywhere, but I didn't care. I knew drugs were destroying my body, but that didn't matter. When I almost died… that was the best high I ever had. I wished they hadn't brought me out of it. They should have just left me alone. Let me die."

"Did you think… no one would care? Or you didn't care if anyone did?"

"No one did," Jocelyn said flatly. She shook her head. "I didn't have anyone, Zachary. I didn't have any family or friends. I had my Romeo, and that was enough for me. He made me feel good, when I was doing what I was supposed to and keeping him happy. As long as I was bringing money in and keeping his clients satisfied, he would give me all the good strokes. Tell me that I was smart and funny and pretty. That he didn't want anything else in a girlfriend. He'd give me new clothes and tell me how nice I looked. He'd bring me drugs, and we'd get high together, and I would feel so good. Why would I want to get out of that?"

"But you did, eventually. What changed your mind?"

Jocelyn stared off into the distance. "There was bad stuff too. Of course. There always is. Clients who weren't happy or who wanted to hurt someone just because they were sadists. So then I'd get in trouble with my boyfriend. And I was getting older. Not in as much demand. They were looking for younger girls, and they wanted me to help bring them up and turn them out. I could never agree with that. I never got on board with bringing someone else in. Seducing them, or punishing them and keeping them in line. It wasn't my thing." She took a long swallow from her cup. "I never liked to see Matt with other girls. I was jealous, but I couldn't show it. He didn't spend much time with me. Neglected me, didn't bring me drugs, left me to my own devices. While he was off partying with the little girls. Getting older isn't as bad for men. Older guys are still sexy. Look at Hollywood. But for women… we just get worn out, tired, ugly. Too fat and flabby or thin and bony. Our bodies change, so we don't look and feel like younger women anymore. Sure, there are some great looking old broads in Hollywood too, but they have plastic surgeons and personal trainers.

They're not getting worn out by the constant demands of men and strung out on drugs all the time."

Zachary nodded, watching her face. It broke his heart to hear all that she had gone through. She was lucky to have survived as long as she had and to have been able to get out without being harmed. But she hadn't left that life behind. It had left its mark on her. And she would probably never recover from it.

But Madison? She was young. She'd only been in the business for a few weeks or months. If there was a chance that he could get her out of there and prevent her from living the life that Jocelyn had, year after year...

"You don't know what it's like, Zachary," Jocelyn said sharply. "You think you can just waltz in there and talk her out of it, and that's not the way it works. She doesn't have the choice to just walk away. It doesn't matter what you tell her; there's a lot more involved than that. Even if you could talk her out of it, she wouldn't get far. They would follow. Track her down. Snatch her if she wouldn't cooperate. They would take her away somewhere where no one knew her. Where she didn't have anyone to ask for help. And they would keep her chained up in some basement until she didn't have any more will to run away."

"Did that happen to you?"

"I seen it happen," Jocelyn snapped, not giving him the personal details. Had it been her, or had it been someone else? Or had there been so many of them that it was a ubiquitous experience? Maybe she didn't even remember anymore what had happened to her and what had happened to someone else.

Zachary resisted growling back at her. That wouldn't help anything. She was trying to tell him what it had been like. He didn't even have any right to know. She had agreed to do it, maybe to help someone else out and perhaps just to try to connect with him and let him know what she had been through.

"So if you were going to get someone out, how would you do it?"

"I wouldn't," Jocelyn said. She stared at him fiercely. "Don't you get it? You can't. There's nothing you can do. You're not a Navy SEAL. You're not some crusader of light rushing in and saving the day. You might think you're all of that, but you're not. These are guys who are not going to be trifled with. You've been lucky up until now, bumbling around and making headlines. That isn't what this is going to be like. Not at all."

"I haven't been... I don't see myself that way. I'm just trying to do what I've been hired to do in these cases. I'm not trying to get in the spotlight. Yes, some cases have made it into the media lately, but it's not about that. It's about helping people. About doing the things I've been hired to do."

"You haven't been hired. Being hired would mean you're being paid. I at least know that."

"Okay... so not hired in this case. Just asked for a favor. But I want to do everything I can for Rhys. And for Madison. I can't just walk away and pretend that she doesn't exist or that I don't know what she might be going through. Could you do that?"

"Of course I could! I do that every day of my life. Turn my face away from all of the other victims and remind myself that I got out. I did. And I can't live anyone else's life. That's up to them. I didn't get out alive just to rush back in there and upset the apple cart. I don't want to bring the whole organization down on top of me."

"I can't do that." Zachary thought about Annie, the girl who had died when he was in Bonnie Brown. He had kept quiet. He had been too afraid of the guards and what would happen to him if he talked, so he had kept quiet. For years he had been silent about what had happened to her. He pretended that he didn't know. He blocked it out. He walled off that part of himself and made himself forget.

Until he had walked through the doors at Summit. And then her ghost had been resurrected and he wasn't able to walk away again without acknowledging her. Maybe someday Jocelyn would have to face her own ghosts and either justify herself or give them a voice.

"I can't do that. It isn't in my makeup to be able to turn my back on Madison and pretend that there was nothing I could do."

"No one is going to care about this one. You make big news because you solve the murder of the child of a public figure. Because you manage to identify a serial killer. Whatever else." She made a brushing-off motion with her fingers as if none of it mattered. "But no one is going to care about one girl being trafficked. No one cares." She said each word as if it were a separate sentence.

"I'm not trying to make the news. And people do care. Her parents care. Rhys cares. I care. Even if no one else does, that's enough. I can't leave her there."

Remembering Summit and thinking about Madison being trafficked and no one caring about it made Zachary think of Tyrza. She had been nothing like

Madison. Young, yes. But black. Autistic. Not able to tell the police what had happened to her.

But her mother had cared. She had made sure that everyone knew she wasn't going to give up until she found her daughter. She was going to make a big, loud, noisy stink. And rather than let her do that, they had let Tyrza go. They had released her. Left her wandering by the side of the road. She had been saved by a mother who hadn't been afraid to be loud and ruffle some feathers.

"Dammit, I can see the gleam in your eyes, Zachy," Jocelyn said in a harsh voice. "I know what that means!"

CHAPTER 27

Zachary turned away from Joss and looked out the window. It was too late. She already knew exactly what he was thinking and had seen the resolution in his eyes. If he had wanted to hide that from her, then he should have turned away from her earlier.

"You can't read my mind," he told her. Like the ten-year-old brat he had been. Like the bratty little brother she had tried to care for and protect. And he'd just continued to break the rules and get into trouble and go the wrong way.

Until he'd gone and sent everything he cared about up in flames. Literally.

"I can too," Jocelyn returned, in that knowing-older-sister voice that was familiar to him even though it was decades later. "I can see exactly what you're thinking.

Why did you even come here today, if you'd already decided what you're going to do? Why not just stay home and jump right into hot water like you always do?"

"I wanted to learn what I could from you. I thought you could help me to figure things out. Figure out the best way to get her out of there."

"There is no best way. There is no way. Unless you're going to kidnap her. And then you'd have to get her out of the state, get her a fake name, hide her away until they don't care about her anymore."

Zachary nodded seriously. "You think that even if she agreed to go home, they would come back after her."

"Of course they would. She's an investment. She's theirs. Anyone who gets in their way, they don't care.

They'll just cut down everything in their path and get her back."

"Her parents, you mean?"

"Anyone who stood up to them. If they went to the police and started making trouble? If you got in their way or tracked her down again? They'd cut you down. They would make sure that you never interfered with their business again."

Zachary thought of the business card he had left behind. That had been stupid. He should have known better than to give them his name and to leave his contact details behind. It was a criminal enterprise. Did he think that they wouldn't care about a private investigator nosing around? What if he had to leave town too? He'd made a life for himself there. He had friends. People he cared about. How was he going to feel if he had to leave everything behind and start over?

Joss nodded, feeling like he was finally getting it. "You can't mess with these guys. Just go home and stay out of it. Pick up a new case. Lose yourself in something else. Go to bed with Kenzie and stay there for a week. Just stay out of it."

Zachary sighed. He took a sip of his coffee, which was starting to cool down. It was rich and bitter and he tried to focus on the aroma and flavor and nothing else. He had to face reality. He wasn't a blow-em-all-up private eye from the silver screen. He was just one guy trying to make a living. Trying to help out a few people along the way.

Madison just couldn't be one of them.

* * *

The rest of the visit with Jocelyn had focused more on the business aspect of the trafficking world. He knew very little about how it all worked, and Jocelyn, of course, knew all about it. She might have been a naive teen when she had started out, who didn't know anything about anything. But she had learned the business from the ground up. From the way that the Romeos targeted and attracted girls to the way that they got them addicted to drugs and the party lifestyle and designer dresses and handbags. The way that they kept them under control with addiction, coercion, blackmail, and love for the boyfriend who had started it all in the first place.

By the time she understood what trafficking was, Jocelyn was in way too deep to get herself out or even to want to. There was only one way to maintain her lifestyle and that was by turning tricks and doing whatever she was told whenever she was told. Only then would she be rewarded.

She knew all of the ways that girls were advertised on Backpage and classified sites and the dark web. Sometimes out in the open, using code words that only regular clients would understand. If a girl was lucky, she'd have a place like Madison had with Noah. If she was unlucky, her lot would be much worse. If Madison could keep Noah and his bosses happy, that was the best that she could hope for.

Madison could continue the fantasy of being in love with her Romeo and lie to herself about what was really happening. And that was the only way she could be happy.

* * *

Zachary begged off of doing anything with Kenzie that night. He needed time to make notes of the things that Jocelyn had said and to process everything. He told her he was tired. He hadn't slept well after their couples therapy and he needed another night to try to catch up.

Kenzie said that she had some work to catch up on and that she was okay with a night on her own. He listened closely to her words and inflection, but she didn't sound upset. Maybe, like he did, she needed some space to herself now and then. She probably had some things to think of after their couples therapy too. Like whether he was the kind of guy that she wanted to spend time with long term. Maybe she should cut it off while she could and Zachary had Dr. Boyle to fall back on and to guide him through the breakup.

"But let me know if you change your mind," Kenzie said. "Or if you want to chat later on. Okay? I'm flexible."

"Okay, thanks. I'll let you know."

He hung up the phone and put some music on in the background, and fought hard to focus on his notes and to remember everything Jocelyn had said, refusing to let it pull him back down into unwelcome memories.

CHAPTER 28

The next day, he worked on catching up on other cases. Paperwork, invoices, collection, passing on information, looking at his schedule to figure out surveillance time blocks. He had plenty of work to keep him busy. He didn't need to be wasting time on cases that didn't pay anything.

Unfortunately, you couldn't save everyone—especially those who didn't want to be saved.

It was evening, and he was watching the clock, wondering if he should call Kenzie or whether she would drop by the apartment. He didn't want to leave it too long between talking to her. He didn't want to make that mistake again and to fall back to where they had been before.

His phone buzzed.

Zachary picked it up, expecting to see a text from Kenzie. Maybe a suggestion that they go out for dinner, or just a note that she was on her way.

But it wasn't. It was a message from Rhys. Zachary tapped it and a gif popped up. An old I Love Lucy shot, with "Honey, I'm home," printed across it.

Zachary frowned, looking at it.

Rhys was at home. Was he grounded? Did he just want Zachary to call him? To stop by the house for a visit? They hadn't talked since Zachary had broken the news to him about having found Madison, but that she had refused to return home.

He tapped the phone icon to see if Rhys or Vera would answer the phone. But before it could connect, there was a knock on the door.

Zachary looked at the door. He ended the phone call.

He walked over to the door, but he already knew who he was going to see through the wide-angle peephole.

Honey, I'm home.

Zachary opened the door for Rhys. He looked back over his shoulder at the living room window, which was dark. He didn't like Rhys being out on his own so late. Vera wouldn't like it either. She would ban Rhys from seeing Zachary if he kept taking off to see Zachary on his own. Zachary shut the door.

"What's going on? You shouldn't be here so late. Grandma will be worrying."

Rhys ignored the question. He tapped his phone busily and turned it around for Zachary to read it.

A message from Madison's account. Please help me.

CHAPTER 29

Zachary drew in his breath sharply. Madison had reached out to Rhys?

Maybe Jocelyn had been wrong. Maybe Madison was ready to get out of the business. Maybe she wanted to get back to Rhys and her friends and school and all of the normal teenage stuff instead of earning drugs and nice clothes through prostitution.

Rhys looked at Zachary, his eyes wide. He gestured to the screen insistently. <u>What do you think?</u>

"Do you know where she is?" Zachary asked. "Is she still in the same place or did they—or did she move somewhere else?"

Rhys shrugged. He used his finger to pull the message up and down, demonstrating that was the only thing Madison had sent to him. Just those three words.

Please help me.

And she could change her mind at any time. They needed to get to her while she still wanted out. Before Noah could return or talk her out of it. Zachary chewed on his lip. He needed to think it through.

But he had already made his decision without weighing any risks. Like Joss had said he did.

"I'll go see if she's still in the same place," he told Rhys. "If she's there, I'll get her to come with me. If she's not… well, I'll scout it out and see what I can find out."

Rhys nodded eagerly.

"You can't come. It's too dangerous. I can't watch my own back and yours at the same time. I can't take a teenager into a situation that might be dangerous."

Rhys looked affronted. He pointed to himself. He pointed to the phone screen. <u>I got the message. She asked me.</u>

"And you came to me. Because you know it's too dangerous to go on your own."

Rhys pointed from his shoulder to Zachary and back again. <u>Both of us together.</u>

"No. I'll take you as far as her street. You can stay in the car and keep lookout. But you can't come up. And if something happens, if I don't come back out or you think something has gone wrong, then you call 9-1-1 and get help. You don't come up."

Rhys considered this, frowning.

"That's my only offer," Zachary said. "I shouldn't even be doing that. I should take you back home and you can wait there until I have news."

Rhys shook his head violently.

"I don't want you to get hurt. I can't risk that."

Rhys held both hands up in a stop position. He pointed to himself then made a steering wheel motion. <u>I'll stay in the car.</u>

"You have to do what I say," Zachary insisted. "If you think anything is wrong, you call the police. You don't come looking for me under any circumstances."

Rhys nodded his agreement.

* * *

Zachary got ready to go, his mind racing a mile a minute. He tried to think through all of the possibilities of what he might be facing. His ADHD brain was good at that. Coming up with all of the possible permutations and hazards and presenting them to him in rapid succession. Slowing down and thinking of just one course of action, that was a lot harder.

Rhys watched him, his eyes still wide. He looked at his phone every minute or two, watching for any further messages from Madison. Zachary noted that he didn't write anything back. He didn't send any gifs or emojis. Just kept checking to see whether she had sent anything else.

"Okay." Zachary blew his breath out in a long stream. It was time to stop preparing and go. Either it would work out, or it wouldn't. He would keep Rhys safe and he would do his best to get Madison out of there. If he didn't succeed, at least Rhys would be safe.

CHAPTER 30

They got to Madison's apartment as quickly as they could, but it was already dark. Zachary looked up and down the street, regretting his agreement to bring Rhys with him. And regretting that they had gone over so late in the day. It wasn't that great a neighborhood. And wouldn't evening be the time that Madison started working? That didn't seem like an ideal time to show up.

But she had asked for help. What if she knew that Noah was going to move her? What if she'd been hurt after Zachary had left? Putting it off might endanger her.

"Okay. You stay here," he told Rhys.

Rhys looked out the window and back at Zachary, his eyes wide. He pointed at Zachary and raised his eyebrows. <u>You okay? You sure?</u>

Zachary opened his door and got out. "Keep the doors locked."

He left Rhys there without looking back. He didn't want anything to stop him. He couldn't show Rhys how nervous he was about trying to rescue Madison.

He wondered as he went up the stairs toward the apartment whether he should have called the police. They had already been there to try to talk her into leaving with them. And who knew what kind of consequences there would be if they came back. She wouldn't go with them. And then the things that Jocelyn predicted would happen. She would be taken away and hidden. Locked up and assaulted.

The police would be too obvious and attract too much attention.

No one would notice one lone private investigator walking into the building. He had been there once before and he didn't look anything like a cop. The guy who had seen him downstairs would think he was Madison's client. Other people, looking at his gaunt face and bloodshot eyes, would assume that he was an addict. He frequently went without shaving, knowing that people would discount him as a homeless person or druggie. Someone that they didn't want to look at or acknowledge, in case he asked them for money or targeted them some other way.

He could slip in, talk to Madison, and get back out quickly, unobtrusively. No one would even know he had been there.

He reached the top of the flight of stairs and stopped and listened for a moment. Making sure that there was no one else in the stairway, breathing and watching for his approach. He couldn't hear anything but his own heart pounding in his ears.

Zachary pushed the door open and slipped into the hallway, still on high alert, looking and listening for anything out of place. It could be a setup. But if it was, then it was Rhys that they were setting up, not Zachary. It was Rhys who had gotten the distress signal.

If they were watching for a young black boy, they weren't going to find him. Zachary could walk right by them and they wouldn't know who he was.

He padded down the carpeted hall, his light shoes making no noise. The only noise he made was the brushing together of his pants as he moved and his breathing, which sounded loud in his ears, but he knew logically it was not.

He stopped outside of Madison's door and listened. He couldn't hear anything going on inside this time. No argument or discussion going on. Maybe a TV way in the background, or maybe that was from one of the neighboring apartments. The walls were not built to be soundproof. There might not even be anyone home, though there was a light under the door. They could have left the lights on. Not everyone was diligent about shutting their lights off, especially kids who had never been responsible for paying electrical bills. Or it might have been left on to make it look inhabited so that it didn't become a target for burglars.

Zachary considered his approach. Send a text message to Madison to let her know he was there? Knock on the door? Which would be safer for her?

He stood there for several long seconds, considering, biting his knuckle anxiously. In the end, he decided it was better that he draw any negative reaction to himself, rather than alerting Noah or whoever might be with her that she was communicating covertly with someone. If Zachary showed up out of the blue, she had plausible deniability. She hadn't called him. There was no evidence that she'd ever reached out to him, because she hadn't. She'd messaged Rhys. And if she were smart, she had then deleted the message from her phone. Rhys hadn't messaged her back. So she was clean. No sign that she had contacted anyone.

Zachary raised his hand and knocked lightly on the door.

Maybe not loudly enough to be heard over the TV, or through a closed bedroom door. But if Noah were the one watching TV, that was probably for the best. It was better if Madison were the only one who heard him.

He waited. The sound of the TV kept going. No one shut it off or muted it, listening for him to knock again. There were no footsteps.

Zachary felt like the acid in his stomach was eating a hole right through it. He wanted something to happen, and he didn't want anything to happen. It took all of his self-will to raise his hand and knock again, a little more loudly.

He didn't hear the footsteps before the chain on the door clinked and the bolt slid open.

Madison opened the door and looked out at him.

Several emotions crossed her face as she recognized him. Relief, curiosity, confusion. Fear and anger.

"What are you doing here?" she whispered.

"Rhys got your message. I'm here to help you."

Her face was blank.

"To help you get out," Zachary said, waiting for the confirmation on her face. "You sent a message to Rhys."

Madison shook her head.

Zachary swore to himself.

Someone else had picked up Madison's phone and sent that message.

Or she might be lying. She might have messaged Rhys and then chickened out. She might be worried that someone would overhear them. She might not trust him. She had sent the message to Rhys, so why had Zachary shown up?

Or it might have been someone targeting Rhys. As Zachary had noted to himself before, Rhys was vulnerable. There were plenty of boys being trafficked too. Some for sex and some for slave labor. Rhys was young and part of a minority population, which made him more desirable. And he was selectively mute, using only a word or two in a day. He couldn't call for help.

"You did," he told Madison firmly, as if he knew she was the one who had sent the message. "You asked him for help." He tried to use his most reassuring voice, soothing Madison like she was a scared puppy. "I'm here to help you, Madison."

Madison shook her head again, stepping back slightly from the door. Distancing herself. Preparing to shut the door. She glanced nervously over her shoulder.

But it was too late, Noah had heard her, and he stepped into the kitchen.

CHAPTER 31

Zachary's mind spun through a hundred reactions and scenarios at once. Reach inside and grab Madison by the wrist. Pull her out of the room and trust that she would run with him once she was out the door. But Noah could be armed. He was undoubtedly faster than Zachary, and probably faster than Madison. They couldn't escape with superior speed. And Noah was in his own territory. He wouldn't hesitate to go after them, to pull a weapon if he needed it. Who was going to report him? One of his neighbors? Someone who had to live with him in the building when he made bail and returned home?

Zachary didn't carry a gun. He might be able to hold Noah off for a minute if he didn't have one, but not for long.

Madison hadn't sent the message to Rhys. Therefore, Noah was the one who had sent the message. He knew that Madison hadn't betrayed him. He had been trying to set Rhys up. Rhys was safe, in the car with the doors locked. Noah's ploy had failed. He had no way of knowing that Rhys was close by. He could see that Zachary had come in his place. As long as Zachary didn't force the issue, he should be able to back out of the situation without endangering himself or Madison. A good guy, but a coward. Someone who fled at the appearance of danger. Not someone that Noah needed to worry about.

"Uh, hi. Sorry, I guess I got my wires crossed somehow. I thought Madison had sent a message saying that she needed help. But she says it didn't come from her. She's fine, and no one needs my help, so I'll get out of here. My wife will be wondering where I am."

Noah continued to approach the door. He nudged Madison back, out of the way, so that Zachary was face-to-face with him, without a target or shield in between them. Zachary was glad that there was no chance of Madison getting caught in any crossfire. He wanted to keep her safe. Or as safe as he possibly could.

"I sent that message," Noah said, staring into Zachary's face, his expression blank, eyes deep dark pools.

Zachary tried to regulate his breathing, hoping that Noah wouldn't be able to hear how hard he was straining for breath or how fast and hard his heart was pumping.

"You sent it?"

Noah nodded. Zachary breathed through his mouth, waiting for Noah to explain. Noah would gloat, tell him that it was all a set-up and Zachary had fallen for it. Maybe it had been Zachary that Noah was hoping would come. Maybe his bosses wanted Zachary out of the way. Noah was hoping to please them by getting an obstacle out of the way.

Noah looked over at Madison. Zachary tried to analyze his expression. Not a threat. Not angry. He didn't see anything but Madison's own fear reflected back in Noah's face. Noah reached over and touched Madison on the arm. Reassuring.

Noah opened the door farther. "Come in. Out of sight."

CHAPTER 32

Zachary's body was telling him to retreat.

Pull back and get away from the danger. Don't march right into the spider's parlor. Get away.

But his brain was at odds with his body. The fear on Noah's face. Madison's confusion. The strange interplay between them that Zachary couldn't figure out. Something didn't make sense. But if he stayed for longer, he could figure it out. He was good at sorting out body language and human behavior.

He stepped into the tiny kitchen. Noah shut the door and bolted and chained it.

The floor was a little sticky. Like the linoleum had softened too much over the years and turned tacky. The kitchen was too small for all three of them to be in there comfortably. Noah motioned for Madison to leave the kitchen first, and she walked into a living room that was almost as small. But there were places to sit. Dark, stained furniture that looked like it had been pulled from the dump. Maybe picked up from a curbside or garage sale. Madison sat down on a rusty-colored, flowery couch with dark wood accents. Seventies? Eighties? It looked like something that Zachary's family might have had in the house that had burned down.

Noah motioned Zachary to a chair and sat down beside Madison. He didn't cuddle up to her, but he took her hand and held it in another gesture of reassurance.

<u>What was going on?</u>

"You sent that message to Rhys? Asking for help?" Zachary asked. His mouth was as dry as cotton. Some of his meds gave him a dry mouth, but it was so bone dry he could barely talk or work up a drop of spittle.

His tongue stuck to the roof of his mouth and felt like it belonged to someone else.

Noah nodded. He glanced aside at Madison and then looked at Zachary again. "You came here to get Madison. Because of Rhys."

Zachary nodded. It wasn't like there was any question of that fact. Why else would he be there? That was why he had come before, and that was why he had come this time.

Madison put her free hand on Noah's back. Like she was comforting him. She shook her head slightly. "Why?"

"You don't belong here. You should get out. You should go with him."

"I can't."

"You have to."

Madison shook her head more definitely. She looked at Zachary, as if expecting him to explain it to Noah. "If I leave, they'll go after him. They'll beat him up. Torture him."

She loved him. She wouldn't do anything that might put him in danger. Even if he was the one who had pulled her into the situation, acted the part of the Romeo and seduced her into something that she would never have thought she would agree to. Now she was stuck, and she wouldn't leave because of the danger to him.

"I hope they kill me," Noah said. "At least then, I wouldn't have to do this anymore. I'd be out of this life."

"No." Madison squeezed Noah's hand more tightly. "No, I won't let anything happen to you."

Zachary looked helplessly at the two of them. "Maybe... why don't you start at the beginning. Noah... I guess I'm being stupid here, but I don't understand. If you want out of the life, then get out. And if you want Madison out... then let her go. Help her to get away. You're the one holding her here."

"I'm not. I already told her to go. I told her she should have gone with you or the cops. If she stays around here... it's just going to get worse and worse."

Zachary could see the same pain in Noah's eyes that he'd seen in Jocelyn's. It felt like a stab to his chest, thinking about how scared and hopeless Jocelyn must have felt for all of those years, feeling trapped and too afraid to even try to get out. Until she was all worn out and no one wanted her anymore. Until she nearly died, and no one had cared.

"How is it going to get worse?" Zachary asked. If they were going to get Madison out, she needed to hear it. She needed to hear all of the gritty, sordid details and to understand what she had gotten herself into and how she needed to get out now, not to wait until she reached the end of the line like Jocelyn had.

Noah swallowed. He looked down at his hands, his elbows leaning on his knees and Madison's hand held between his. How old was he? Studying his face close up, Zachary wondered if he was even nineteen. He'd looked older. He'd acted older. But in the dim light of a yellow lamp, he looked very young. He didn't have any stubble on his face. His skin was smooth as a child's.

"You don't want to be in this kind of life," he told Madison without looking at her. "I've told you that. But I haven't… I haven't told you everything."

"What is it? Tell me now."

Noah looked up, across the room, across the kitchen, to the locked front door. Reassuring himself that he was safe from intruders, that there was no one else there to hear his confession.

Zachary's phone vibrated in his pocket. He suddenly remembered Rhys, sitting out there in the dark, cold car, waiting for Zachary to return. He pulled it out and glanced at the single character on the screen. A question mark.

"Give me a second," he said. He quickly tapped out a message to Rhys that he was okay and would get down as soon as he could. But Rhys was to sit tight for now. Then he slid the phone back away and looked at Noah. "I'm sorry. Just a check-in to make sure everything is okay."

Noah nodded.

CHAPTER 33

"I was thirteen when I started," Noah said. "I don't know. Maybe twelve. I don't remember exactly when the first time I saw him was."

"Him?" Madison repeated.

"Connor." Noah's voice cracked. "The one who recruited me."

He didn't look at Madison. She stared at him, trying to understand what he was talking about.

"Connor said I was special. He said... I had a beautiful face. I'd never... I'd never been with anyone. Never had anyone give me attention like that. Never had anyone say a kind word to me."

Madison made a little noise of protest.

"I was living with my grandma. No one wanted me. My parents died. But they'd never wanted me around anyway. I bounced back and forth between them and different steps or uncles or whatever. And my grandma. She was the only one who ever gave me any kind of stable home. A place where I could sleep and not be afraid of who might show up in the middle of the night, or what kind of a mood people might be in. She was good to me, but she was old, and her health wasn't good, and it didn't help to have everyone always messing with her, disrupting things and dumping me there without a word of warning."

"And she died," Zachary filled in, remembering what the man at the bodega had said.

"Yeah," Noah agreed. "And… I was lost. I didn't know what to do with myself. Where to go or how to feel better. I drank, I did pot, I hung out with guys who broke all of the rules. Because I didn't have anyone else to go to. At least they put up with having me around. And then Connor..."

Zachary shook his head, his stomach flipping.

"He said he loved me," Noah said, eyes glistening. "He said he would help me. Take care of me. But it was just a sham. Just like they would teach me to do later, to bring other kids in. Other boys. And girls."

He looked at Madison. Her eyes were wide. Maybe it wasn't until then that she realized that she'd been intentionally targeted. Like Jocelyn had suggested, Noah would tell her that he just needed her to do something for him to help keep the leg-breakers off of him. Just one favor. And just another. And someday, when they had paid off all of the debts and had enough money, they would live an idyllic life with the two of them sharing a little house somewhere, safe and comfortable and able to put the hard days behind them.

She thought that he really did love her. That he was her boyfriend. She'd caught his eye, and he had been drawn toward her. It had been fate. Cupid's arrow. Not an act coldly crafted to draw her in and seduce her until she was willing to do whatever he asked her to.

"But… no." Madison breathed. "No. That's not what it was like."

Noah let go of her hand and put his hands over his eyes. "Yes. That's exactly what it was like. I found your social profiles online. That's how we identify who we're going to target. See where you go to school. What your schedule is. How much time your parents are away or doing their own thing. What you're posting online. We work up a profile. What kind of a person you are and what we'll use—what I'll use—to lure you."

Madison's breath rasped loudly. She stared at Noah, shocked and distressed, still not believing that what he was telling her was true. Despite everything she had done, she had thought she was doing it for him. To help him. Keep him safe. To get his love and approval and all of the good feelings that went with doing what he wanted her to. He was supposed to love her. Zachary had no doubt that Noah had told her that he loved her. And she had believed it with all her heart. She would do anything for him. Just like he felt about Bridget.

"You're not the first one." Noah's voice was strangled. "I turn out a couple new kids every year. You don't know what kind of... what a piece of crap I am."

"But..." Madison shook her head, tears starting to run down her face. "Why? Why would you do that?"

"Because I have to do the same thing as you... to keep my boss happy. And it's not enough to just turn tricks. That only earns so much money. I need to keep bringing in fresh meat. And each of them, eventually, will have to do the same. You move up in the organization, or you don't survive."

"And your boss is... Connor?"

Noah took a deep breath. "No. No... Connor died years ago. He had someone over him, and they had someone over them, and on up. When he was gone, then the person over him took over his stable."

In reading up on trafficking to verify what Jocelyn had told him, Zachary had come across an article that said that each person being trafficked earned their pimp in the neighborhood of three hundred thousand dollars per year. If Noah was turning tricks and bringing in two new kids each year, then he was bringing in almost a million dollars a year for his boss. And if each of those two new kids stayed in the business and also started targeting a couple of new girls—or boys—each year... it was no wonder traffickers were bringing in billions of dollars across the country every year.

And no wonder they didn't want to lose any of the victims to do-gooders like Zachary or police stings and would fight to get them back, forcing them to keep earning money until they were worn out and useless.

Or dead.

"Who's over you?" Madison asked. "Is it someone I've met?"

Noah nodded.

"Who is he?"

"She," Noah corrected. "Peggy Ann."

Madison's jaw dropped. Her eyes could not get any wider. She shuddered. "I knew... she was scary. I thought... I don't know what I thought. Just that she was... not someone to cross, I guess."

Noah nodded. His right hand went to his opposite shoulder, rubbing his bicep. Madison pushed the sleeve of his t-shirt up, revealing puckered burn marks. She smoothed them gently with her finger.

"Did she do that? Peggy Ann?"

Noah's eyes were far away. "I don't remember."

"You don't remember? How can you not remember who did that to you?"

Noah looked down at the scars. "There have been a lot of people. A lot of punishments. It's best... not to think about it."

Madison leaned into him, resting her forehead against his shoulder. Noah rested his cheek on the top of her head and he stroked her back gently.

"You do care," Madison said, slightly accusing.

"Of course I care," he murmured. "That's why I get in trouble. That's why he's here." Noah nodded to Zachary.

"So you want me to... take Madison away. Is that it?"

"Yes. Take her away. Make her parents go away with her. And if they won't go away, then she has to go by herself. She can't stay around here."

"My sis—my friend says that she'll have to change her name and move out of state to keep them from finding her."

"Yes. Do that." He held the back of Madison's head, pressing her against himself. "Get far away from here so Gordo can't find you."

Madison sniffled. "Who is Gordo?"

"He's… the top boss around here. I don't know if there's anyone above him, but I don't think so. I think everything goes back to Gordo. All of the money flows up to him. And… all of the information."

"You need to get out too," Zachary pointed out. "If you don't, they'll just come after you. Peggy Ann and Gordo and all of their enforcers. You'll be killed."

Noah nodded tiredly. "Yes."

"So you need to get out," Zachary repeated. "You can't just stay here and wait for them to find out."

"It won't take them long." Letting go of Madison, Noah rubbed his eyes and then pulled out his phone to look at it. "You need to get her out of here. Before they come looking."

Zachary's heart started pounding faster again. He had settled down, listening to Noah and realizing that he wasn't the enemy. He wasn't there to shoot Zachary or kidnap Rhys. He wanted Madison to be safe. After all of the boys and girls that he had turned out in the past five or six years, he couldn't do it again, and he wanted Zachary to take Madison somewhere safe.

But the fact that Noah wanted to help didn't mean that the danger was gone. It had just transformed into a different shape. Into Peggy Ann, who Zachary pictured as a tall, Amazon-like redhead, and Gordo, an enormous Mexican man, both of whom would do whatever they had to in order to keep their hooks in Madison, and would torture and kill Noah for letting her escape.

They were both out there, getting closer. Maybe looking in through the windows of Zachary's car, parked down on the dark street, seeing Rhys there waiting.

Zachary stood up, shaking off the inertia. They had to move. Sitting there talking about it wasn't going to do anyone any good.

"Come with me. Both of you."

Madison looked at Noah, waiting for him to agree. Noah shook his head.

"Yes," Zachary said firmly. He gestured for Madison to get up. A snappy, brisk command. She got to her feet.

Zachary reached for Noah's arm and gave it a little tug. "Come on. You're coming with us."

"No. I don't want to. You go ahead."

"We're not leaving you here."

"I'm tired. I just want it all to be over."

Zachary pulled harder. "I know what it's like to be depressed," he said. "I know what it's like not to want to put in the effort to survive."

Noah nodded. "Then leave me alone."

"No. Other people pulled me through. Just because you can't see the light at the end of the tunnel, or imagine ever having enough energy to live again, that doesn't mean it's the end. Things can change. Now come on."

One more insistent pull. Madison grabbed Noah's other arm and, between the two of them, they got him to his feet.

Zachary juggled his phone out and messaged Rhys. Coming now.

He and Madison walked Noah to the door. Once they got him moving, the momentum seemed to keep him going. They didn't have to force him, but both still held on, guiding him, unwilling to release him and take the chance that they wouldn't be able to get him moving again. He wasn't big or heavily-built, but Zachary suspected that he and Madison did not have the strength it would take to move him if he were a dead weight.

Out of the apartment. They shut the door, but no one bothered to lock it. Down the hall. To the stairs.

Zachary felt his phone vibrate. They coaxed Noah down the stairs. Zachary's heart was pounding.

When they reached the bottom, he pulled his phone out again. It was a stupid thing to do. He needed to get Madison and Noah out to the car without being distracted by whatever else happened to be going on.

Rhys, of course. Zachary stopped in his tracks.

A gif of a rotating red light.

Madison looked at him, still pulling Noah forward, but now Zachary was anchoring him on one side instead of helping to direct him and keep him moving. "What is it?"

Zachary turned the phone around to show her.

Madison scowled. "Dammit, Rhys, use words!"

Zachary felt the same way. Clearly, Rhys meant there was an emergency. But did he mean that the police were there? That someone was hurt? That the bad guys were there? Zachary didn't know whether to keep going, to hide, or to go back up the stairs.

CHAPTER 34

When he looked at the stairs, he knew that wasn't going to happen. There was no way that he and Madison would be able to get Noah back up the stairs again. And it was probably the worst thing they could do. Going back up to the apartment would just mean that they were cornered. Unless they went up farther, to another floor, in the hopes that whoever was coming after them wouldn't expect them to be higher up in the apartment building.

But they couldn't make it.

Zachary looked out the narrow window in the door between the stairway and the lobby. There were no flashing lights out on the street. No police out there, waiting for them. At least, not police with a car with its lights on.

"This way." He jerked his head, and he and Madison hustled Noah through to the hallway Zachary had taken the first day. The domain of the man with the bathrobe. Zachary hoped not to run into him again.

Anyone who saw them in the hallway would think that Noah was drunk. Maybe they were trying to take him home. Though anyone who lived in the building would know that they were on the wrong floor. Zachary tried to think of a way to explain that, but couldn't come up with anything. Too many scenarios were running through his head and he couldn't find one that worked.

When they were on the other side of the lobby door, Zachary stopped and looked back. He stayed as far to the side as he could, so they wouldn't see his face blocking the window if they looked in his direction.

The lobby remained empty. He stayed there, watching, waiting for someone to enter the building. Maybe it was a false alarm. Maybe Rhys had been wrong. Worried by something that wasn't anything to do with Madison and Noah.

The inner lobby door opened, and a man and woman walked through. Zachary studied them. The woman was not the tall, well-built redhead that he had envisioned. She was rather petite, with dark hair, probably in her forties. Her face was not unattractive, but was hard. Sneering. She wore fashionable clothes with a red leather jacket.

Was she Peggy Ann? The woman who had scared Madison so badly? Who had burned Noah? Noah wasn't a big guy, and Zachary couldn't see the small woman being able to overcome him by physical force.

But maybe she hadn't needed to. There had been other threats, other ways to coerce him. And she didn't need to be strong to punish him for his failings.

The man was not big either. Nor fat. Probably not Gordo. Which made sense, because why would Gordo, the top boss in Vermont, or maybe in all of New England, be there to see Madison and Noah? Zachary backed away from the window. He looked at Madison and Noah.

"Is that her? Or someone looking for you?"

Noah didn't move. Madison moved in close to Zachary and peeked out. "That's Peggy Ann. I don't know who the guy is." She turned to look at Noah. "Is he one of your friends? I mean…" She had to shift her thinking, "One of your clients or bosses?"

Noah didn't move. Zachary took a step back so that they weren't all crowding around the door. Madison put her hand on Noah's arm to encourage him forward. Noah reluctantly looked through the window. He withdrew, pressing himself against the wall so he couldn't be seen through the door.

"Jorge," he said. "He's..." Noah hesitated, searching for a word. "A troubleshooter. He must have heard about you." His eyes met Zachary's. "Or about the police coming. He's come to... take care of things." Noah's eyes darted back and forth, worried. "Sort out any problems."

Goosebumps rose on Zachary's neck and arms. He looked through the narrow window, a quick peek to map the progress of the couple across the lobby to the stairs. As soon as they were on their way up the stairs, Zachary, Madison, and Noah would need to get across the lobby and outside. They could get to the car and get out of there before Peggy Ann and Jorge knew that Madison and Noah were missing. If they would even know there was something wrong. Maybe they would think that the two had just gone out for food or to see to a client.

Except that they'd left the door unlocked. Did they usually lock it when they left? They might not have a lot of money in the apartment, but Madison's clothes were pricey.

He waited a few more seconds, then took another peek through the window. They were disappearing through the door to the stairs. Zachary watched through the sliver of window, waiting for them to mount the stairs. That would be his signal to move. He didn't see them on the stairs, and wondered if he'd missed it. They might have been too far to one side and he just hadn't been able to see them. His heart was jumping all over the place, telling him that it was time to move, but he hesitated, wanting the confirmation that they were on their way up to the apartment. It wouldn't make more than a few seconds' difference one way or the other, but he wanted to be sure.

Still nothing.

Zachary put his hand on the doorknob, getting ready to lead the others into the lobby. Clearly, he had missed the couple climbing the stairs, and to wait any longer would be detrimental to their chances of making it out of there in one piece.

Then the door to the stairs opened. Zachary froze. Jorge, the troubleshooter, stood in the doorway. He looked around the lobby, eyes sharp. Zachary moved slowly to the side. Any sudden movement would attract attention, even if Jorge hadn't been specifically looking at the door to the ground floor apartments. He hoped that by fading gradually to the side, Jorge wouldn't see him, and they would avoid detection. He waited, frozen, not even able to breathe. He didn't hear footsteps walking toward them, and in a moment heard the snick of the other door closing again. He was afraid to look. Afraid that as soon as he put his face to the window again, he would see Jorge looking straight back at him, just waiting for him to make a mistake.

But if Jorge had gone on, they needed to get out. Zachary moved over again, very slowly, looking past the edge of the window with one eye, exposing no more of himself than absolutely necessary.

CHAPTER 35

He did not see Jorge. There was no one in the lobby. He didn't want to see them going up the stairs this time. He'd been hiding for too long. Either they would go up or they would not, and Zachary believed that the last look around the lobby was Jorge's final look. He wouldn't stay down any longer after that.

"Let's go."

Madison stuck close to him. Noah was looking dazed. Zachary wondered for a moment if he were dissociating. Not even consciously with them any longer. He nudged Noah's shoulder, and the three of them moved through the lobby. Madison was dragging back, looking around, too worried that there might be someone hiding there. But if there were, it was too late. They were going to get caught. There was no way to avoid it once they were out of the hallway.

"Come on, keep moving. We need to get out of here."

"It's not going to work," Noah intoned. "We're never going to be able to get away from them together. You should go ahead. I'll stay back, try to convince them that I've moved Mad somewhere safe. I can keep them distracted, give you a chance to get away."

"You're coming with us," Zachary said firmly.

Madison looked at him, nodding her gratitude. She still had feelings for Noah, even if he had betrayed her. She hadn't had enough time to reconsider the impact of what he had told them. She kept operating on the same level, as if he were her boyfriend and she needed to protect him.

Zachary hit the release for the inner lobby door and hustled Madison and Noah through it. He followed them through and out the second door to the front of the building. They turned toward him, not sure which way to go.

"My car is down there," Zachary gestured toward it, in too much of a hurry to sort out his left from his right. They kept moving. They looked around the neighborhood with bright eyes, as if they had been released from a long prison term. The cold air and the darkness were startling after having been inside.

Zachary hurried, trying to press Madison and Noah forward faster. They still had time. Peggy Ann and Jorge wouldn't have figured out that they had run yet. They weren't yet in pursuit. But it wouldn't be much longer. They would arrive at the apartment and find the door open. They would look around, but it would be immediately obvious that Madison and Noah were not there. They wouldn't know how long it had been since they left, but they would run down the stairs anyway, they would look up and down the street trying to spot them.

"Come on. Come on."

Zachary could see, as they approached, that there was a cop standing beside his car. His heart sank.

* * *

Dealing with the police force was never quick. And if he didn't get out of there right away, Peggy Ann and Jorge were going to see them all together, and they would know who was behind Madison's and Noah's disappearance.

Madison and Noah stopped stock-still at the sight of the police officer. As if he might not see them if they didn't move and didn't get any closer. Maybe just because they didn't know what to do. Retreat? Run? Wait?

Zachary forced a friendly smile at the officer, getting closer and studying his face in the dim streetlight to see if it were someone he had worked with before. But it was just a beat cop or someone on traffic, not a detective that he had worked with. Not one of the administrative positions that Zachary might have had the opportunity to meet with and talk with before.

"Hi. Is there a problem, officer?"

The policeman looked Zachary over. He had a notepad and pen in his hand. Writing a ticket? It didn't look like a ticket clipboard to Zachary. Just a regular notepad.

"Is this your car, sir?"

"Yes." Zachary scanned the signs along the street for one that said he wasn't allowed to stop or park there. He didn't see any. The curb wasn't painted a different color. There was no fire hydrant close by. He couldn't see any reason the cop should be there making inquiries. Nothing that would have tipped him off that Zachary's car didn't belong to a resident. "Is there a problem?"

"Is this… your son?" The cop looked mildly uncomfortable asking the question. Zachary was clearly white and Rhys was not. Even darker in the shadows of the car. But there was no reason that a white man couldn't be the father of a black boy or responsible for him by some other relationship.

"No." Zachary gave Rhys a little wave, trying to look casual and unconcerned. So that Rhys wouldn't be anxious and the policeman would see that there was nothing wrong and would let Zachary drive away before Peggy Ann and Jorge came back out of the building. "Just a friend. I was just running inside to get the others." He indicated Madison and Noah. "I hope you weren't waiting long. You know how long kids can take to get ready sometimes." He smiled, inviting the cop to agree. To laugh about how long it took his kids to get ready. Though he didn't look old enough to have teenagers. Maybe he had younger siblings or cousins or could remember the days when he would take hours to get ready for a date or a dance or even just to go out to hang with other guys.

The cop didn't look too sure of this. He didn't laugh or give Zachary a knowing look. "I'd like you to open the car, sir."

"Of course." Zachary's key fob didn't always work, and he didn't want the car to flash its lights when he unlocked it, advertising his presence. So he walked around to his door and unlocked it manually. He hit the switch to unlock the rest of the doors.

"Would you ask your friend to get out of the car, please?"

"Sure," Zachary said agreeably. "But can I ask... if something is wrong? We have a thing that I'm supposed to be getting them to, and I didn't want to be late."

"I want to talk to him."

Zachary bent down to talk to Rhys, inside the car. "He wants to talk to you. It should just take a minute."

Rhys's eyes were wide and worried. He wanted to know what was going on. Wanted to know why Noah was there and what had taken Zachary so long. He knew enough to be worried about talking to the cop.

He had grown up knowing that cops could stop him at any time, and they wouldn't like the fact that he was black and was refusing to talk to them.

As Rhys got out of the car, his hands raised to his shoulders to show that he was unarmed and wasn't planning to attack anyone, Zachary stepped back from the car, walking a couple of steps around the hood to have an unobstructed view of him. But he stopped there, not wanting the cop to think that he was being pincered between the two of them.

"You should know that Rhys is selectively mute," he explained calmly. "That means that he won't be able to talk to you out loud."

The cop didn't like this. He looked at Rhys suspiciously. As if he might be some kind of monster or predator and was trying to keep the cop from figuring it out.

"How does he communicate, then? Does he use sign language?"

"He uses a combination of gestures and text or pictures on his phone. He's not going to cause you any trouble; you just need to know that it is going to take longer than usual to establish communication. And we do want to be getting on our way."

The cop ignored the last part of Zachary's statement, making no indication that he would move things along.

"Can we get into the car?" Madison asked. "It's kind of chilly out here."

She wasn't wearing a coat and the cop was. So was Zachary. The car would be warmer, and sheltered from the breeze. The cop looked at Madison, his hand at his hip. He looked her over, and his eyes spent even longer on Noah.

"You, I know," he said, looking at Noah.

Noah stared down at his feet, nodding.

"You pimping them out?" the cop demanded, eyes going back to Zachary. "I'm not going to put up with that on my watch."

"No. No sir. I'm trying to get them out of here. Away from all that. That's why we're here." Zachary looked back toward the apartment building. Peggy Ann and Jorge could be coming out the front door any time. "And why we need to get on our way. Soon."

"Turn out your pockets," the cop told Madison and Noah. "Put the contents on the car. Then put up your hands."

Noah obeyed. Madison didn't have any pockets. She looked at the cop for a moment, then slid a couple of fingers down into her bra and pulled out her phone. She put it on the car. They both raised their hands.

"Stay there," the cop told Rhys. He went over to the other two and felt their pockets and other key areas to satisfy himself that they weren't carrying any weapons. He opened the back car door and used his flashlight to check the back seats, footwells, and under the front seats. He ran one hand along the crack in the back of the bench seats. He finally nodded. "Fine. Get in. But if you cause me any trouble, believe me, you'll never get a break out of me again."

Madison and Noah got quickly into the car, bumping over each other and getting settled into place. The policeman looked at Rhys.

"Are you okay?"

Rhys nodded.

"Did he bring you here?"

Rhys hesitated, looking at Zachary, then nodded his head.

"Why did he bring you here?"

Rhys pointed at Madison.

"To get her?"

Rhys nodded again.

"Are you two turning tricks? Is he taking you to some party to make some money?"

Rhys shook his head violently, eyes wide.

"Why, then?"

Rhys frowned. He pointed at Madison, then he made a roof-and-house motion with both hands.

"To take her home?"

Rhys and Zachary nodded. Zachary was itching to explain the whole situation himself in a couple of brief sentences so that they could get into the car and get out of there before Peggy Ann and Jorge came looking for Madison and Noah. Madison and Noah were ducking down, making themselves as invisible as possible. Sheltering behind the seats where they wouldn't be as easy to see. Peggy Ann and Jorge would come out of the apartment building, and see the cop there with Rhys and Zachary. Maybe they wouldn't get close enough to see that Madison and Noah were there too. They wouldn't connect the two incidents.

But he knew that if he tried to help the conversation with Rhys along, the policeman would just view him as more suspicious. He couldn't speak for Rhys, but had to let him explain himself without interruption.

"How do you know her?"

Rhys considered. He pointed to his pocket and made a 'telephone' hand-shape beside his ear.

The cop nodded. "You can get out your phone."

Rhys nodded and lowered his hand slowly to take his phone out with two fingers. He held it up, making sure that the policeman could get a good look at it before changing his grip on it. Rhys tapped and swiped his phone to find a photo, then held it up for the cop. Madison sitting at her desk. One of the photos he had shown to Zachary.

The cop looked at it. "You know her from school."

Rhys nodded. He looked at the apartment building, and tapped his wrist where he would wear a watch. He looked back at the car where Madison and Noah were sitting. They were hunched down out of sight, which was good, but it would be better if they were out of there.

But the policeman wasn't sure he wanted to let them go yet. He wanted to be sure of what was going on before he let them take off. Better not to be the guy who had let a pimp operate right under his nose. That kind of thing never looked good when it hit the papers. People didn't understand that the police couldn't just arrest someone on a gut feeling.

"I want your name and contact information. ID if you have it."

Rhys nodded. He indicated the cop's pen and notepad. The officer handed them over. Rhys put the notepad on the car to write his information down. He handed them back when he was done and pulled his student bus pass lanyard out of his shirt. Turning it over, he displayed his student ID card. The policeman compared the information Rhys had written down with what was on his card.

"You can get back in the car."

Rhys got in. The cop went through the contents of Noah's pockets, which were still on top of the car. He wrote down detailed notes. Zachary was sweating with his anxiety over getting out of there. They had been there much too long. Peggy Ann and Jorge were probably watching the drama from inside the apartment building. Maybe making phone calls to have Zachary followed or to call in hired guns. He knew the cop was just doing his job, but if it ended up with Madison and Noah being retrieved by their cartel and Zachary and Rhys in the crosshairs of some criminal intent on making sure that they didn't interfere again…

The officer handed Noah his possessions back, other than his phone, and didn't give Madison's phone back either. He left them side by side on the top of the car, face up, keeping an eye on them.

Then he turned his attention back to Zachary. "Now I want your information. And I want ID and your car registration and insurance."

Zachary nodded. He glanced along the street again for any signs saying he wasn't allowed to park there. He still didn't spot anything. If there was a sign, it was out of sight and he could challenge it in court. The cop wanted him for more than just a traffic violation, but if that were all he could get, Zachary was sure he would go for it. Then he would have an official record of who he had stopped. He would be able to show his superiors that he had done everything in his power to curtail any criminal activities.

CHAPTER 36

Zachary slowly removed his wallet from his pocket and removed the items that the policeman wanted to see. His hands were shaking violently. The adrenaline was having an effect on him. Walking into the apartment not knowing what situation he was going to face, being confronted by Noah, trying to make a run for it and trying to avoid Peggy Ann and Jorge. Trying to deal with the cop when every fiber in his body was telling him to get out of there.

Closer to the cop, he could see his name bar. Burkholdt.

"Tell me how you got involved with this," Burkholdt said. "This is exactly the type of situation that we don't want civilians caught in the middle of. You shouldn't be here."

Zachary swallowed and looked down. That was probably true. He had considered whether to call the police before going to see Madison, but he had been afraid that she would just refuse to cooperate if he showed up with officials. And in retrospect, he was sure that instinct had been correct. He wouldn't have been able to make any kind of progress if he'd shown up there with the police, or if the police had gone there without him. Madison was not the one who had sent the message asking for help. She would have just looked blankly at them and refused to go. She would have denied knowing anything about that message. She would say that she hadn't sent it. Because she hadn't.

He told the cop about being a private investigator. About Rhys coming to him to help with finding Madison, and then returning for more help when he'd received her message asking for help. He left out the details about Madison not being the one who had sent the message or about Noah's involvement in the whole thing. He hoped that if he kept it simple, the policeman would finally agree to let them go.

"She was reported as a missing person?" Burkholdt asked.

"Yes."

"So if I called in asking for confirmation, I would be told that there was a report made?"

"Yes. Joshua Campbell was assigned to the case. I spoke to him."

"You did, did you?"

"Yes. I always let law enforcement know if I've been retained on a case that the police have had some involvement in. Or if they should know about it. I always cooperate with local law enforcement."

"Sure you do."

"You're welcome to call him. I have his numbers if you need them."

Burkholdt studied him closely, considering this. Eventually, he nodded. He wrote down all of Zachary's information.

"How is the other boy involved in it?"

"Noah?"

For a moment, the policeman looked blank. Then he shrugged. "Whatever name he gave you. He's been around here for a long time. I know him. Just how is he mixed up in this?"

"He was just… helping Madison out. Took her under his wing. Felt sorry for her, I guess."

"Figured he could turn her out, more likely. You can't trust him. If I was you, I wouldn't take him with me."

Zachary nodded. "I know… but I need to. I can't explain all of the details right now, but I think it's safer to have him with me than not."

"Don't count on it. He's more likely to call his pimp with her new location than he is to help her out. People like him don't change. He's not going to suddenly go from being a hooker to being the savior of a runaway. He's just looking for a higher paycheck. A way to move up in the organization. As soon as he knows where she's going, he'll tell them."

Zachary swallowed back the acid that rose in his throat at this suggestion. He had to admit that Burkholdt had a good point. What were the chances that Noah was really looking to help Madison out, after putting months into getting her established in the business? What were the chances that even if he had altruistic feelings toward Madison, or was feeling guilty for what he had done, that they would last?

Joss had talked about walling off her feelings. Compartmentalizing. So that she didn't have to think about the things she was doing. She could keep those parts of herself separate and not have to acknowledge them.

He was sure Noah would rather not admit what kind of person he was and the things that he had chosen to do to get the money or drugs that were dangled before him like a carrot. He would rather think of himself as a fair and compassionate person. The kind of guy who would help a teenager get back to her family. But when it came down to it, who was he more likely to be loyal to?

He started to regret having insisted that Noah come along. He had been affected by Noah's story and his tears. But Noah probably had a hundred different stories and could turn the tears on and off at will. He was playing them. Getting Zachary and Rhys right where he wanted them. Once he'd confirmed their intentions and found out everything he could about them and lulled them into a false sense of security, they would turn back to his supervisors. To Peggy Ann and the rest of them. That was what he had been trained to do for the past five years. If that part of his story was true.

The cop handed Zachary's ID back to him loose, leaving him to put everything back into his wallet.

Zachary shivered with cold while at the same time, sweat dripped down his back.

"Listen to what I tell you," Burkholdt said again. "Leave the boy here. Don't take him with you and trust him not to report everything he sees."

"I can't leave him here."

Burkholdt looked into his face, lips tight. "You need to leave him here."

Zachary took a deep breath. "Are you arresting him?"

"I don't have any cause to arrest him. But I know this kid. I've arrested him before and I know what he does around here. You should listen to someone who knows."

Zachary nodded. He looked at the driver's seat of the car. "Thank you for your concern. Am I free to go now?"

The cop's jaw muscles stood out as he clenched his teeth. He nodded. "You're free to go." He handed Zachary the two phones.

Zachary's knees wobbled. He tried to keep himself together. Keeping tight control over his body, he managed to walk back around the car and to get into the driver's seat. He was looking around, charting his escape route, before he even got into the seat. The keys were still in the ignition. Before he even had his door shut or his seatbelt on, he was shifting into gear. He put it into reverse, backing up over the curb onto the sidewalk and then throwing it into drive and performing a tight U-turn to get them turned around and heading back in the direction they had come. The cop had jumped back out of the way when he had backed up onto the sidewalk. Madison gave a little shriek as they were thrown unexpectedly around the car. None of them had been braced for Zachary's maneuver. But he was desperate. His body was throwing up all kinds of signals that he was in danger and he wasn't going to ignore them. He wasn't going to sedately perform a three-point turn or drive forward until he came to an intersection where he could get himself turned around properly. If the cop jumped into his car and came after him, then Zachary would deal with it. But not until he had put some distance between him and the people who were after them.

Noah swore, hanging on to Rhys's seat in front of him and trying to stay upright. "Who taught you to drive? We're going to have that cop right back on our tail!"

"I'm getting us out of there," Zachary snapped. "I'm not staying around to see if they managed to get a tail on us while we were trying to get away from that cop. We were sitting there way too long."

He looked in his rear-view mirror, watching for any suspicious vehicles. He was going fast enough that they would have to make themselves pretty obvious if they were going to keep up with him. He was aiming to put as much space between him and any pursuers as possible.

When he got to a straight stretch of road, he opened and slammed his door to make sure that it latched properly, and pulled his seatbelt around himself and clicked it into place.

"You might want to put on your seatbelts too," he told his passengers.

Rhys was already pulling his out, grinning. Madison and Noah complained as they put theirs on.

"Do you want to get out of there safely, or not get out at all?" Zachary demanded.

He had a bad feeling. He'd missed something. He knew that there was a problem, but he couldn't think of what it was. Something had been off. His ever-vigilant PTSD brain had caught it but hadn't passed the message to his conscious brain.

"We need to go somewhere safe," he told his passengers.

He waited for the suggestions. First on the list, of course, was to Madison's parents. But he immediately discarded that idea. There were others in the organization who would know how to find Madison's family. They knew what school she went to. They knew her name. It would only take a few minutes to find out her address, if they didn't have it already. Her home was too dangerous. He was going to have to convince her parents to leave their home and make massive changes in their lives if they were going to be able to keep Madison alive and out of Peggy Ann's stable. He didn't know how he was going to approach that. How he was going to convince them of anything.

He needed to take Rhys home and to make sure that he was safe. Vera was sure to be wondering where he was and worrying over him. But he didn't want to take Noah to Rhys's house either. Though he supposed that Rhys's grandmother was just as easy to find as Madison's family. His only hope was that Noah and Madison hadn't told anyone who had come after Madison and how he knew about her. If they didn't know that Rhys had asked Zachary to look into it, then Rhys would be safe. If Peggy Ann and her crew knew who Zachary was, he was going to have to plant enough disinformation for them to believe that he had been hired by Madison's parents rather than by Rhys.

"We could stay with someone," Madison suggested. "What about Jeff? Or Roxanne?"

Noah shook his head. "Can't be anyone in the organization or known to it."

"But they're not part of… they're just friends."

"No."

"They're just people we hung out with. Friends."

"I don't have any friends, Mad. Anybody we've hung out with. Anyone we've partied with. They're all part of it. Or they're known. Clients or prospects."

Madison made a noise of protest. She looked at Noah, her face lined with anxiety and pain. "Noah… I don't understand this. I don't believe it. Tell me it's not true. You're just teasing. You just want me to go home."

"It's too late to go home. I want you to be safe, and you won't be safe there."

"This doesn't make sense. I love you, Noah."

"No, you don't. You've just been... conditioned. It's what we do. It's how we get people to do what we say." Noah cleared his throat, but his voice was still unsteady. "Praise and love when they do what they're supposed to. Consequences and punishment when they don't." He turned away from her to look out the window. "You think you're making your own choices, but you're not. You're doing what they want you to do. Whenever they want something, they tell me, and it's my job to get you to do it. Whatever it takes. If I can't, there's a consequence."

There was a long silence. Zachary glanced over at Rhys, who was playing with his phone, listening to the others.

"Where are we going to go, then?" Madison asked. "One of my friends from school? I know they're not mixed up in this."

"They'll look for you at the school. And if you're not with your parents, they'll start checking out your friends at school. You can't stay here, Mad. It has to be somewhere else."

"What do you mean, somewhere else? Where?"

Noah looked at Zachary in the rear-view mirror. "Did you have any kind of plan? Or were you just going to take her home?"

"We were still working that out. Your message took me by surprise."

"Where then?" Madison asked in frustration. "We can't just drive around all night."

"A hotel?" Zachary suggested. "Somewhere we can stop and regroup and figure it out? They're not going to find you if it isn't somewhere you have been connected with before."

"What hotel?" Noah grumbled. "We have people at hotels. They'll be on the lookout. She'll be seen."

"They can't have people at all of the hotels all of the time. We'll pick somewhere they're not watching."

Noah shook his head, but didn't argue it any further.

CHAPTER 37

Zachary breathed a sigh of relief when they were all in the hotel room. He had watched carefully for a tail and was pretty sure that they couldn't have been followed. Every now and then, his ability to drive fast came in handy. He had a good eye for detail and noticed things in an instant.

The kids all seemed to be relieved too. Noah had been vigilant as they approached the hotel and looked around the lobby, watching for anyone that he knew or anyone that might be looking at them the wrong way. But he had gradually relaxed and, by the time they got into the room and closed the door, he was ready to crash. He went into the bathroom, and when he came back out, he lay down on one of the beds and buried his head.

Madison still hadn't been able to reconcile herself to the fact that Noah was not her boyfriend and had not necessarily had her welfare in mind for the past few months. She sat down and put her arm around him and, after rubbing his back for a few minutes, curled up against him and closed her eyes. Zachary wasn't sure whether either of them was asleep, so he tried to be careful what he said. He sat down on the one chair, beside the other bed where Rhys was sitting. Rhys slid closer to him. He pointed at Noah, raising his brows.

Zachary knew there was more to explain than he could manage there, especially right in front of Noah and Madison. He considered what to tell Rhys. "I'll have to explain it all to you later," he said softly. "But… he was the one who messaged you. He was the one who wanted out."

Rhys's eyes widened and he raised his brows. He hadn't been expecting that. More likely, he had figured that Madison had refused to leave without her boyfriend and, rather than trying to fight it, Zachary had just agreed to bring him along.

Rhys looked at Noah, pondering this. He pointed at Noah, looking at Zachary again. He did?

Zachary nodded. "Yeah. He's got a good story. But... we can't trust him. Not yet." He was mindful of what the cop had said, warning Zachary not to take Noah with him.

Rhys nodded his agreement with the sentiment. Zachary still had Madison's and Noah's phones, and he took them out and laid them down on the desk. They were both locked, of course. He hadn't expected otherwise. He pressed the button to bring up the lock screen on Madison's. It was set for a four-digit numeric passcode. Zachary looked sideways at Rhys. "What do you think her unlock code is?"

Rhys rolled his eyes and pointed to Noah.

Zachary tapped in 6-6-2-4. The phone unlocked. Zachary chuckled. He wasn't bad at guessing passcodes, but he didn't usually get them the very first try.

He poked through a few screens, checking out Madison's call log and most recent messages and texts. She had a number of social networks set up on it, some of them with accounts that Zachary had been able to find, and others that he had not. The racier ones did not include her picture on the account summary or public feed. There were plenty of pictures on private feeds, but Zachary didn't have any desire to see them and quickly switched back out of them.

Rhys picked up Noah's phone and tried a couple of unlock codes on it before he put it back down again. He watched Zachary. After a few minutes, he tapped Zachary's knee.

Zachary looked up to see what he wanted. "Yeah?"

Rhys held up his phone, showing Zachary the gif he had sent earlier, the rotating police light.

Zachary nodded. "Yeah, thanks for the heads-up. We managed to avoid Peggy Ann and Jorge going into the building because of your warning."

Rhys raised his eyebrows and put his head forward. <u>Huh? Who?</u>

Zachary frowned. "Peggy Ann and Jorge. The people who were coming after Noah and Madison. To take care of things."

Rhys shook his head. He pointed at the police light again.

Zachary realized all at once that Rhys hadn't been warning him about the approach of Peggy Ann and Jorge at all, but had been telling him about the policeman standing outside the car, trying to talk to him. "Oh. Of course. You didn't even know about them. You were just warning me about the cop."

Rhys nodded. He raised his brows again, looking for more information.

"Your timing couldn't have been better. Because you messaged me, I looked out in time to see Peggy Ann—that's Noah's boss—was coming into the building. And Jorge, some kind of enforcer. 'Troubleshooter,' Noah called him. So we ducked into another hallway so they wouldn't see us and, once they were going up the stairs, we came out. I was trying to get away before they could come back down and see us. But the cop wouldn't let me go."

Rhys nodded slowly. He held up two fingers.

"Two? Two what?"

Rhys made a curvy shape with both hands.

"Two people. A woman and a man. Peggy Ann and Jorge."

Rhys pinched a lock of hair between his fingers and showed it to Zachary. Then he pointed to his eyes. Then ran a finger over his skin.

"Hair, eyes—oh. What they looked like?"

Noah nodded.

Zachary did his best to describe the couple to Rhys. He had only seen them briefly, but he was observant and had trained himself to notice people and to be able to describe and remember them for later.

Rhys leaned back a little. He pointed at himself, then pointed two fingers at his eyes.

"You saw them? Before they went into the building?"

Rhys nodded.

It made sense that he had seen them. There were only two directions that Zachary would have expected them to approach from, so it was fifty-fifty that they would walk by Zachary's car where Rhys could see them.

Rhys showed Zachary his phone again.

"The cop?"

Rhys nodded.

"What about the cop?"

Rhys held up two fingers again.

"Peggy Ann and Jorge."

Rhys made a duckbill motion with his hand, opening and closing it.

"Talking?"

Rhys held up the phone.

"The cop."

Rhys waited. Zachary put it together.

"Peggy Ann and Jorge were talking... to the cop?"

Rhys pointed at Zachary, nodding. You got it.

Zachary breathed out slowly, juggling the pieces in his mind. But he didn't have enough information yet.

"They were talking to the cop… how? Did he confront them? He said that he recognized Noah. Did he recognize them as troublemakers? People he didn't want around his neighborhood?"

Rhys shook his head.

"Why was he talking to them? Was it just casual?"

He shook his head again, insistent.

Zachary didn't like where the conversation was going. He swallowed. "He was friendly with them? He knew them?"

Rhys nodded and pointed at Zachary.

The cop had known Peggy Ann and Jorge. Maybe that was why he had detained Zachary and his group. He had been waiting for them to come back down. To come out and see who he had cornered.

The last thing that he had done before Zachary left was to try to convince him to leave Noah behind. He had said that Noah would betray him, which was probably true, and that Zachary should leave him behind so he couldn't expose them.

But he was friends with Peggy Ann and Jorge. Maybe not friends, but he knew them and was on speaking terms with them. So he hadn't wanted Zachary to leave Noah there so that he wouldn't be able to tell them where Zachary took Madison.

He wanted Noah there to hand him over to Peggy Ann and Jorge. He wanted Noah to have to face his boss and the enforcer. To face the music. They could torture him, withhold his drugs, force him to tell them who had come for Madison and where to look for her.

Zachary swore under his breath. He looked at Noah and Madison, apparently asleep on the bed. On one hand, it was strange that they would be able to settle down and sleep when they were in so much danger. But Zachary had experienced the same phenomenon before, when his brain and his body would want to shut down in times of stress. Rather than melting down, like he had at Dr. Boyle's office when he had forced himself to stay and deal with his anxiety, he would just turn off. And there was nothing that he could do to stop it. Madison and Noah weren't sleeping because they felt safe to do so, but because they had been on high alert for too long and couldn't deal with it anymore. The body enforced rest sooner or later.

If they were really asleep, and not just watching and listening to see what he was planning.

There was no reason for Madison to turn on Zachary and Rhys. They had only done what they had to protect her, and she wouldn't turn them in to the organization.

Noah was another story. Despite the fact that the cop had been trying to mislead Zachary, what he had said was true, and Zachary had recognized it from the start. Once Noah was away from the criminals he was used to associating with, he would start to regret what he had done. He would realize that burning his bridges was a bad idea if he wanted to survive. He would remember he needed them. Like Madison, he had been conditioned to obey. He knew there would be consequences if he did not. He had suffered through their torture and punishments before. He knew that Peggy Ann and Jorge would not hesitate to hurt him or to hurt Madison. He would want drugs and easy money and, after five or six years, he had learned only one way to get it.

That's what Joss had tried to tell him. That it didn't matter what Zachary did and whether he managed to get Madison out or not. There would be people who would not stop at anything to get her back. Her friends would betray her, including her Romeo. That was Noah's job. To make sure Madison did whatever the bosses told him.

CHAPTER 38

Zachary got up off of his chair and walked around the bed that Noah and Madison were lying on, so that he was standing behind Noah. The two were spooning. Zachary watched Noah's profile, the skin around his eyes and mouth, especially. He listened to the even inhalations and exhalations. If Noah was awake, he was a pretty good actor.

"Noah," Zachary said softly.

Noah didn't move.

"Noah."

The boy still didn't move. He looked very young, asleep there like that. Closer than ever to Madison's age. Tricking since he was twelve or thirteen? Under the control of a criminal enterprise for that long? He acted like an adult. He'd been forced to mature much faster than Rhys, who was still mostly boy rather than man. He had been on his own dealing with horrific people who put him through all kinds of abuse. Zachary's chest was tight. He felt for the boy.

He couldn't help it.

Ignoring the emotions, Zachary reached out and touched Noah's neck gently. He half expected Noah to stir or to strike out at him. Either pretending that he had been asleep, or actually startled out of sleep. But Noah didn't move. Zachary felt for his pulse, settling two fingers over the spot.

If Noah were awake, then his pulse would be racing, despite his pantomime of sleep. He could calm his outward body functions, making himself look relaxed and breathing slowly, but he couldn't control his heart. Not that well, anyway.

His pulse was slow, not fast. Like he was in a deep sleep.

Madison shifted. She didn't uncurl or get up, but Zachary thought that she might be awake. He kept his fingers over Noah's pulse, waiting for a burst of speed as Noah too woke up and remembered the situation he was in.

Madison turned over. She opened her eyes and looked at Zachary. A frown quickly replaced the relaxed, slightly parted lips. "What are you doing?"

"Checking on him."

Madison looked at Noah, then at Zachary's face. "Why?"

"I was surprised he was asleep. His pulse is very slow."

"He's sleeping," Madison said with a shrug.

"Why?"

"Because… neither of us has slept very much the past few days. With you coming around, and the cops, and dealing with everything else from his… well, from other people in the organization, I guess… it's been very stressful. Neither of us has slept very well."

"But he shouldn't be that much more deeply asleep than you. You're still worried about someone finding you, right? You're still feeling threatened. Like you need to be alert."

Madison rubbed her forehead, frowning. Eventually, she shrugged. "Yeah, I guess. But he's more tired."

"Why isn't he waking up with us talking over him?" Zachary gave Noah's shoulder a shake, then put his fingers back over Noah's pulse again. No increase in speed. Noah's heart still plodded away, too slow. Way too slow. "What did he take?"

Madison shook her head. "I don't know. How would I know if he took anything? I don't know that."

"Look at him. You know he did. And he's depressed. Giving up. Feeling people closing in behind him. What does he use?"

"Little of everything," Madison admitted. "It just depends. I don't know what he had on him. I don't know what he might have taken. I thought… he just needed to sleep. I need to sleep."

"I don't think you're going to get much sleep tonight. We're not here to sleep; we're here to talk strategy, somewhere we won't be seen."

Madison rubbed her eyes, smearing her mascara. "Come on. Just let us sleep tonight. We can figure it all out tomorrow."

"Tomorrow, you might change your mind. And he might be dead."

Madison's eyes widened in alarm. "Dead? What are you talking about?"

Zachary was looking at Noah's face. "His lips are getting blue. Do you know what that means?"

"He's not... Noah's always careful. He wouldn't overdose. He always knows how much he can take. He said..."

Zachary waited, brows up, for Madison to complete the thought. "What did he say?"

"He said you can always take more later, if you need it. That you can't take it back once you've taken it. There's no backing up."

"Do you have Narcan?"

"Umm..." Madison trailed off, shaking her head. "I don't need to. Noah always said, if you're careful, you don't need it."

"Then it wasn't an accident."

"No!" Madison shook her head. "He wouldn't do that. He was always careful. He told me what to do. He would never just... he would never just overdose like that on purpose."

"I think he did. Either way, it doesn't matter." Zachary pulled out his phone and started to dial emergency.

Rhys threw his school backpack down on the bed next to Noah. He unzipped one of the front pockets quickly, and handed Zachary a small black kit. Zachary opened it, knowing what he was going to find.

There wasn't time to ask Rhys why he was carrying Narcan. It was a nasal inhaler, and it was several doses. Maybe enough to keep Noah alive until the paramedics could get there. Zachary tossed his phone to Madison. "Get an ambulance here."

"But you've got the Narcan."

"It might not be enough. Get them."

Zachary positioned the inhaler inside one of Noah's nostrils and squeezed. He heard it puff, and waited for a reaction from Noah. He lay there still, breaths coming in very slowly. Lips dusky.

Zachary switched nostrils and tried another puff. Noah made a noise and pulled back. Zachary watched him, hoping that would be enough. But Noah remained still.

Madison babbled into the phone, trying to describe the situation and to tell the paramedics where they were. Rhys grabbed one of the keycard folders that they had been given on check-in and held it in front of Madison's face. She told them what hotel they were in, the address listed on the folder, and the room number handwritten in the blank. Her eyes on Noah's face, she sobbed and explained that they thought he might have overdosed. The dispatcher spoke to her reassuringly, and Madison nodded and answered the dispatcher's questions every now and then.

Zachary gave Noah another dose. And another. He shook the dispenser, but it was empty. Noah stirred and complained. Zachary felt his pulse. It had picked up a little bit and his face was pinker than it had been.

Rhys went to the hotel room door and opened it, looking down the hallway toward the elevator. Zachary could hear voices getting closer. Rhys stood with the door open and, in a few moments, he was stepping out of the way of the paramedics.

"Let's get some room here," one of them ordered. "Can the rest of you go sit on the other bed, please?"

Zachary slid off and caught Madison by the arm. "Come on."

She resisted, but eventually joined him, leaving Noah alone on the bed.

She sat with her face in her hands, sobbing. Zachary took his phone back from her. The other two phones still lay on the desk beside him.

"I gave him four doses," Zachary said, when one of the paramedics picked up the inhaler and looked at it.

"Okay. Good job. You kept him alive long enough for us to get here. That's the most you can do."

Zachary shook his head. There had to be something more that he could do. It was ridiculous that all he could do was sit there and give Noah four doses of Narcan, and it wasn't enough. He should be carrying the stuff himself, like Rhys. He should have it with him wherever he went, but especially when he was working on a case that involved young people and drug addicts. He should have known that and planned ahead.

He watched the paramedics working over Noah, giving him carefully measured shots. Noah grew more and more lucid with each dose, eventually blinking himself awake and pushing the paramedics away from him, complaining and telling them to go away.

"You need to go to the hospital, buddy," one of them told him. "You have an overdose and someone needs to keep an eye on you for a while. Your body could still be processing the opiates and you could lose consciousness again. You need to be under supervision."

"Just leave me alone," Noah growled. "I'm fine."

"You're not fine. Not with how many doses of Narcan you needed. Your condition is very serious."

Noah shook his head. "I'm fine. I'm not going to the hospital. You can't force me."

The paramedics looked at each other, then over at Zachary. But he didn't know how to convince Noah to go to the hospital. He was usually on the other end—trying to get out of the hospital when they didn't want to release him.

"Just give me the form to sign," Noah said, waving his hand at the paramedics. "I'm not going anywhere."

It took a few minutes to get everything straightened out. The paramedics continued to monitor Noah's vital signs for a few minutes but, eventually, they had to leave. Noah waited until the door was closed behind them, then looked at Zachary.

"So, what's your brilliant plan?"

CHAPTER 39

Zachary's thoughts kept going in circles, but every time he thought he had a solution, he found a way to talk himself out of it. He needed some time to think it through, maybe to talk it over with someone who was not so closely involved with the situation.

At first, he had felt like they were moving too slowly, Noah and Madison sleeping and Zachary not able to get anywhere without their cooperation. But now that Noah was awake again, Zachary felt rushed, pressured to act without knowing for sure what to do. He needed to come up with a working solution.

"I need to make a call. I need to figure this out."

"Who's stopping you?" Noah asked. "Go ahead."

It would help if Zachary knew who he was supposed to call. He tapped his phone restlessly, trying to figure it out.

Rhys touched Zachary's arm. Zachary looked over at him. Rhys's lips pursed, and he gave a soft kissing sound.

"Kenzie? No dead bodies. Not really her area." Zachary exhaled, frustrated.

Noah was sitting on the bed. He leaned back against the wall and closed his eyes. "We gonna be here all night? If we are, I'm gonna go to sleep."

"I don't want you passing out again. I want to know you're okay. Keep him awake, Madison."

Madison held Noah's hand, looking into his face. With all that Noah had said and done, it was hard to believe that she was still so in love with him. It just went to show how well conditioning worked. It was going to take a long time to unwind all of the lies he had told her and to figure out what her true feelings were. Zachary was still trying to sort out his feelings for his parents, for Bridget, and for others who had harmed him under one guise or another.

Zachary unlocked his phone and looked at the recent calls list. He'd missed a couple of calls from Kenzie. Rhys said to call Kenzie. Maybe it was a sign. Zachary tapped her name. It rang a few times before Kenzie answered it.

"Zachary? Where are you? I thought you would be at home."

"Yeah, sorry. I thought I would be too, but I had to go out..."

"What happened?"

Zachary didn't want to say too much in front of Madison and Noah. "It's… the case I closed. Things… didn't turn out quite the way I expected."

"Are you okay?"

"Yes. Everyone is fine. Rhys says hi."

"Rhys is with you? Are you sure everything is okay?"

"Yeah. I want to get him back home, but I don't want to lead anyone there. Would you let Vera know he's fine and I'll get him back to her as soon as possible?"

"Sure. She's going to be scared, though."

"He's fine. So am I. I just need… I don't know what to do. I need to talk it through with someone who can help."

"The police? Have you called them?"

"No... there might be one of them involved on the wrong side, and I don't want to tip him off."

"A dirty cop?"

"Yeah. Maybe. No proof, just suspicions."

"Tell Campbell."

"I will. When I know more. Until then, I want to stay below the radar."

"You are not supposed to be doing stuff like this on your own."

"There's no danger right now. We're okay. I just have to figure out where to take them on a more permanent basis."

"Them?"

"Yeah, we kind of got a two for one deal."

"Another girl? One of Madison's friends."

"No."

"Not… oh. Not Noah…?"

"Yes."

"Sheesh. You can't trust him."

"No. I don't. But I still need to figure out what to do."

"Anywhere is better than where they've been."

"But it's like Joss said. The organization isn't going to let them go as easily as that. We've lost them for now, but they're going to be looking everywhere I can think of to take them."

"Where does Joss think they should go?"

"I haven't talked to her," Zachary explained. "Just before, when we had coffee. She said we need to get—her—out of the city and give her a new name and live that way. But how do you do that? Where do you take her and how do you set her up so that she's safe and independent?"

"And doesn't turn around and run back to them."

Zachary glanced over at Madison, still talking to Noah and holding his hand. Kenzie and Joss were right. If they weren't able to get through to her, Madison was going to go right back to them again.

"I imagine you have as many skills as anyone at getting her off the grid," Kenzie said.

"What do you mean?"

"I mean, you know how to find people. So you do the reverse. Make her unfindable."

Zachary thought about that. Could he hide her well enough that no one would be able to find her? Kenzie had a point.

"Why don't you call Joss and find out what she recommends?"

"She uh… may have told me to stay out of it. That was her recommendation."

Kenzie snorted. "Well, if she knew anything about you, she should have known that wouldn't work."

"Yeah, I think she had a pretty good idea."

"She's the one with the experience, so you might want to give her a call."

In the back of his mind, Zachary had known this, but he hadn't wanted to call Jocelyn again. Disregarding her advice and then expecting her to bail him out… he had a feeling she wouldn't appreciate that.

"I suppose."

"Do it. And then hurry up and get back to me. I don't want to be worrying about you all night."

"Okay. And you'll let Vera know?"

"I suppose."

Zachary said his goodbyes, and then hung up. Rhys looked at him, probably understanding a lot more of what was going on than he was meant to. He pointed at the phone and rolled his eyes about them having to call Vera.

"Well, you can't just disappear and not tell her anything," Zachary pointed out.

Rhys shook his head at Zachary's naivete. Zachary wondered what he had told Vera or how he had managed to sneak off without Vera knowing what was going on in the first place.

CHAPTER 40

"Hi, Joss."

There was a huff of frustration from Jocelyn before Zachary could even tell her what was going on. "What did you do now?"

"I didn't do anything wrong," he protested, feeling again the like ten-year-old who was always in trouble for something. If all of the kids got in trouble, he could count on Jocelyn to blame him for it. She was the one who was in charge and supposed to keep them all in line, so he supposed she probably got the most severe punishment when she failed to do so. But he ended up getting it from her and from their parents, so he got punished twice when she only got punished once. And it wasn't always even his fault. Most of the time, maybe, but not all of the time, and it always stung the most when he was blamed when he hadn't done anything wrong.

"You're not just calling me for coffee again."

"Well, no."

"You got yourself into some kind of trouble. I told you that you were going to get into hot water, and you went ahead and did it anyway."

"I didn't. I let the case go." Zachary kept his voice low and turned away from the kids. They were talking to each other and had turned on the TV, so he had a measure of privacy.

"You let it go."

"Yes!"

"So you're calling me about something completely unrelated."

"Well, no."

"Then what happened?"

"She asked for help."

"She asked you for help."

"No, she asked her friend for help, and he's the one who came to me. So I had to—"

"You didn't have to. You're allowed to say no. And you should say no when it's something like this. I told you that you shouldn't have anything to do with it, and now you got yourself into some kind of trouble."

"I'm not in any trouble."

She was silent, waiting for him to explain why he was calling her if he wasn't in trouble.

"I'm not in trouble, but… I need to help them to find somewhere safe…"

"Them?"

"Well, yes." Zachary kept his voice low. He was turned away from them, but really didn't want them overhearing. He should probably have gone outside to talk. But he would have attracted attention pacing outside while talking on the phone. They were trying to keep a low profile and not give people any reason to notice them. "Madison and Noah."

"Who is Noah?" Joss groaned. "Oh, no! Tell me you didn't take her Romeo too!"

"Uh…"

"I warned you! I told you they're just going to get her back again. And especially if you're going to take one of them with you! You have to dump him." She swore angrily. "I'd tell you to slit his throat and leave him under a bridge somewhere, but you wouldn't do it, would you? How could you, Zachary!"

Zachary cupped his hand around his mouth and the phone receiver to try to keep his words from carrying. "It turned out that he was the one who sent the plea for help, not her. He was the one who wanted out. She does too, of course, but he wanted to get Madison out of there. And I need somewhere safe to take them. I can't take them back to my place."

"Obviously not. This guy's got you wrapped around his finger, Zachary. He's telling you stories. I know how it is. They get really, good at it. They could talk the socks off a kitten. But it's all lies. None of it is true. None of it."

"I know that he's probably telling me a bunch of stories. But I can tell how he feels. And I know that when he starts feeling better, he's going to panic and want to call back and turn them both in. I know. But right now, he needs somewhere to go, and I'm the only one who can help."

"You can tell how he feels?"

"I… yes. I can tell. He's depressed and suicidal, and I can't leave someone like that to his own devices."

"He's just reading you and reflecting your own feelings back. That's the best way to get someone on your side."

"He's already OD'd. I need to get him somewhere safe."

"He OD'd?"

"Yes. An intentional overdose. So I know... he's not just reflecting my mood. He got Madison out of there, and now he can't see the light at the end of the tunnel. He doesn't know where to go or what to do. He knows he's burned his bridges. They won't take him back now, after what he's done, and he doesn't have anywhere to go."

"You're some piece of work, Zachary."

"Is there any way you can help me? We're stuck here in a hotel and we can't stay here forever. I don't know how long it will take them to track us down. It's not exactly the big city. There are only so many places to look."

"Yeah," Jocelyn's voice was soft, as if she were suddenly afraid of being overheard.

Zachary looked at his watch. It was late, so she shouldn't be at work. She couldn't be worried about being overheard on the phone by a boss or coworker. But he hadn't asked her if it was a good time or if she were alone. He had no idea whether she had a boyfriend or was the type to seek out company when she was feeling down.

"Is someone else there?"

"What? No. Who else would be there?"

"Oh. Sorry. It just sounded like you were trying to avoid being heard. My mistake."

"I told you before, Zach, you gotta get her far away from there. She needs a new name and to stay away from anyone from her old life. Everyone she associated with before Romeo and everyone she's associated with since. She can't talk to any of them, even if she doesn't think they have any connection to the syndicate. They can get to anyone."

Zachary opened his mouth to disagree and say that they couldn't get to him, that he would never put Madison at risk, but then he closed his mouth. He had called Jocelyn to ask her for her experienced opinion. How was arguing with that opinion going to get him anywhere?

"Okay. So... how far away to I need to get her?" He ran through different possibilities in his mind. "New Hampshire? That would be away from their territory, right?"

"It's not like they have to follow state borders."

"Noah said that he thought that Gordo was the head man over Vermont. So I assume that means that if we can get them out of Vermont..."

"Gordo?"

"Yeah."

"I can't believe you're dragging me into this." Joss's voice was suddenly angry and biting.

"I'm sorry. I didn't know who else to talk to. You're the one who has experience with this stuff. Kenzie said I should go to the police, but..."

"You already saw how the police handle this. They ask her if she needs help, and she says no, so they stay out of it. And you don't know how many people inside the police department might... be easily bought."

"Yeah. Actually, I might. Do you know this guy? This Gordo?"

"I know him." Joss was quiet for a minute. Zachary thought it best not to disturb her thoughts. She would have plenty to think through. "Would he know me? No. Maybe he would know my street name, but he doesn't know me as Jocelyn Goldman. I left that name behind years and years ago. I don't think he would know my face. I don't exactly look like I did when I was working for him."

"How... were you that high up in the organization? Do you mean you worked for him personally?"

"I've... I know him. He doesn't know me. I'm just another girl. He wouldn't take a second look at me. Not now."

Zachary shifted uncomfortably. He took a quick look at Madison and Noah, but they were still distracted, staring at the TV and talking to each other. Zachary hadn't expected Jocelyn to know Gordo's name. He supposed Vermont was still a pretty small place. Jocelyn had been in the business for a lot of years and she would know a lot of the players.

"If I find someone in New Hampshire, do you think that would work? I might be able to make some connections there."

"You'd be better off sending her to Canada."

The Canadian border wasn't that far away but, in order to get Madison into Canada, they would have to smuggle her across. She wouldn't have the passport she needed to get over the border. Even if she did, she would be traceable. She needed to get somewhere without documents.

"We can start for the Canadian border," he suggested to Jocelyn. "And then circle around. Backtrack and go for New Hampshire. They would think we were going one way, when we were really going the other."

"Which would work especially well if you could dump Noah at the border. Especially if he's got more drugs on him. Throw him out and let the drug dogs get him."

She had a nasty imagination.

"I'm going to do it. Make a run toward the border, that is, not leaving Noah to the dogs. With any luck, they'll waste their time searching for data on who has crossed the border and not search in other directions until they've exhausted the possibilities."

"Okay. Whatever."

Zachary looked again at Noah. Noah saw the look and raised his brows. His lifted his hands palms-up. "What is it, bro? You got somewhere for us to go yet?"

"Maybe," Zachary told him.

Noah rolled his eyes and looked back at Madison, dramatizing his impatience. "This guy rolls in acting like he knows everything and is the big man, and he doesn't have a clue. I should never have called him."

Madison looked as if she might agree. She was looking tired and worn, her makeup smeared or rubbing off, her eyes tired and bloodshot. She hadn't, as far as Zachary could tell, had any drugs since they left the apartment and, if they had gotten her addicted to something, she was feeling it.

They were probably both thinking that they had made a mistake and should have just stayed with the organization.

"Get your stuff together," Zachary said. "We'll be leaving in a couple of minutes."

Everyone just looked at him. It wasn't like any of them had any luggage to pack. They had just run; they didn't have anything to get ready.

"Use the bathroom, splash water on your faces, whatever you need to do," Zachary said. "We're going to be in the car for a few hours and I don't want to have to make rest stops."

Noah got up. Zachary met Madison's eyes. "You'd better keep an eye on him."

"I can use the potty by myself," Noah growled.

"Last time you went in there you shot up. I don't want that happening again."

"I used up what I had."

"I don't know that. I'm supposed to believe you?"

"I don't have anything."

Zachary looked at Madison. "Unless you want a repeat, I'd keep an eye on him."

She looked ready to argue. Zachary turned away from her, focusing his attention back on the phone.

"You have a plan?" Jocelyn asked dryly. "That's your brilliant plan? You'll just start out toward Canada and then turn around for New Hampshire. And somehow, you'll know somewhere to drop them once you get there. It will all just magically turn out."

"I have more in mind than that. But I'm not going to tell <u>him</u> what it is."

"Well, that's something, anyway," Jocelyn conceded. "Do you really have somewhere to take them?"

"Well... we'll see," Zachary said. "I have an idea, but I need to think it over while I'm driving."

"It's pretty late to be driving. I don't want my baby brother falling asleep at the wheel."

"I won't fall asleep."

"That's what everyone says. Right before they fall asleep."

Zachary hung up the phone.

CHAPTER 41

Before using the hotel bathroom to freshen up and prepare for the drive himself, Zachary told Madison and Noah about his plan to help them to escape over the Canadian border.

"You've gotta be kidding me," Noah protested. "We don't want to go there."

"It will be safe. Gordo's territory doesn't extend that far, right?"

"For good reason! It's freezing up there. Even worse than here. And there's nothing to do. It's all just igloos and dogsleds. They don't even have the real Netflix."

"You want to be safe or not?"

"How are you going to get us across the border?"

"I know a guy at Newport. I called him to see when he'll be on shift, and he'll be there if we leave now. He'll let me across without checking everyone's papers. For anyone following us, it will be like the two of you were ghosts. The trail will stop at the border."

"You know a guy."

"Yes."

"And how are you going to deal with all of the rest of the border guards? It's not just one person, you know. Everybody is going to see us crossing, and they're going to know something hinky is going on."

"Trust me. Madison trusts me, don't you?"

Madison looked back at Zachary, just as skeptical as Noah.

"And Rhys trusts me. Right Rhys?"

Rhys blinked at Zachary, then gave a nod and pointed at him, making a pulling-the-trigger motion. <u>You da man</u>.

"You see?" Zachary shrugged. "It's no problem. I know how to get things done. That's why Rhys came to me."

He went into the bathroom and gave them plenty of time to talk things over before returning.

"Great, everybody ready to go now?"

None of them seemed very excited. But Zachary was confident in his plan. It was going to work.

At least, he had some confidence in his plan.

It was a good plan.

It had at least some chance of working.

* * *

Zachary took a quick look around the hotel parking lot as he waited for Madison and Noah to get into the car. Rhys was quick, grabbing the shotgun seat, but Noah and Madison seemed to be moving very slowly, a lot of looks passing between them.

He had a bad feeling.

He'd been confident when he was still in the hotel room. Or at least, he'd had as much confidence as he could have in the half-baked plan, but as he stood there in the parking lot, he felt exposed and uncomfortable, sure someone was watching them.

He looked for security cameras. Shapes in parked cars. Cars that had too many antennae. But he couldn't see anything out of place. Not consciously. That didn't mean that his brain hadn't picked up on something, subconsciously. Something had alerted him to the fact that he was 'off.'

"Just get in," he told Madison and Noah, as they discussed which side each wanted to sit on.

They both looked at him, surprised at the sharpness that had crept into his voice.

"Get in," Zachary repeated. "I don't like being so exposed. Something… there's something wrong here. So get in and be quiet."

Noah gave Madison a 'he's cracking up' look, and then slid into the seat behind Zachary. Madison waited for him to move in and, when he didn't, she went around the car and climbed in on the other side, rolling her eyes at Zachary.

They could give him as much attitude as they liked, as long as they did what he said.

As Zachary got into the driver's seat and started the engine, there was a loud bang.

Everyone jumped. Rhys clutched his hand to his chest, gasping and laughing at himself. "Backfire."

But Zachary knew his car, and it was not a backfire. He looked all around, but couldn't spot any attackers.

"Get your heads down," he warned, still scanning for danger.

He hadn't turned the headlights on and, if it had been an old model car, he would have been able to roll out of the parking lot without lighting up, but it was a new car, and it had automatic lights. Drawing the eyes of anyone within a couple of blocks.

Zachary pulled his door shut as he put the car into drive and let it creep forward.

There was another bang and breaking glass.

Madison started to scream.

Rhys looked wildly over his shoulder into the back seat, the whites of his eyes glistening in the streetlights. He made a loud moaning noise, a panicked noise of alarm. Zachary reached over to touch him reassuringly on the leg, at the same time pressing the gas pedal to the floor. He withdrew his hand to grip the steering wheel and make a tight turn out of the parking lot, tires squealing all the way. The passengers were all thrown from side to side as he navigated quickly through the dark streets, turning this way and that, hoping to lose any pursuers in the maze.

He had a picture in his mind of the city streets. He didn't know every street in the city, but he had a pretty good mental map. He knew where he was relative to his apartment, the highways, and other familiar landmarks. He knew which direction was north and, after hopefully losing their tail, he pointed the nose of the car in the right direction on the highway and kept the gas pressed down.

"Everyone okay?" he asked, searching the rear-view mirror for any sign of a car that was following too close behind them. There hadn't been any headlights behind him for the last few turns, but that didn't mean they couldn't send cars in every direction to find him again. It was a big organization, if Noah and Jocelyn were right, and he didn't see any reason they would lie about it.

He patted Rhy's leg again.

"Rhys? Okay, bud?"

Rhys was still making a throbbing groan, checking anxiously behind them and looking all around for any other dangers.

"How about back there? You okay now, Madison?"

He spared a glance in the mirror at Madison. She was no longer screaming—that had only lasted for a moment—but she was definitely still scared. Probably regretting that she had ever let herself be talked into walking away from the organization that could either protect her or harm her. Better to do what she was told and to be protected.

"Noah?"

There was no answer from Noah. Zachary couldn't see him. He looked at Madison again.

"Is Noah okay?"

"He's hurt," Madison finally managed to get out. Zachary twisted around to see Noah. He could only take his eyes off of the road for a split-second, and then he was looking out the windshield again, part of his brain driving while the other part processed the image. One quick flash, and then his mind filled in the details as if he were developing a print from a negative.

Noah was slumped to the side like he had fallen asleep with his head against the window. Like a tired toddler who couldn't make it home. There was blood on his face. It was his window that had broken.

"Can you look at him, Madison? Turn him toward you and tell me whether it's broken glass or...?"

Madison sobbed. He could see, out the corner of his eye, that she was trying to do as he said, awkwardly moving in the confines of the back seat to turn Noah's body and head around so that she could get a better look at it.

"I don't know," she said in panic. "I can't tell. It's all bloody. He's bleeding so bad!"

"Head and face wounds bleed a lot. Lots of blood vessels close to the surface. It doesn't necessarily mean that it's a serious wound."

Zachary turned his face slightly toward Rhys, keeping his expression a calm, reassuring mask.

"Rhys, can you see? Can you tell whether he's been hit, or whether it is just the broken glass?"

There was a break in Rhys's moaning. He started to turn his head to look, but then stopped, as if he had encountered a wall. He seemed not to be able to turn his head past a certain angle. Had he been hurt? Maybe he got whiplash with Zachary's reckless driving. A fine thing if he ended up having to take Rhys back to Vera injured. She would never let him see the boy again.

Rhys moaned. He covered his face with his hands and hunched forward.

CHAPTER 42

Zachary was holding back the panic.

He was usually pretty good in an emergency. His own inner thoughts and anxieties could turn him to a pile of mush, but confronting actual physical danger, his thoughts sped up and he processed everything at lightning speed.

That didn't always translate to being able to convince his body to react quickly. He often felt like he was moving in slow motion because his body just couldn't keep up with his revved-up brain.

Rhys was incoherent, but then Rhys was usually mute and unable to answer any questions out loud. It really wasn't that much of a change. But Zachary knew that this was far beyond Rhys's usual muteness.

Madison was crying and bordering on hysteria, but she seemed to be unhurt. The bullet must have come from the other side of the car, breaking the glass on Noah's side and lodging somewhere rather than hitting Madison or exiting through her window. Not a level shot, then, but something pointed down, maybe a sniper on a building. Zachary didn't think it could have come from a low angle. He would have seen or heard someone close to the ground.

"Madison. I need you to calm down."

"I can't!"

"I need you to calm down so that you can help Noah. I need to know if he's badly hurt. I can't stop in the middle of the highway."

"I don't know. I can't tell. There's so much blood, and it's dark out, all I can see is black."

Zachary had processed more than that in his one quick glance, but Madison was not a trained observer.

He remembered Dr. Boyle helping him, coaching him through his panic attack. "You need to calm down. Take a few deep breaths. Make sure that you're pushing all of the air out." He knew what Madison was going through. He knew how hard it was to stop when everything was falling apart in front of her eyes.

"Count your breaths. Ten seconds in. Ten seconds out. Just hold it for a moment. It will be okay, Madison."

He was looking for an emergency turn-out. He didn't want to stop; he wanted to keep moving so that whoever had been waiting for them in the parking lot or on top of one of the nearby buildings could not catch up with them. But he had a wounded child in the car. Maybe more than one. It would be irresponsible to keep going without evaluating them.

He found a place where the shoulder was wide enough to pull over and slowed the car, signaling, sliding over until they were rolling to a stop. He put the car into park and opened his door.

He had to be careful, because there was a lot of traffic zooming by, and there really wasn't a proper turn-out. Open his door or step out incautiously, and a passing vehicle might take him out. He watched the traffic and started to slide out of the car, looking back at Noah.

There was another crack like lightning striking, and Zachary jumped backward in alarm. He tried to spot the source. Where was the shooter?

"Call 9-1-1," he told Rhys.

But Rhys didn't move. Zachary strained back and forth, trying to see the shooter in the traffic behind them.

A car slowed as it approached them. Because it was the shooter, or just because someone was being cautious and didn't want to accidentally hit Zachary's car or an opening door?

The other phones were all with Zachary. He had hung on to them to make sure that Madison and Noah would not be able to call to warn anyone where they were going until he was ready for them to. Sooner or later, he would need to give Noah the opportunity to reach someone in the syndicate, to tell them that Zachary was headed for the border. But he hadn't expected a shooter to attack them right as they were leaving the hotel. He had thought that they would have plenty of time and not have to worry about a physical attack until they were much closer to the northern border.

Zachary shifted into drive and screeched into the driving lane without even shutting his door. The movement of the car slammed it shut.

Madison was shrieking and sobbing, all semblance of calm, reasonable thinking gone.

"Rhys. Your phone. Get it out."

Rhys kept his hands over his face and didn't move.

Zachary hit the car's Bluetooth button, but didn't get the answering tone that said it was listening to him. He pressed it again. He held it in, willing it to connect to his phone, but it didn't.

The other phones were in Zachary's pockets. He would have to drive, trying to avoid the pursuer, and get out one of the phones and place an emergency call, all at the same time. Maybe another driver who saw him driving recklessly or heard the gunfire would call it in.

Maybe Zachary would be surrounded by police cars in a couple more minutes.

But he was not so lucky.

Zachary pulled one phone out and looked at it. Madison's. Using Noah as her unlock code. Not very secure. And Noah had sent Zachary a message from her phone, not his own, so he knew the password. He had probably given her the phone in the first place.

Both phones had probably come from the same source. The trafficking syndicate. So that they could reach their workers at any time, night or day.

Zachary swore. Even if Noah and Madison didn't answer any incoming calls or messages, the organization could still track their positions.

He transferred Madison's phone to his right hand, which was also holding the steering wheel steady, so that he could find the button to roll down the window with his other.

Tracking the phones. He should have thought about it earlier.

He had picked out a hotel where the traffickers didn't have anyone installed, but they didn't need anyone at the hotel to tell them where Zachary and his young charges had gone. All they needed to do was to follow the phone signals.

He should have thought about it. He knew better. He'd tracked phones and he'd had to outsmart others who were tracking them.

The technology was not new. It wasn't hard. It could be used by mothers to check on the location of their children, or professionals to track down their phones if they were lost or stolen. Certainly, a big organization like Gordo's trafficking ring would have plenty of resources for tracking employee cell phones on the fly.

With the window down, Zachary transferred Madison's phone back to his left hand, then tossed it out the window.

There were screeching tires behind him. Maybe he'd manage to hit the pursuing car with the cell phone. Two for the price of one. He looked into his rear-view mirror at the black van. Nice and anonymous. Invisible.

He knew what he was looking for this time. The next time, he wouldn't. That meant he had to lose his tail and not be caught again.

He worked another phone out of his pockets. This one was his, so he dropped it into the center console. He felt for the last phone. It took a while to locate which pocket he had shoved it into. He was always temporarily losing his phones. Kenzie told him if he always put it in the same pocket, he would always know where it was.

But she lost things in her purse, so who was she to tell him how not to lose his phone?

He transferred Noah's phone to his left hand and chucked it out the open window too. Then he rolled the window up.

"Now they can't track us," he told the others. "Watch out the back. Tell me if anyone else is following. I'm going to do my best to lose them."

Rhys was still holding his hands over his face. Madison turned her head to look out the rear window, but she was still crying and trying to tend to Noah, and Zachary didn't know if she would be any help.

He needed to lose the tail and keep them from picking him up again, and he wasn't going to have any help from the teens. He put on blinders, hyperfocusing on driving and escaping anyone following him.

He couldn't worry about Noah or Rhys or Madison. He would be no help to them if he didn't ditch the traffickers. So he shut it all out, focusing just on losing any tails. When he thought he had managed to lose anyone who was following him, he pulled over to the side under an overpass, getting out of the roadway. He took his foot off of the pedals and turned off the ignition. He sat there in the sudden quiet, heart pounding, watching every vehicle that went by. He watched for any of them to slow down, looking for him or for anyone taking notice of the car pulled over under the bridge. He watched any nondescript vans or SUVs. He looked for any windows that were open or broken. They sat there for what seemed like a long time,

Madison still crying and Rhys moaning something under his breath.

As he watched, Zachary deliberated about what to do next. If he showed up at the emergency room with Noah, they were going to have a lot of questions. The police would get involved and word would get back to Burkholdt, the policeman who had stopped them at Madison's apartment building. He had written all of their information down. He would be watching for any reports that included their names.

Zachary turned around and craned his head around his seat to look at Noah. The boy was still unresponsive, even though Madison had been shaking him and trying to rouse him. It was too dark for Zachary to be able to see any details other than that his face was streaked with blood tracks.

Noah needed medical attention. And Zachary needed to make sure that everyone else was okay. Just because they didn't look like they'd been hit, that didn't mean that they hadn't been. Sometimes people didn't even know that they had been injured until the adrenaline burned off and they were out of danger.

Thinking about that, Zachary did a quick self-assessment, checking his hands, arms, and chest for any injuries. He quickly felt his head and his shoulders and back, as far as he could reach. He seemed to be uninjured by any of the flying glass or bullets. That was lucky.

"Rhys, are you okay?"

Rhys was murmuring something under his breath. Zachary had never heard him say more than a word or two at a time, and strained to make out what he was saying.

"Just stop it. Just stop it." Rhys kept repeating the words over and over again.

Zachary's heart gave a painful squeeze. He remembered Vera telling him about Rhys's traumatic reaction to his grandfather's murder. He had been in the house and had witnessed what had happened.

"Just stop it," Vera had said. "That's all Rhys would say for days after it happened. Just stop it. Just stop it. Any time anyone tried to ask him about it, that was all he would say."

"But eventually, he stopped saying that too," Gloria, Rhys's mother, added. After that, he had suffered a breakdown that had left him institutionalized for some time, and he had never regained the ability to speak or communicate in the usual way.

The gunshots had clearly thrown Rhys into a flashback of his grandfather's murder.

"Rhys. It's okay. You're safe. The shooting has stopped, and you're okay. Can you tell me what you can see and hear? What can you hear right now? The traffic driving by the car. The wind. Madison. Do you hear that? You're here, Rhys. In the car with Zachary. You're not back there."

He could see Rhys nod, his head bobbing up and down in the shadows. He reached toward Rhys.

"I'm going to touch you, okay? It's just me. You're safe."

He rested his hand gently on Rhys's shoulder. "It's okay now. Can you look around? Tell me what you see?"

At first, Rhys didn't uncover his face. He just hunched there, curled up into himself, like the little boy he had been when his grandfather had died.

"Look around, Rhys. I'm going to pull out soon, but I want you to see that you're safe. They're gone. Whoever was shooting at us, they're gone now. Look around."

Rhys slowly pulled his hands away from his face and raised his head slightly. He looked ahead of the car, then out Zachary's window, and his head swiveled to look out his own. He grasped at Zachary's fingers, still resting on his shoulder, squeezing them, holding himself anchored. He swallowed and nodded.

Then he turned his head and saw Noah in the back seat, and that was a mistake. Zachary should have anticipated it. Zachary's grandfather had been shot in the face, and Noah slumped in the back seat, face covered with blood. Rhys went rigid, letting go of Zachary's hand. He gave a squeal like a hurt animal and again buried his face, sobbing.

"Oh, Rhys..." Zachary squeezed Rhys's shoulder. But he couldn't delay any longer, hoping to be able to get Rhys into a better mental space. Noah's injuries might be critical. Zachary couldn't delay seeking treatment. He restarted the engine. "Okay. We're going to pull out now. Everybody be calm. We don't want to attract the attention of other drivers. Try to look natural."

Hopefully, no one would look into the car, because there was no way that any one of the three teens was going to act naturally. All he could do was to hope that no one would notice the broken window and the boy slumped over with blood running down his face.

"We're on the move now. Hang in there."

Rhys continued to sob, as did Madison. Zachary could feel everything spinning out of control. He tried to hang on and act like an adult who knew what he was doing. He pulled out from under the bridge, merging into the traffic, and tried to match the speed of the traffic around him. Nothing that would attract attention. There was nothing about his car that would attract attention, other than the broken window. Nothing that the bad guys would be able to see from far away. Hopefully, no police who had been called about the gunfire would notice it. It was just a detail on an otherwise nondescript car.

Picking up his phone, he held down the home button and told it to call Kenzie. Shutting off the engine seemed to have rebooted the Bluetooth, and he heard it ring over the car speakers.

"Zachary," Kenzie picked up after half a ring. "How did it go?"

He remembered he was supposed to have called her back after speaking with Jocelyn. But events had overtaken that resolution.

"Uh… things are getting complicated. Where are you?"

"I'm at your apartment."

"Can you go home?"

"You're not going to be back tonight?"

"I'll come to your house. Can you open the garage for me so I can drive in?"

"And where am I supposed to park my baby?"

"On the street. Just for a few minutes. I can't make it up to my apartment."

Even taking Noah into Kenzie's house was going to be complicated. Usually, he parked on the street and walked across the lot to get to the door.

"Are you okay, Zachary? What do you mean, you can't make it up to your apartment?"

"I'm okay. But... we have a casualty."

"A casualty? How bad? Go to the hospital."

"Too dangerous. They're going to be watching the emergency room. And the police will get called."

"And you think you've got a dirty cop."

"Yes."

"This is not a good idea, Zachary! I'm not qualified to be treating serious injuries. And if it's… something that has to be reported to the police, then I'm required to report it too."

"Can we just meet at your house? We can discuss it there."

"How bad is it? Are you putting lives in danger?"

Zachary looked in his rear-view mirror at the slumped, unmoving body. "No."

Kenzie let out a long breath, then grudgingly agreed. "Okay, I'll meet you at the house. But you'd better not be lying to me."

Zachary grimaced. She wasn't going to be happy when she saw Noah. But he had to do everything he could to protect the teenagers, and he didn't think he could do that by taking them to the emergency room. He needed to split them up. Kept in a group, he would just put all of them in danger.

"I'll see you there."

CHAPTER 43

Neither Rhys nor Madison said anything to Zachary about lying to Kenzie on the phone. Neither seemed to be in any shape to talk.

He kept a close eye on the mirrors for any more gangsters or the police. A couple of other drivers gave him odd looks, but no one seemed to be paying too much attention to the little car with the broken window. Luckily, with the way that Madison had pulled Noah's face toward her, he was facing away from the broken window, hidden by shadows.

It seemed like it took much longer than it should have to get to Kenzie's house, like the timeline was stretching out, getting tight and thin as a rubber band. As promised, Kenzie had left her red convertible parked at the curb and the garage door open for

Zachary. The interior lights were on. Zachary drove straight in and slammed the gearshift into park.

He jumped out of the car, ignoring the weakness in his knees, and walked past Noah's door in order to open it. Kenzie opened the door that connected to the house.

"Zachary?"

"Close the garage door."

"You said that you'd park by the curb."

"And I will. But for now, you need to close the door."

She looked like she would argue with him, but instead, she reached over and clicked a button beside the door. The motor ground and the chain clanked and the big door started to lower into position.

Zachary unbuckled Noah's seatbelt and retracted it, looking for any sign of a bullet hole or bleeding on

Noah's torso. He turned Noah's head toward him and quickly evaluated his facial injuries in the light. It seemed to mostly be superficial cuts from the glass, but there was a long, straight, blackened line from his chin to his ear that Zachary thought was a bullet track. He gave the headrest a quick once-over for a bullet hole, but didn't see one.

"Times like this, I wish I'd done weight training," Zachary muttered. He tried to pull Noah out of the car and pick him up, like he'd seen done on hundreds of action movies on TV but, despite the teen's slight frame, he was a dead weight and Zachary couldn't get good leverage to lift him. "Rhys, can you come around here and help me?"

Rhys pulled his hands away from his face, but his expression was such a mask of grief and pain that Zachary knew he couldn't expect any help from him.

"Madison, can you shift him from your side? If you can push him up toward me, and I can get my arm underneath him..."

As he wrestled to get a proper purchase on Noah, he was aware of Kenzie coming around the car for a look, and braced himself for her objections and criticism.

"Oh, boy," Kenzie said from behind his shoulder. "Hold on a minute, just hold him there."

Zachary couldn't see what she was doing but, in a moment, heard something rolling across the concrete floor. She came around the car with a dolly; the kind that could be used as a vertical hand truck for a stack of three or four boxes and had a hinged section that could be pulled down to the horizontal to move several stacks of boxes at the same time. Kenzie wheeled it over to a wall of plastic storage boxes arranged in a grid and laid four boxes across the support rods of the horizontal section. Then she pushed it over to the car door.

"Okay, move out of the way."

Zachary frowned, confused. How exactly did she think Noah was going to get from the seat to the dolly unless Zachary pulled him out? Noah wasn't conscious; he wasn't going to crawl over there himself.

"Just do it," Kenzie insisted.

Zachary hesitated for a moment, then moved slowly back, keeping one hand on Noah to keep him from falling out. Kenzie moved into position beside him. She moved too quickly for him to anticipate what she was going to do. In a few seconds, she had rearranged Noah and somehow managed to pull him out of the car and lay him down on the layer of boxes.

She smiled at Zachary's stunned expression. "I help move bodies around all the time," she pointed out. "I know a thing or two about how to handle them."

Zachary shook his head and couldn't think of a clever comeback. He'd think of one in a day or two. In the meantime, he was just stunned at how effortless she had made it look.

Kenzie pushed the dolly over to the door, which luckily was level with the floor of the garage and not up several steps. She opened the door and pushed the dolly through it into the house. Zachary scrambled after her. Madison climbed out of her side of the car, wiping her eyes, and followed her boyfriend through the door.

Zachary stopped and opened Rhys's door. "Come on, bud. Come inside and we'll get this all sorted out. It will be okay."

With some encouragement, Rhys got out of the car. Zachary guided him into the house.

* * *

Despite all of his reassurances to the others, Zachary entered the house and followed Kenzie with a lead ball in his stomach. He was waiting for the recriminations from Kenzie. He had lied to her and he knew he should have taken Noah directly to the hospital. But he was too concerned about the safety of the other teens. They needed to be protected too.

Kenzie was in the kitchen bent over Noah, examining his face and torso, and then turning him on his side to look at his back. The boxes on the dolly were too low for her to work comfortably like she could over a gurney, but she made no complaint about the circumstances.

"How does he look?" Zachary asked anxiously.

"It all looks superficial. Lots of blood, but it always looks like more than it is, and facial wounds bleed like the dickens. He hasn't lost a significant amount, and I don't see any other injuries. Were you shot at?"

Zachary nodded. "Yeah. I think that one along his jaw is a bullet track."

"Looks like it. But it just skimmed the surface. Lucky for him." She continued to examine Noah. "There are cloths and towels in the linen closet at the end of the hallway. Bring me stacks of both, and fill a couple of bowls with warm water."

Zachary obeyed without asking more questions. He fetched the towels first, and then looked through the kitchen cupboards for large bowls.

"The most concerning thing is his loss of consciousness. A bullet certainly has enough force to knock a person out if it hits the right place. I don't see any entry point, so I don't think we have any internal trauma, but if the blow causes swelling to the brain, that is a dangerous situation."

Zachary nodded. Kenzie took a bowl of water from him and started to wipe blood from Noah's face. She worked in silence for a few minutes. She looked over at Madison and Rhys, huddled close by watching, both faces streaked with tears.

"Why don't you guys go wait in the living room. Zachary will make you some coffee."

Neither moved at first. Then Madison touched Rhys's arm and encouraged him to move out of the kitchen into the living room.

"Hot and sweet," Kenzie told Zachary. "Good for shock. Make enough for all of us. I don't think we need to worry about falling asleep tonight."

Zachary nodded. "Yeah. Sure."

He worked with the single-cup coffee machine on Kenzie's counter to produce one cup of coffee at a time and stirred copious amounts of sugar into them.

"He's so young," Kenzie murmured as she cleaned the blood off of Noah's face, revealing his smooth skin and rounded jaw.

"I know," Zachary agreed. "He says he's been doing this since he was twelve or thirteen. I don't know if it's true," he added quickly, anticipating her answer, "but

I'd say he's been in the business for quite a while. He's pretty... skilled at what he does." Zachary's face heated as he realized how she might interpret that. "Managing Madison, I mean," he explained. "I don't have any experience with his <u>other</u> skills."

Kenzie looked up at Zachary briefly, laughing. "Oh, man, Zachary. I wasn't even thinking that!"

"Good."

Kenzie patted Noah's face with the towel, leaning close to see if the lacerations were continuing to bleed.

"So... he's okay?" Zachary asked. "I mean, as far as you can tell? Other than not knowing if he'll have a concussion?"

"I think you can count on him having a concussion. But his vital signs are all strong."

Zachary breathed a sigh of relief. He carried two cups of coffee into the living room and gave them to Rhys and Madison, then returned to the kitchen.

"Now," Kenzie said, "we need to figure out what to do next. What did Jocelyn say?"

CHAPTER 44

At Kenzie's suggestion, Zachary hired an Uber driver to take him and Rhys to the Salters' house. Then his car could stay out of sight in the garage, and Rhys didn't have to be subjected to the sight of the bullet-damaged car again.

"Make sure Vera knows enough to understand that he's been through a trauma. That he's having flashbacks. She'll want to get him in to see a therapist right away. Probably keep him company tonight, rather than letting him go to bed by himself."

Zachary nodded.

"It's probably best if she doesn't know all of what happened," Kenzie said, looking toward Noah, "I don't want her worrying about these guys coming after them, but..."

Zachary sighed. "If everything works out, then we won't need to worry her about that, but..."

"Just get him home," Kenzie said, seeing the Uber car arrive in front of the house. "We'll worry about the rest later..."

Vera was waiting at the door when Zachary and Rhys arrived. Her face was drawn and tired. She looked Rhys over worriedly, reaching out to give him a hug to reassure herself that he was okay.

"What's wrong, Zachary? What happened? He was supposed to be at a friend's..."

"He came to me," Zachary said uncomfortably. "Let's go inside..."

She took Rhys into the house. Zachary stood outside for a moment, looking for anyone keeping surveillance on the house.

He joined them inside.

Zachary cleared his throat and tried to think of the best way to explain it all to Vera. Memories of all of the times he'd had to explain to foster parents or school officials what he'd done wrong came rushing back to him. He hated disappointing them. He hated explaining that he'd broken a rule or done something on impulse that, on reflection, he should have known was a bad idea. He waited while Vera and Rhys sat on the couch, then sat in the easy chair across from them.

The Rhys he knew was absent. Rhys was always present and engaged, focused intently on Zachary to be able to communicate with him. The boy sitting on the couch with Vera was a thousand miles away, sucked into the past, drowning in fear and confusion.

"Madison messaged Rhys asking for help. Rhys came to me."

"He should have come to me. We could have called the police." Vera looked at Rhys, frowning over his lost expression. "But what... why didn't you go to the police? What happened? Kenzie said that he was with you, but she didn't say what had happened."

"It's been a long night. We went to help Madison and her boyfriend Noah. But a lot of things happened. It was... Rhys had a bad flashback to when his grandfather was killed."

Vera rubbed Rhys's back. "What did he say? How do you know that? He never talks about..."

"He was saying 'just stop it, just stop it,'" Zachary explained. "You told me that's what he said after your husband was killed."

Vera's brows drew down. She nodded, eyes shining with tears. "Yes, that's right." She tried to look into Rhys's eyes. "Sweetheart... you want to tell me about it? Rhys?"

He didn't look at her.

"Kenzie said... you probably want to get him to a therapist right away. And stay with him tonight. So he's not alone."

"Of course," Vera agreed. "He was alone that night." She hugged Rhys close to her. "When we came home, he was in his bed, and Clarence was in the kitchen," she choked up, "dead. We thought at first that maybe Rhys had slept through it, but..."

But he hadn't. Zachary had a pretty good idea that he'd seen everything. And despite what Vera said, Rhys hadn't been alone with his grandfather that night.

"Just stay with him tonight," he repeated. "And get in to see his therapist. Whoever has been helping him."

Vera nodded. She ruffled Rhys's hair like he was a little boy. "And later, will you tell me more about what happened tonight?"

"I don't know how much I'll be able to tell you," he evaded. "You know, client confidentiality..."

"Oh. Of course. Do you... need anything? Some tea, or... is there anything I can do for you? I appreciate you taking care of Rhys and bringing him home."

"No. I've got to get back to Kenzie's. There's more work to be done tonight."

Vera nodded. "Okay. But call me. Tomorrow, if you can. Soon."

"I will. And I'll come back and see Rhys." Zachary looked down at his feet, unable to meet her gaze. "If you want me to."

"You're always welcome here," Vera said.

But he was sure it was just words. She was being polite and, once she'd had a chance to think about it and to see how badly he'd traumatized Rhys, she would have second thoughts.

* * *

Step one was taken care of. Rhys was back with Vera, safe and sound. Out of the way of any further retaliation by the trafficking syndicate if the rest of the steps went according to plan.

When Zachary returned to Kenzie's house, he found Madison asleep on the couch. Noah was still lying on the boxes on the dolly and, despite the hard, uneven surface, appeared to be resting comfortably. Kenzie had cleaned up the bloody towels and everything looked neat and tidy. Noah had a couple of adhesive strips pulling together cuts on his face, and Kenzie said he wouldn't need stitches. As long as she monitored him and he didn't have any unexpected brain swelling, he would make a good recovery. Concussions could cause long-term problems, but Kenzie hoped that he was young enough to bounce back from it quickly.

"You need to go take care of your car," she told Zachary. "There are some basic supplies on the tool bench beside the storage unit. Tape up some plastic over that broken window so you don't get pulled over by the police. Then you'd better get on your way." She looked at the clock on the wall. "It's getting late. Or early."

Zachary managed to find everything he needed in the garage and temporarily covered the window. He looked over the car and found several nicks and holes from bullets. It was going to need some body work when he was done. At least he had money in savings from a few recent cases.

Once the car was ready, he went back into the house and woke Madison up.

"We need to get you to the safe house," he told her. "Let's get moving."

Madison groaned and rubbed her eyes. "I don't want to go anywhere. Why can't I stay here?"

"It's not safe here. I don't want to put Kenzie in danger if anyone manages to track you this far. We need to get you out of here."

"Where's Noah?"

"He's still in the kitchen."

"Is he awake?"

"Not yet," Kenzie advised. "I'm still waiting for him to come around."

"Then we can't go yet."

"You're not going together," Zachary told her firmly. "We need to separate the two of you to make you harder to track. And to make sure that Noah can't turn you back in to Peggy Ann and Gordo."

"He wouldn't do that."

Zachary remembered how sure Jocelyn had been that he would do just that, sooner or later. "We can't be sure of that."

"He wouldn't!"

"We need to get you somewhere safe, Madison, and we need to do it right now, before Peggy Ann can find you. Do you want her to find you here?"

Madison's eyes widened. "No."

"Do you want them to target Kenzie, because she gave you safe shelter? You think that's a good way to repay her for what she's done for you and Noah?"

"No!"

"Then you need to get out of here before they can trace you. They were already tracking your phone. They know all of your friends and family, because Noah gave them all that information and they can look up anything they want to about your friends at school or on your social networks. I have a safe house for you, but you need to come with me and do what I say and not argue or ask questions."

Madison looked uncertain. Zachary stood there, looking as stern as possible, trying to channel all of those 'mom looks' he'd gotten from his various mother figures over the years. In charge and unmoving.

Madison nodded, dropping her eyes. "Yeah, okay," she agreed in a small voice.

"Go to the bathroom and let's get out of here."

"Okay."

He nodded and watched her retreat down the hallway to get ready to go. Kenzie smiled at Zachary. "I'm seeing a whole different side of you today!"

"Did I do okay? Do you think she'll listen?"

"No guarantees," Kenzie sighed. "I've heard that it's pretty hard to get these girls out of the lifestyle, once they're in. Their whole outlook is distorted. But all you can do is your best. Stick to the plan and hope that she can hang in there."

Zachary nodded. They waited a couple more minutes, and then Madison came out of the bathroom.

"Can I say goodbye to Noah?"

"Make it quick," Zachary said. If everything came together the way they had planned, then it would be the last time she saw him. They might as well give her one last moment with him.

Madison tiptoed into the kitchen and looked down at Noah. Her eyes shone with tears. Zachary wondered how much of it was true emotion and how much was being exhausted and coming down from the adrenaline and whatever drugs she might have taken earlier. She'd been through a lot, but her feelings toward Noah were strong. She'd been manipulated by an expert with plenty of experience.

She murmured a few words to him, promising him that she would see him again soon, and gave him a kiss. She looked at Zachary and Kenzie, awkward.

"You'll take good care of him, won't you? And he'll be okay?"

"I'll do my best," Kenzie agreed. "I'm just worried about his head. He really should have woken up before now."

Madison squeezed Noah's hand and reluctantly let go.

"All right," Zachary said. "Let's get on our way."

CHAPTER 45

It seemed like it took a long time to get to their destination. Zachary was a little anxious about how it would all work out. He had only met the Creedys briefly before. That was one of the reasons they were a good choice for a safe house. His connection with them was very tenuous. It would be almost impossible for anyone to figure out where he had taken Madison.

He wasn't sure how they would respond to Madison or how long she would be able to stay there. Once she was settled, he would contact her parents and see if they were willing to pull up stakes and move away to start a new life with her. Even if they did, he wasn't sure it would work out. Madison had had a taste of independence, money, and drugs and, once most girls had been in that life, it was pretty hard to make a break from it and just go back to living at home with their parents and dealing with the normal responsibilities of teenagerhood.

Madison slept most of the way, so Zachary didn't have to worry about keeping a conversation going. Had she taken something, like Noah, while she was out of sight? Between being shot at and the coffee and his anxiety over Rhys's trauma and getting Madison somewhere safe, Zachary wasn't going to be able to sleep for some time. It might be days before he was able to calm down enough to get a good sleep.

Madison awoke as they entered the city, with the pink light of dawn peeking over the horizon and the abrupt stops and starts at traffic lights. She snorted, straightened, and rubbed her eyes, looking around.

"Are we there?"

"Almost."

"Where are we going?" She hadn't expressed much curiosity about his plans until then. "I'm not going to some kind of rehab or lockdown."

"No. It's just a couple that I know from another case. Not an institution."

"I don't need some kind of therapy or retraining."

Zachary shrugged. Opinions on that matter would vary. He knew there were a lot of people who would insist that the only way to keep Madison off of the streets and away from individuals who would harm her was to put her into a program of intensive behavioral therapy. He had been in enough institutions and programs to recognize that if the target of the therapy didn't buy into the program, there wasn't much point. She would pretend to be 'converted' and follow the program until she found a way to escape, and then she would run. If she were going to overcome the life she'd been lured into, that decision was going to have to come from her, just like Joss had said.

Madison sat there looking sullen for a few minutes, then apparently decided that it wasn't getting her anywhere, and relaxed her confrontational attitude. "What are they like, then? Who are they?"

"They're older than your parents. They lost a daughter a few years ago to a drunk driver. They have a set of twins. Grown. Empty-nesters."

"And they take in fosters, or what?"

"No. This isn't something they normally do. I just asked them for a favor. Be nice to them. They don't have any ulterior motives and aren't judging you; they don't know much about your situation. They're just giving you a place to stay for a few days while we sort things out."

"That's it?"

"That's it. An older couple doing a nice thing for you."

Madison stared out the window. She nodded. "Okay."

It didn't take long for Zachary to make his way across town to the Creedys'. He looked at Madison one more time.

"Be nice," he reminded her. "We want to keep you safe. That's why we're here. Not because anyone is trying to save you."

"Yeah, I hear you. I know."

They walked up to the house and Zachary rang the doorbell. It was Mrs. Creedy who answered the door. An attractive older woman with dark strawberry blond hair. Zachary didn't know if it were natural or dyed. He suspected it might be dye, but it was the same color as it had been the last time he had seen her.

"Mr. Goldman, come in." She gestured for them to enter and Zachary stepped up and into the house, with Madison behind him.

"It's Zachary. This is Madison, Mrs. Creedy. Thank you again for offering a roof over her head for a few days."

Mrs. Creedy studied Madison curiously. "Of course. I couldn't turn her down knowing that she wouldn't have anywhere safe to go. How are you, Madison; are you okay?" She touched Madison's arm, looking concerned.

Madison pulled away. "Yeah. I'm fine."

"You must be tired. It sounds like you've been up all night. I'll show you to your room."

Madison shook her head. She folded her arms, looking back and forth between Zachary and Mrs. Creedy. "This is really nice of you. I'm just… not sure about it all. I slept in the car, so I'm okay for now." She looked anxiously at Zachary. "Do you think you could call Kenzie? See how Noah is doing? I want to know…" She trailed off. She wanted to know what Noah would tell her to do, if Zachary guessed correctly. She was used to doing what he told her to and was adrift without him managing her life.

"Kenzie is going to call when she knows something. I don't want to interrupt her when she may be getting some sleep or be busy with Noah's care."

"Yeah… I guess…"

"Why don't you sit down, and you and Mrs. Creedy can get to know each other. You can tell her about school. What you like to do, your best subjects..."

Madison sat down, but she shrugged at Zachary's suggestion. School had not been her priority for a few months. Even though she had been attending up until her disappearance, she had been mentally absent. Sleeping through classes after spending her nights partying or servicing Noah's clients. Waiting for the end of the day when he would pick her up again. Her grades had been plummeting, and she had been completely disengaged.

Which was exactly why Zachary wanted her to talk to Mrs. Creedy about school. He wanted her to start thinking about school again. How important it was to her future. How normal it was for a girl of her age to be going to school, not hanging out with her boyfriend and turning tricks.

Madison scratched her ear, looking at Mrs. Creedy.

"I don't know. I'm not really into school."

"It can be hard for young people," Mrs. Creedy said generously. "I found it was a lot harder for my twins. Hope was different. She really loved school. Loved learning, and socializing with her friends. She got good marks, went on to college. I really thought she was going to turn out to be something great. A doctor or professor. Maybe something else. But..." Mrs. Creedy trailed off.

Madison looked sideways at Zachary. "Zachary said you had a daughter that died."

"Yes. She showed so much promise, and then... she was taken from us so suddenly. I don't know... how someone recovers from that. One day she was in our life, and the next, she was gone. I hope you're good to your parents. Don't ever think that you don't matter to them. Nothing matters like your children."

Madison pulled her feet up onto the couch, her bent knees in front of her chest. She looked pensive.

Zachary didn't speak up. It was what Madison needed to hear, and she needed to hear it from someone other than him. He would never say anything so absolute. He knew very well that children were not the most important thing to every parent. His biological parents hadn't wanted kids around. They had dumped their children when things got too hard. That freed them up to pursue their own lives, whatever it was they had wanted. Zachary had a hard time picturing what they had gone on to do after he and the other children were gone. He assumed that they had broken up. There were only two ways that his parents could have gone. Either they had separated and divorced, or one of them had killed the other. They hadn't gone on to live happily ever after, that much he knew.

And he'd had plenty of foster parents who hadn't given much thought to the children they were raising either. Sometimes they loved their own bio kids and treated them differently from the fosters. And sometimes there was no difference. They just treated them all like something unpleasant tracked in on their shoes.

But Madison's parents did care about her. Deeply. She needed to be reminded of that. Kids tended to think that their parents didn't love them because they had strict rules and expectations. Because the kids didn't want responsibility and their parents wanted them to grow up to be productive adults and, somewhere in between, they had to stand firm in order to shepherd their kids into the right path.

"I'll be talking to your parents," Zachary reminded Madison. "They're going to want to talk to you and to come and see you. But we have to be careful that they can't be tracked here. So it might take a few days to get everything arranged."

Of course, he was planning on Madison's parents agreeing to leave their lives behind in order to reunite with her and have her for a couple more years. That might not happen. Or it might not happen in the 'few days' that Zachary was promising. Zachary didn't know how long Mrs. Creedy would be agreeable to putting Madison up, or how long Madison would stay there before she got tired of it and ran.

He was hoping he'd be able to fit everything together like a puzzle and it would all come smoothly together.

But that wasn't always the way that things worked out. His life had not turned out that way.

"Yeah, I know," Madison agreed. Maybe she had doubts that it would all be roses. After everything she had done to disrespect her parents and their rules, the way that she had broken their hearts by running off, maybe the reconciliation wouldn't be as easy as that. Maybe they wouldn't want Madison back.

"What do you like best about school?" Mrs. Creedy asked, returning to the topic that Zachary had introduced.

"I don't know. I like seeing my friends. I haven't seen any of them for a long time. But... I guess I won't be able to see them at all now."

"Oh, I'm sure you could still reach out to them," Mrs. Creedy assured her.

"No," Zachary said firmly. "Not in the near future. You don't want to be tracked through them. You're going to have to wait until you're safe. That's going to be a while."

He didn't want to suggest that it might be years before Madison would be able to see them or talk to them again. He didn't know how long it would be before the traffickers stopped looking for her and watching her friends.

Mrs. Creedy looked like Zachary had said something impolite. Her lips pressed together and she shook her head slightly. But Zachary had told her. He had explained that Madison was in danger if she tried to reach out to the people in her old life. Mrs. Creedy had to understand that. They both had to get it.

Zachary's phone rang, making him jump. He had left the ringer on, which he didn't usually do when he was with clients. He pulled it out and looked at the screen. Kenzie. He tapped the speaker button.

"Kenzie. Hey, how's it going? How's Noah?"

There was a pause before Kenzie answered. Long enough for Zachary to look at Madison and meet her eyes, and to see the worry there. Why did Kenzie hesitate? Noah had been doing well. She had said that his injuries were superficial. Teenagers were fast healers; he'd bounce back in no time.

"Zachary, can you take me off speaker?" Kenzie suggested.

Zachary pulled his eyes away from Madison's anxious gaze to tap off the speaker button on the screen. He put the phone up to his ear.

"Kenzie? What's going on? Is everything okay?"

"There have been some... unexpected developments."

Zachary stood up and looked around, trying to decide if he should leave the room. He took a couple of steps toward the door. He lowered his voice slightly.

"Unexpected developments? What does that mean?"

"Well, you know I was worried about brain swelling."

"Yes. Because of the way the bullet knocked him in the head. But he was doing pretty good when we left."

"He was... I wasn't expecting him to go downhill that fast."

"What happened?"

"I'm sorry, Zachary..."

Zachary looked at Madison, wondering how much she could hear of what Kenzie was saying. She would have to piece the rest together from his side of the conversation.

"Sorry... for what?"

"He turned so fast. He seemed like everything was just fine, and then his vitals went all to hell. I don't know if it was swelling in his brain or maybe he had an embolism... but it all happened so fast; there was nothing I could do."

"You had to take him to the hospital?" Zachary suggested.

"No, Zachary. I lost him. I know this makes things more complicated with Madison... I did everything I could. It was just too fast."

"No."

"I'm sorry."

Zachary looked at Madison. She was clearly following the conversation. She had gone completely white and stared at Zachary with wide eyes and a slack jaw.

"Madison," Zachary said, his voice rough.

"No! No, don't tell me! Don't tell me that!" Madison shrieked, going from calm a moment before to nearly hysterical with nothing in between. "Noah is okay! When we left, Kenzie said he would be okay. We just had to wait for him to wake up!"

"It was unexpected..."

"No! No, no, no!"

There were no tears yet. She was too shocked and horrified to work up any tears.

They would come later, when it all started to sink in.

CHAPTER 46

"Oh, Madison." Mrs. Creedy moved over beside Madison on the couch. "It will be okay. I know it doesn't feel like it now, but you'll go on with life. It doesn't seem possible right now, but your life will go on."

She was speaking about her own life, of course. She had no way of knowing how Madison was going to take the news. She didn't know what Madison's choices would be. Maybe she would go back to confront Peggy Ann. Maybe she would have a breakdown. Maybe it was something that she'd never be able to get over and would stick with her for the rest of her life. Mrs. Creedy couldn't know how it would affect her.

Madison first pushed Mrs. Creedy away, and then fell against her, clutching her tightly and protesting in words that were so fast they were unintelligible.

But the words didn't matter. The fact that she was grieving and was accepting comfort from Mrs. Creedy mattered. She would bond to Mrs. Creedy, lean on her and depend on her to help her to make decisions. And maybe that meant she would be able to make the right decisions, ones that would lead her back to her family instead of farther away from them.

Zachary said a few more words to Kenzie that no one listened to, and then returned to sit on the chair he had been sitting on. He watched Madison. It hurt to see her so upset. His empathy and compassion for others was one of the things that drove him to do the things he did. Mr. Peterson had suggested to him a long time ago that maybe he could make some money with his photography by becoming a private investigator, but Zachary would never have done it if he hadn't cared about people and wanted to help them and to ease their pain. It was painful to see how upset Madison was. She had put her whole life into Noah's hands, and now he was gone. What was she going to do with herself now that he was gone from it?

* * *

Eventually, Zachary left the Creedys'. Mrs. Creedy had her hands full with Madison, but she seemed to take to the role eagerly. She'd lost one of her daughters, but here was a child who needed her. A way to exorcise her demons, to spend all of the compassion she had on someone else. She would take good care of Madison until Zachary could get her parents there, hopefully for the beginning of a new life.

He was exhausted and keyed up at the same time. He wanted to go home and go to bed, but he didn't know whether he would be able to sleep even after a few more hours of driving. He got into the car and started on his way back. He told his phone to call Mr. Peterson and listened to it ring a few times as he headed back onto the highway.

"Zachary," Mr. Peterson sounded cheerful, as always. Happy to hear from his former foster son. "How are you?"

"I'm okay. Just wanted to hear your voice."

"I'm happy to talk to you at any time. You sound tired."

"Tired... and not. Got a drive ahead of me still."

"Maybe you should take a break and catch some Z's. Not a good idea to drive tired."

"I'm not sleepy. Just... wrung out. It's been a difficult day."

"The sun is barely up. How has it been that tiring already?"

"I haven't slept. I meant... the last twenty-four hours. It was kind of crazy."

"Oh. You want to talk about it?"

"I don't know." Zachary watched the cars ahead of him, thinking about what he would tell Mr. Peterson if he shared the story. He couldn't tell him everything. And he didn't want to say anything that might be a breach of Madison's privacy. "I was helping out some teens who... were in pretty bad circumstances. It's been tough."

"Do you think things will turn out all right? It can be hard with kids... sometimes no matter how much energy you put into it and how good your intentions are… you can't make things better for them." He might have been speaking of his own experiences with Zachary. He had been an important father figure in Zachary's life, despite the fact that he had not officially been one of his foster parents for more than a few weeks. He had stayed involved, and there had been plenty of times when he had given Zachary advice or tried to help him to get onto a better path. But Zachary had rarely listened to him. Or been able to follow through on the things that Mr. Peterson had suggested even when he knew the advice was good.

"Yeah. I don't know what she's going to decide, or if she'll be able to get herself onto a better path."

"It can take years. Sometimes there's a lot of damage and trauma to get through."

"Tell me about it," Zachary agreed.

Mr. Peterson gave a muffled laugh. "Longer for some kids than others."

"Yeah." Zachary made some quick lane changes and watched behind him for any tails. He was sure that no one had been able to follow him to New Hampshire. But he still needed to keep an eye out. If someone had managed to get a tracker on his car or his phone, it could wreck all of their plans. "How's Pat doing?"

"He's... on the way back," Mr. Peterson said finally. "I think he's stabilized on the antidepressants, and he likes the therapist that we've been working with."

"So you think..." Zachary wished that he'd had better results for Pat. If only he'd been able to find Jose alive... "You think he'll be okay."

"I know he'll be okay, Zachary. You don't need to worry about that. It's just taking him some time to work through the grief... and the guilt."

And Zachary felt guilty for Pat's guilt. He had made stupid decisions, and the consequences had been disastrous. As usual. Pat had felt guilty for involving Zachary in the first place. Guilt that he wouldn't have had to deal with if Zachary had been able to tamp down his impulsivity and act like the professional private investigator was supposed to be. Instead of still acting like the ten-year-old who ran into everything full-bore without considering the consequences.

"Well, say 'hi' to him for me."

"Sure will. How is your family?"

Zachary didn't answer immediately, trying to sort out an answer for himself. The problems with Jocelyn were not going to be resolved any time soon. She had a lot of trauma to work through herself, and a lot of that was also Zachary's fault. He didn't know if she could ever forgive him for the choices he'd made that had impacted the rest of her life. Or if she even should.

"How's Kenzie?" Mr. Peterson prompted. "Everything going okay there? It was so nice to see the two of you together again, but I understand that things don't always turn out the way you want them to, even when you're working on it as hard as you can."

"No, things with Kenzie are going good." Zachary was glad to be able to report this. "I think... we're closer now than ever. We went to our first couples session."

"Yeah? How did that go?"

"It was... horrible. And good."

His foster father laughed. "Oh yeah? Horrible and good?"

Zachary couldn't help chuckling at his own description. "I had… bad anxiety. Thought I was going to die. But… we stuck it out, and I'm glad. And we went for ice cream."

"Of course. Ice cream makes everything better."

"Well, if you ask Kenzie. And… I don't know if I can argue. It did feel pretty good."

"That's great. So you'll keep going?"

"Yeah. She'll kick my butt if I don't. So I know I have to. And that… we can get through it, even if it's hard."

"Sometimes the most important things are the hardest."

"If it will help me communicate with Kenzie, and work through… our issues… then it's worth it."

"Attaboy. I'm proud of you, Zachary. Good for you."

CHAPTER 47

Despite Mr. Peterson's encouraging words, Zachary couldn't face Kenzie when he got back in town. He was just too worn out emotionally to deal with her feelings and his at the same time. He went back to his own building and shot her off a text to let her know that he was home before heading to bed. He sat in his car in the parking lot for some time, looking for any sign of trouble. As far as the traffickers knew, he had been headed for Canada. Even if Noah hadn't passed that message on to them, they knew he had been traveling north before they lost him. It would take them a long time to thoroughly check border crossings for any sign of the teens. They didn't have any reason to be surveilling his apartment, but it was still important to be careful. And if they were watching him to figure out where he had stashed Noah and Madison, he wasn't going to lead them back to Kenzie's house.

Zachary knew he couldn't sleep without help, and that sleep was the thing he needed most. So despite his resolution after the incident at Mr. Peterson's that he wouldn't take any more sleep aids, he went straight for the medicine cabinet. It was okay for him to take something, as long as he was careful not to mix his meds and to take the proper dosage. The mistake he had made then would not be repeated. He would stick to that part of his resolution.

He took the recommended dose and lay down in bed, closing his eyes and waiting for the pill to take effect.

Usually, while he was waiting for it to kick in, he would check his email or his social networks, or just play with his phone browsing popular videos until he started to feel drowsy. But he didn't even want that distraction. He wanted to think of nothing until he woke up again.

Thinking of nothing wasn't an option. The hamster that was his brain was running full-tilt on the hamster wheel, turning as fast as it could and getting nowhere. He second-guessed everything he had done in the past twenty-four hours. If he'd made better decisions, things might have turned out differently. But better, or worse? And which decisions would he have changed?

He pressed his fingers to his temples, trying to slow the hamster down and get rid of all of the worries pinging around in his brain.

It seemed like he would lie there awake forever.

* * *

He was feeling a lot better when he awoke a few hours later. He was still groggy from the meds and still short on sleep, but the deep emotional exhaustion had lifted, and the hamster-thoughts pinging around his brain had slowed down, back to a normal pace.

Time to move on to the next step of the plan. Zachary had a drink of water and wondered when he had last eaten. He munched a granola bar over the sink, then sat down at the table with his phone and dialed the number he knew by heart.

"Campbell here. Zachary?"

"Yeah. How is it going?"

"About usual. How about with you, Zach? Don't tell me you already have another case you need my input on."

"No, not exactly."

"What's up, then?"

"I'm wondering about getting a rumor started."

There was a long pause as Campbell considered this. Then he heard Campbell's chair squeak as he leaned far back at his desk. "Exactly what are you talking about?"

"I have a young lady who could be in some danger, and others who could be collateral damage. Unless we can convince some bad guys that she is out of the picture."

"Out of the picture how?"

Campbell would know who he was talking about, of course. Zachary had only talked to him about one young lady recently. "I've moved her out of state and she should disappear without a trace, if I've done my job. And if she doesn't rebel and decide to go back to the old life. But... I don't want certain people putting pressure on her family and friends to find out where she disappeared to."

"I'm not sure how I can help you with that."

"Let's say... there may be someone in your department who has a line of communication into certain quarters."

"An undercover agent?" Campbell jumped to the wrong conclusion.

Zachary considered it. What was the difference if Campbell thought that an undercover fed might be in position, rather than there being a dirty cop in his precinct? If the rumor were convincing enough, then it wouldn't matter which was true. Everyone involved would get the message, either way.

"Could be."

"Hmm. And what exactly is the rumor that you want spread around?"

"There were some reports of gunfire on the highway last night."

"Uh... yes, there were."

"After that incident, two teens that the police department was aware of dropped out of sight. There were reports that one or both teens were hit."

"Madison Miller and...?"

"A kid known as Noah. He probably has a number of different names on the street. He was involved in prostitution and in turning out new young girls and boys."

"Her pimp?"

"Yeah. Her boyfriend, as far as she was concerned. A Romeo, in the business."

"So Madison and this Noah might have been hit in this shooting last night," Campbell said, sounding concerned.

"Yeah. The police can't get confirmation of this, but word on the streets is, that's who was involved in the shootout, and both of them might have been hit."

"Might have been?"

"The rumor is that they were both killed. Again, the police are unable to verify any details. No bodies have turned up in the morgue. No injuries treated in emergency centers. But Vermont has a lot of wild, wooded areas, and the ground is soft enough to dig now."

Campbell snorted. "Can I just say that if you were ever discovered to be digging graves in the woods, I'm not going to be standing behind you?"

"You won't need to. So... do you think that rumor might get around?"

"I know a couple of people who like to share gossip around the water cooler. One would only need to plant a couple of details. Not even rumors, just... speculation."

Zachary nodded. "Exactly."

"And these rumors or speculations are not going to come back to bite us?"

"I've looked at it from all angles... I don't see how it could be a problem. But if the word leaks out to these bad actors, it might save the lives of anyone remotely connected with the former prostitute. They aren't going to be looking for someone who is dead. They'll just move on."

"No retaliation?"

"I don't see it. She was an asset, that's all. If she's gone, there is no point in wasting resources on retaliation. That won't bring in more money."

"No, that's true."

"I appreciate it. I don't want her family and friends to be harmed."

"I'll plant a little speculation, and we'll see what happens. I can't promise the results you're looking for, but it sounds like a reasonable plan."

"You're a lifesaver. Thanks again."

CHAPTER 48

Zachary didn't know whether he should call Vera or just show up on the doorstep. If he called her, there was less chance of confrontation, and she could just tell him not to bother contacting them again.

But if he showed up on the doorstep, he was there, and it wouldn't be as easy for her just to shoo him away. Maybe he would get in to see Rhys one more time. Or she would concede that he couldn't have foreseen what would happen when Rhys had come to him for help.

Or she could punch him in the nose.

She was a kind, Christian lady, so that seemed like it was only an outside possibility, but still one that had to be considered.

In the end, he decided that despite the risk of confrontation, he had to chance it. He had to see Rhys one more time if he possibly could.

That didn't make it any easier to stand on the Salters' doorstep and force himself to press the doorbell.

Eventually, he was able to do it and, a few minutes later, Vera opened the door.

"Oh, Zachary!"

She stood there for a minute while they both considered how she would respond to his unannounced visit. Finally, she stepped back and let him into the house.

"Come sit down," she directed, pointing to the living room.

Zachary sat down in his accustomed seat. "Is he here? Or…?"

Zachary didn't want to hear that Rhys had been institutionalized again. But if that was the only way for them to help him, then it was the best place for him to be. Zachary scratched at the knee of his jeans, waiting for the accusations. Waiting for Vera to tell him that he had set Rhys back ten years and that chances were, he was never going to be able to recover again.

"He's sleeping right now." Vera looked at her watch. "He's been sleeping a lot lately. His therapist said that it's normal and not to push him too fast. Sleeping is apparently good. A way for his brain to try to process what happened and to start healing."

Zachary nodded. Some therapists subscribed to this theory. Others believed that it was best not to let patients sleep any longer than eight hours, but to get them out of bed on a strict schedule and get them to group therapy or whatever was the treatment of choice.

"I'm sorry," he said, shaking his head. "I didn't mean for anything to happen to him that night. I should have brought him straight back here. I should have been more responsible. Just called the police and let them deal with it..."

"When Rhys came to you begging for help?" Vera stared off into the distance, thinking about it. "I may spoil the boy, but I don't think I could deny him whatever help I could give him if he asked me for something."

Zachary shrugged, still looking down. "But I put him into unnecessary danger. That wouldn't have happened if I had just called the police and brought Rhys home."

"But would that have helped Madison?"

"Well... no, probably not. She wouldn't have accepted any help from the police. And it might have had a negative consequence for her, having the cops show up on her doorstep."

"Rhys really likes Madison. I know it's just puppy love; he isn't romantically attached to her, and she doesn't have those feelings for him, but he was... it felt like he was the only one who cared enough to help her. Even her parents, they weren't able to do anything to get her back."

"Yeah."

Zachary was silent, considering her reaction. "So... how is he?"

"I honestly don't know. It's so hard to tell with him, with the communication barriers. I was afraid when you brought him back… he was so distressed… and when you said that he'd had a flashback and been saying that… it took me back to how he was after Clarence died. And he just slipped away from us."

Zachary nodded. "I was worried that… he'd regressed all that way again."

"Me too. But he has been… he's still communicating. As much as can be expected. He's worried about Madison still, but I keep telling him that you would do everything you could for her. That he had to trust you to do what was best."

"Thanks… I don't know what she'll decide. So many of these girls just go right back to the life. All we could do was… give her a fighting chance."

Zachary finally looked up at Vera. She looked him straight in the eye, sharp and discerning.

"Can you tell me what happened? What it was that upset him so much? Made him go back to Clarence's death?"

She still had a hard time calling it murder. How could Rhys get better if she denied what had happened?

"I don't know… I don't think you'd be quite so kind to me if you knew what had happened. I had the best of intentions… I never meant for it to play out like it did. I didn't realize… I didn't think about them being able to track Madison's and Noah's cell phones. I should have known. It was stupid not to realize it. I know plenty about tracking technology. But…" Zachary shook his head. It was hard to believe that he had been so stupid. He could blame it on how complex the situation had been, on adrenaline, on trying to deal with three teens who wanted three different things. But he should still have realized that Peggy Ann and her crew would be able to track the phones they had given to Madison and Noah.

"All of that technology." Vera waved it away with one hand. "I would never have thought of it. I'm getting better at all of these gifs and emojis, because of Rhys, but I really haven't got a clue how it all works."

"I do, and I should have realized."

"Just tell me, Zachary. How can I help him if I don't know what happened? He can't tell me. If he tells his therapist, if he's able to, then the therapist still can't tell me. I think I need to know. Don't you?"

Zachary swallowed. He took a deep breath in and blew it back out.

What was the worst that could happen?

The worst was that Vera would tell him he could never again have anything to do with Rhys. And if he were going to make such huge blunders, then that was probably the best thing for Rhys. It might hurt Zachary, but he had to do what was best for the boy, not what felt best to him.

"Okay… we had gone to a hotel to hide and to work out a plan of action. Somewhere safe, where we wouldn't lead the guys who were after Madison back to you or to Kenzie or to Madison's family. We didn't want to bring other innocent parties into it."

Vera nodded. "And that's when you talked to Kenzie. And told her to call me to let me know that Rhys was okay."

"Right."

"That was the first I knew that anything was wrong."

"I'm sorry about that. I didn't want to worry you... but I didn't know if you already were..."

"It was the right thing to do."

"So... after we'd had a chance to rest and to put together a plan of action, we headed out again. And that was when... that's when they attacked. They must have had a sniper on the roof, and they had cars ready to tail us. It was a very dangerous situation. I should have seen it before we walked out there."

"How could you?"

"I should have known."

Vera dabbed her nose with a crushed tissue. "What happened?"

Vera had probably already guessed. He had, after all, said 'sniper.' What else did she think that meant?

"They tried to ambush us. I managed to get everyone in the car and to get out to the highway, but they were still following the cell signal, and they attacked again there. In the whole thing… Noah was hit. Mostly it was just flying glass. And he was knocked out. But you can imagine how it seemed to Rhys…"

Vera didn't say anything for a long time. Zachary waited.

"So they were shooting at you," Vera said finally.

"Yeah."

"And this Noah… he was okay?"

"He was knocked out. And he had blood on his face. So for Rhys…"

"It was just like when Clarence was shot. The sound of the gunfire. Hit in the face."

Zachary nodded. "I'm so sorry. I had no intention of putting him in any danger."

Vera shook her head. "That poor boy. That poor, poor boy."

Zachary stared down at his hands. It was probably time for him to leave. Vera wouldn't want him hanging around there. She shouldn't have to tell him it was time to leave. She was so polite, she would keep being nice to him even when she wanted him out of the house.

"I guess... I should..." He started to get up.

Vera shook her head. "No, no. Let me wake Rhys up. He'll want to see you. He'll want to know how everything went. He's been asking after you."

Zachary hadn't received any messages from Rhys and thought maybe Vera had forbidden it. He was relieved that Rhys was at least communicative enough to ask for him.

Vera got to her feet. "You just stay right here. It might take me a few minutes to convince him to get up."

* * *

Zachary waited, concentrating on breathing and trying to keep his anxiety at bay. It hadn't gone as badly as he had feared. Rhys hadn't completely regressed. Vera hadn't kicked Zachary out and told him not to return. Rhys still wanted to see him, and Vera was willing to let him. But he couldn't shake the anxiety that Rhys or Vera was going to blame him for everything that had happened and for re-traumatizing Rhys.

He could hear Vera talking in Rhys's room and, eventually, the two of them came out. Rhys went directly to Zachary and, as Zachary stood up, took him in a bear hug.

Zachary was startled. He froze, unsure what to do, and it took him several seconds to process Rhys's reaction and hug him back.

Rhys released him after a few more seconds and stepped back far enough to look him in the face. He gave Zachary a searching look.

"She's okay," Zachary said immediately. "I don't know if she'll stay with her parents. They're trying to work things out. But she's safe, and we've fed back false information to the organization that she was killed in the shoot-out. So they won't be looking for her."

Rhys nodded seriously.

"Rhys, I'm so sorry, I never meant anything like that to happen. I'm so sorry that... you were there, and you saw what you did, and that it made you flash back to when your grandpa was killed. I'm so sorry about that."

Rhys took Zachary's forearm in a strong handshake, squeezing tightly. He met Zachary's eyes and gave a slight nod.

Zachary let out his breath. He looked at Vera. She nodded.

"Well, why don't I put something in the oven for supper? You'll stay, Zachary?"

EPILOGUE

The visit with Rhys had turned out well, better than Zachary had dared hope, but he had a pretty good idea that his visit with Jocelyn wasn't going to go nearly as well. He had the highway drive to sort out his thoughts and prepare himself, but he still didn't feel mentally prepared for what was bound to be an awkward and possibly angry meeting.

This time, it wasn't at a coffee shop or other neutral location, but at Jocelyn's house. It was a tiny house, but picturesque and carefully-maintained. It wasn't a dirty, rat-infested apartment. It was probably better than anything she had lived in while she'd been in the trafficking business. Her own place.

He didn't have to force himself to press the doorbell. Jocelyn was watching for him and opened the door as he approached.

"Hey," Zachary greeted.

She nodded. "Hi, Zach. Come on in."

Zachary entered. He took a quick glance around and opened his mouth to compliment her on her home. But he didn't get the chance.

Noah emerged from the kitchen into the tiny living room.

He was looking much better than he had the last time Zachary had seen him. The cuts on his face were starting to heal. He had good color instead of being pasty white. The bullet track along his jaw was still ugly, but Zachary suspected he was probably proud of it. A sick-looking war wound.

"Noah. Wow. How are you doing?"

Noah shrugged. "I'm… doing okay. It's weird. I don't know what to do with myself."

Zachary nodded. Living in the tiny house with Joss instead of turning tricks in the city; that was a pretty big change. He suddenly had choices. And that might be pretty frightening.

"Sit down, you goons," Joss said irritably, motioning to the furniture. "That's what the furniture is here for."

The men meekly obeyed.

"Coffee?" Jocelyn asked sharply.

"Always," Zachary agreed.

She didn't wait for Noah's answer, but disappeared into the kitchen.

"Do you… know how Madison is doing?" Noah asked

tentatively.

"Part of the deal is that you don't have anything to do with her."

"I know. And... I'm not going to try to contact her. I just wondered if she's okay."

"She's okay," Zachary said neutrally. He wasn't going to give Noah any details.

That was the deal.

Just like they weren't going to tell Madison that Noah had woken up with only minor concussion issues. The plan was to give her no reason to go back to the life. Noah wanted out of the business and he wanted Madison to be free to go back to a normal life. That meant completely severing their ties.

"That's good," Noah said contentedly, surprising

Zachary by not pushing for more.

"She owes you a lot for getting her out of there."

"No, she doesn't. I'm the one to blame for her getting pulled in to start with. You're the one who got her out."

"Not without your help."

Jocelyn returned with a round of coffee. "Luke is in a rehab program," she informed Zachary without him asking anything. "Hopefully, he'll stick with it, and be able to get into some kind of training, get himself a good job."

Zachary nodded. "Luke?"

The boy shrugged. "New life, new name." He sipped his coffee and stared out the window.

"That's good. Is it... I just wondered if it is your real

name. I know that Noah probably wasn't."

"It's my real name now."

Zachary shrugged. It didn't matter what Noah's name had been before he'd been trafficked.

All that mattered was what happened next.

ABOUT THE AUTHOR

Award-winning and USA Today bestselling author P.D. (Pamela) Workman writes riveting mystery/suspense and young adult books dealing with mental illness, addiction, abuse, and other real-life issues. For as long as she can remember, the blank page has held an incredible allure and from a very young age she was trying to write her own books.

Workman wrote her first complete novel at the age of twelve and continued to write as a hobby for many years. She started publishing in 2013. She has won several literary awards from Library Services for Youth in Custody for her young adult fiction. She currently has over 50 published titles and can be found at pdworkman.com.

Born and raised in Alberta, Workman has been married

for over 25 years and has one son.

* * *

Please visit P.D. Workman at pdworkman.com to see what else she is working on, to join her mailing list, and to link to her social networks.

* * *

If you enjoyed this book, please take the time to recommend it to other purchasers with a review or star rating and share it with your friends!

Lightning Source UK Ltd.
Milton Keynes UK
UKHW032224211220
375683UK00007B/732

9 781774 680056